Other books by Ruth Warburton

A Witch in Winter

Author's Note

Many texts helped in the writing of *A Witch in Love*
but I'd like to mention a few in particular which
I mined for direct quotes.
The first is the *Malleus Maleficarum* by Heinrich Kramer
and Jacob Sprenger, which is quoted by Anna's
guards in chapter nineteen.
The dedication in the front of the John Donne
collection – which Seth gives to Anna – contains lines
taken from Donne's poem *The Good Morrow*.
And finally, the poem quoted in Anna's mother's letter
is a condensed extract from a sermon by Canon Henry
Scott Holland, part of the passage sometimes called
'Death is nothing at all'. I've abridged it, and added
one line not in the original to suit my own purposes.
The Bible quotations are all taken from the
King James version.

A WITCH in LOVE

RUTH WARBURTON

A division of Hachette Children's Books

Copyright © 2012 Ruth Warburton

First published in Great Britain in 2012
by Hodder Children's Books

1

A Catalogue record for this book is available from the British Library

ISBN 978 1 444 90470 3

Typeset in Berkeley Book by Avon DataSet Ltd,
Bidford on Avon, Warwickshire

Printed and bound in Great Britain by
CPI Group (UK) Ltd, Croydon, CR0 4YY

The paper and board used in this paperback by Hodder Children's Books
are natural recyclable products made from wood grown in
sustainable forests. The manufacturing processes conform to the
environmental regulations of the country of origin.

Hodder Children's Books
a division of Hachette Children's Books
338 Euston Road, London NW1 3BH
An Hachette UK company
www.hachette.co.uk

For my dad.
And for Meg, Kate and Eleanor.

CHAPTER ONE

'Merry Christmas,' I said, and leant forward to kiss him. As our lips met I felt a small flurry of snowflakes swirl around our heads.

'Damn.' I pulled back, feeling my cheeks flush scarlet with a mixture of anger and embarrassment. The snow fell on Seth's dark curls and melted on the restaurant table-top. None of the other diners had noticed and Seth only smiled his wide, devastating smile. I didn't smile back. Instead I shook my head at him, my cheeks still hot.

'Don't smile – I've got to get this under control, Seth.'

'Sorry. It was just so beautiful.'

Beautiful was hardly the point. My slips could get us both into serious trouble – perhaps even killed, if I didn't get a grip. Seth saw my expression and took my hand under the tablecloth.

'It's getting stronger, isn't it?'

I nodded.

It was rarely the same reaction – sometimes the plants nearby would burst into bud, sometimes the sun would come out in spite of the pouring rain, sometimes all the lights would dip, just for a second, as if there'd been a fault in the power supply.

'Don't worry,' Seth said. 'No one noticed.'

I looked around the dimly lit restaurant. It was true, all the other tables were full of chatting couples and families reunited for the Christmas holidays, far too preoccupied to notice two out-of-towners, still less the little swirl of snow at their table. I'd been lucky. This time.

I turned back to Seth. He was watching me quietly, the candles reflected in his slate-grey eyes. He'd dressed up for the night, discarding the usual worn jeans and ripped T-shirt that he wore out sailing for a crisp white shirt – ironed, no less – open at the neck, revealing the line of his throat and a triangle of skin, deeply tanned from day after day spent out on the water. He was distractingly beautiful and I still couldn't quite believe that we were a couple, even six months on – but I tore my mind back to the important issue.

'Someone will notice one day. What about the time I scorched all the grass under our feet? If it hadn't been

2

a rainy day that could have been a forest fire there and then.'

'But it *was* a rainy day,' Seth pointed out. 'So no harm done. You've got it under control, more or less.'

More or less. It was the *less* that was the problem. I put my head in my hands.

'This doesn't happen to Emmaline.'

'Emmaline's had seventeen years to get used to being a witch. You've had six months and your power's building all the time. It's not surprising you're taking a bit of time to get used to it. You'd have to be superhuman to handle all this straight away.'

'And I'm not superhuman. Depressingly average in fact.'

'There's nothing average about you, Anna,' Seth said fiercely. 'And you *can* handle this. I know you can.'

'I hope so.' I swallowed against the weight in my chest and tried to smile. 'Whatever made you think it would be a good idea to have a witch for a girlfriend, hey?'

'I *love* having a witch for a girlfriend. Snowfalls, electrical disturbances and all. I wouldn't swap any of it.'

'Oh really? Not even in the constant worry over whether you really love me or our relationship is just a very long side-effect from an accidental spell?'

'Anna . . .' Seth said, and there was a warning note in his voice, 'Not this again. For the last time, I *don't* have any worries on that score. If you do, you've got to get over them. End of.'

I bit my lip, sorry I'd raised the subject and soured the happy atmosphere. Seth was right. I'd made my peace with those fears, I'd *had* to. I'd broken that spell every way I could think of – and as far as Seth was concerned it was over and done with, its magic snapped.

I couldn't go on inflicting my doubts on both of us, punishing us both for one long-ago mistake. And anyway, for six months I'd been living the life of an ordinary seventeen-year-old girl, albeit one with an extraordinarily lovely and good-looking boyfriend. No spells. No magic. Well, I corrected myself, thinking of that swirl of snow, *almost* no magic.

And it was working. We were fine. Everything was fine. As long as I could hold myself in check, everything would be fine.

Oil and water, whispered a treacherous voice in my head as I lifted the last forkful of dinner to my lips.

I pushed the plate away, suddenly full to nausea.

As if on cue, the waiter bustled up and began clearing.

'Dessert, mademoiselle, monsieur?' He began brushing crumbs with a little silver knife. 'Coffee? Tea?'

'Not for me, thanks.' I looked at Seth. 'Do you want anything?'

He shook his head. 'Just the bill, please,'

The waiter gave a little half-bow and disappeared.

'So what're your plans for tomorrow?' Seth asked as we waited for the bill. 'Want to come out for a sail? I'm trying out the new rudder.'

I shuddered at the thought of the icy grey water and biting December sea wind, but only said, 'I can't; I'm taking Emmaline up to London for some Christmas shopping.'

'Are you mad?' Seth looked horrified. 'Only, what, three shopping days until Christmas and you're going to brave the London shops? It's as much as I can do to cope with Winter on a Saturday.'

'We'll cope. You're all right anyway; you're the only person I've already bought something for.'

'I don't mind.' Seth took my hand and kissed the soft skin inside my wrist. 'I don't need anything else, as long as I've got you and my boat.'

It was true; I had never met anyone less attached to material possessions than Seth. At the look in his eyes my breath caught in my throat and I gave a shaky laugh.

'Well, you have to put up a good show on Christmas

Day. I'll be mighty peeved if you forget to open your presents and go sailing instead.'

Seth grinned and was about to reply when there was a tap on his shoulder from behind.

'Excuse me . . .' It was a gorgeous flame-haired girl from the table behind us, where she was sitting with a group of friends. 'Don't I know you?'

'I don't think so.' He smiled pleasantly but shook his head.

'No, I do,' she insisted. 'Aren't you the barman at that pub in Winter – what's it called, the Crown and Anchor?'

'Oh, yes.' Ever since he'd turned eighteen a couple of months ago, Seth had been helping his mum out behind the bar on nights when they were short-staffed. 'Yes, I am. You might have seen me there.'

'Do you remember me?' She smiled at him flirtatiously, completely ignoring my presence. I would have been annoyed, except that Seth was so transparently uninterested.

'Sorry, no.' Seth shook his head again. The girl looked a little piqued and then tossed her hair.

'Oh well, you will next time. It's Zoe, by the way. See you next time I'm in Winter!'

Seth only shook his head and laughed, and at that moment the waiter turned up with the bill. We paid and turned up the collars of our coats and then plunged into the cold night air waiting outside the restaurant door.

We'd had to park quite a way away, but I was so full that I didn't mind the walk, and we strolled slowly through the back streets of Brighthaven, hand in hand, looking at the lighted windows of the shops. They all had their Christmas displays out, twinkling lights and fake snow frosting, and it gave me a warm inner glow. All my life I'd loved Christmas, every moment of it, from the first feel of the lumpy misshapen stocking in the darkness of Christmas morning, through to the last turkey sandwich, stuffed with leftovers, on Boxing Day night. This year would be our first at Wicker House. Dad was putting up the tree tonight, and I could already imagine how beautiful it would look against the dark Tudor beams of the living room, decked with our old-fashioned decorations, the firelight glinting off the coloured glass. It would also be my first with Seth. In fact, everything was pretty close to perfect. Oh, I could moan about A levels and revision, but at bottom I was so happy it almost hurt. Sometimes I wondered what I'd done to deserve all this – it almost felt too good to last.

I was so wrapped up in thought that it was only the increasing pressure of Seth's arm on mine that warned me something was wrong. I looked across at him; his face was set in anxious lines and his pace had speeded up to an almost uncomfortably fast walk.

'What is it?' I asked.

'Shh,' he said, almost under his breath. 'Don't look round, but there are two men following us.'

In spite of his warning I turned and, sure enough, there were two men in hoodies walking casually behind us.

'They're probably just going our way,' I whispered back. Seth looked uneasy.

'Maybe, but they're going a very odd route. We've zigzagged around like anything, looking at the shops, and they've followed the whole way.'

'Let's turn back here,' I suggested, indicating a very small side street that led back in the direction of the restaurant. 'There's no way they could be going that way by chance. It's pointing directly back the way we came from. If they follow us down here we'll know for sure and we can knock on a door or something.'

Seth nodded and we turned down the alley. The two men behind turned too, one with a quick glance up and down the main street to see if anyone had noticed. Coldness coiled in the pit of my stomach and I suddenly got the feeling we'd been very, very stupid to turn off the beaten track. It was only when I heard Seth swear under his breath with a note of panic in his voice, that I realized quite how stupid we'd been. The alley was a dead end.

As we reached the end I felt Seth squeeze my hand. There was nothing for it. We'd have to face them. My stomach clenched as if the ground had shifted beneath our feet, and we turned around.

'Give us your phones,' said the taller of the two, his voice hissing from beneath his hood.

The words should have scared me, but instead I sighed with relief. They were only ordinary men – boys really. Not what I'd been fearing since I saw the shadows of their faces, dark beneath their hoods. And I could give them what they wanted. I fumbled in my bag, happy to hand over anything that would get us out of the alley.

'And yours.' He nodded at Seth.

Seth sighed and yanked his phone out of his pocket.

'Wallet.'

'You can have the cash,' Seth said, getting out his wallet and opening it, 'but not the wallet.'

'Shut up and hand the thing over.'

'Look, it's worthless. It's just a cheap leather wallet.' Seth held out a handful of notes. 'This is sixty quid cash – but leave me the wallet. You know I'll cancel the cards anyway.'

My heart was in my mouth and I had to clench my teeth to stop myself from screaming, 'Hand over the wallet, you idiot!' but I knew why he didn't want to – it was his dad's, one of the few things Seth had left since he died four years ago.

'Hand. Over. The wallet,' the bigger hoodie said, spitting each word like an insult. Seth shook his head. Then the smaller one sprang.

I screamed. For a short eternity there was a struggle, the sickening sound of fists hitting flesh and bone, and then the attacker staggered back and collapsed to the ground, blood pouring from his nose. Seth was panting, wringing his knuckles with pain from where he'd decked the boy, but otherwise unhurt. With his hood back it was clear the kid was a just a scrawny sixteen-year-old, pale from too many hours spent in front of the TV. He was no match for Seth, who spent every spare hour on the sea hauling on ropes and cables.

I was just about to run to Seth when I felt someone grab my hair from behind. There was the press of something cold at my throat. Seth went suddenly still, pale with fury, every muscle in his body tensed.

'Hand over the bloody wallet or do you want your girlfriend breathing out of a different hole?' the bigger guy whispered, the quiet hiss more frightening than any shout. I kept very still, feeling the chill of the blade against my throat as Seth took out the wallet and held it silently out. The guy let go of my hair to grab it and I stumbled forward to Seth.

'Tosser,' spat the hoodie, and he turned to leave. As he did, the knife flashed again. This time towards Seth.

Everything seemed to happen in slow motion. I saw the flash of the blade towards Seth's ribs, heard the rip of cloth and Seth's gasp of pain as he doubled up against the blow. Blood blossomed on his shirt. And I felt my power, so long suppressed, rise and boil and explode within me like a scream.

'*NO!*'

There was a flashing white blast, like a bomb blast, a rippling circle of power that pulsed outwards. The two hoodies were flung backwards, crashing against the alley walls with a sick smack like the sound of roadkill. The searing light burnt an image into my retinas: ragdoll bodies splayed against rough stone. Then darkness flooded back. As my eyes adjusted to the dim light I saw them both, lying quite still on the ground, bleeding from their nostrils and ears.

I staggered, my legs weak with the sudden expulsion of power, and then Seth was beside me, hugging me, gripping my face and my shoulders with fierce strength.

'Anna, Anna, are you all right?'

'I'm fine,' I gasped. 'Are you?'

He looked down at his shirt, torn and stained with blood, and then lifted it to inspect his ribs. A bloody gash crossed his side.

'It'll heal.'

'Ugh!' I sobbed. 'How could they? How could they? I was so frightened . . .'

We both looked down at the bodies and a new fear came over me.

'Do you think . . . ?'

'I don't know,' Seth said. He knelt gingerly beside the older boy and touched his neck. 'He's got a pulse.' He touched the other boy. 'They're both alive, thank God. I think you just knocked them out.'

He picked up the knife and wiped it clean on his bloody shirt, and then extricated his wallet and the phones from the older boy's grip. Then, from quite close by, we heard a police siren start up, and we both stiffened as if any movement might attract the car. It passed, heading on up the high street, and I heard Seth's shaky gasp of relief echo mine.

'We need to get out of here,' Seth said. 'Is there anything that could lead them back to us?'

'Just the knife, your blood . . .' I wiped it again

12

and then rinsed it in a puddle. It wouldn't help if they bothered with forensics, but I prayed it wouldn't come to that.

'Hopefully when they come to they'll just think they had a fight they can't remember,' Seth said, buttoning his coat over the bloodstains.

'*If* they come to.'

'They'll be *fine*,' Seth said with fierce emphasis. 'Anna, listen to me – they're both breathing; they'll be OK. Now come on, let's get out of here.'

We walked swiftly up the alleyway. The high street was empty as we left, and we made our way as quickly and inconspicuously as possible to the car. My hands were shaking with spent adrenalin.

In the car Seth started the engine. He was about to move off when I suddenly said, 'Wait, wait a sec . . .'

There was a phone box in the corner of the car park and I ran over to it and dialled 999.

'Ambulance,' I said breathlessly in response to the operator's question, and then when I was put through, 'Please send an ambulance to the alleyway off Brighthaven high street. I don't know what it's called, but it's a little dead end between Topshop and Milly's Tea Room. There are two men; they've been in a fight. They're unconscious but breathing.'

'Right. Can I take your name, please?' the operator asked.

I hung up and ran to the car.

In the car on the way back I was silent, trying to keep myself under control. Seth looked at me sideways in the darkness, and I could feel his concern.

'It's OK, Anna,' he said at last. 'It'll be OK.'

'You don't know that.' I stared into the golden tunnels of the headlights; a frightened rabbit leapt into the hedge with a flash of white scut. 'I ruined our evening; I ruined everything.'

'*Don't* say that,' Seth said angrily. 'You didn't ruin anything. Those blokes could have killed us both. You got us out of there the only way you could. Would we be having this conversation if you'd hit them over the head with a rock?'

Probably. But anyway there was one massive difference, and Seth knew it. I was a witch and the two boys were just ordinary people, outwith, with no powers to defend themselves. I'd used an illegal weapon in an unfair fight – and put myself and Seth in danger.

Ever since my run-in with the Ealdwitan last year I'd promised myself, once and for all, never to use magic again and, so far, it seemed to be working. I'd had no more terrifying visits from the Ealdwitan's grey-suited 'employees', no more back-door recruitment attempts, only a dry, official letter with an embossed crow crest, regretting 'an unfortunate incident in June of this year, in which certain of our personnel exceeded their responsibilities and committed certain errors of judgement'.

Those 'errors of judgement' had resulted in the death of one of our friends, the flooding of Winter town, and the destruction of most of Winter Castle. And it all stemmed from my inability to keep my powers under control.

The Ealdwitan's letter had promised 'no further action, providing our previous terms and conditions are adhered to'. Which meant, in plain English: no casting spells on ordinary people and no practising magic. It wasn't only the actions of the police we had to fear over tonight's outburst, but the fury of the Ealdwitan too, if they ever got to hear about it.

The drive back from Brighthaven was a longish one, and I'd got myself under control by the time Seth bumped down the wooded track to Wicker House. He drew up in front of the house and took my hand.

'Want me to come in?'

I shook my head, thinking of his bloody shirt and Dad's probable reaction.

'Better not. Your shirt. You know. Dad would ask questions.'

Seth nodded.

'OK. But listen, Anna, please don't fret about this. You did what you had to do. No one needs to know about this.'

I nodded soberly, but Seth must have read my unconvinced expression, because he pulled me to him and kissed me very hard.

'I love you, Anna. Please, please don't beat yourself up. Promise me? Sleep well, have a good day with Emmaline tomorrow and put this out of your head. Promise?'

'I promise,' I said, a lump in my throat.

CHAPTER TWO

I tried to keep my promise to Seth the next day, but I couldn't stop myself tuning to the local news at breakfast. Dad came down to find me listening to Coast FM and making toast on the Aga, and did a comical double-take in the kitchen doorway.

'What's this? Up before ten in the school holidays? And what's happened to the *Today* programme?'

'I fancied a change,' I said uncomfortably. 'And I'm up early because I'm going to London with Emmaline today, remember? I'm meeting her at the station at nine.'

'Of course, I'd forgotten. Do you need a lift?'

'I'll cycle,' I said, and then broke off as the news came on. Dad was chatting about the preparations he still had to make for Christmas: picking up the goose, cutting the holly and so on; but I wasn't paying attention. Instead I was listening desperately for any mention of two bodies found in an alleyway in Brighthaven. Nothing came up though, so at least they couldn't be dead. There was precious little real crime down here, other than small-scale shoplifting and kids dealing the odd bit of weed. One death, let alone two, would have kept the local news occupied for weeks. As the bulletin ended I gave a silent sigh of relief and turned my attention back to Dad.

'Sorry, Dad, what did you say?'

'I said, it's half eight. If you're going to make that train you'd better get a move on.'

'Cripes!' I looked at the clock above the Aga. 'I'd better fly. Bye, Dad.'

I kissed him and ran for the door, stopping only to grab my cycle helmet and rain mac. It looked like it was due for a downpour.

Emmaline was waiting on the platform when I ran up, hot and panting. She lowered her spectacles as I approached and stared at me haughtily over the lenses like a school teacher.

'Sorry, sorry,' I said, as she tapped her watch meaningfully. 'I got sidetracked.'

Emmaline snorted. 'You mean you slept in! Did you and Seth stay up too late declaring your undying love for each other?'

'Not exactly,' I said crossly, and told her about the scuffle in the alleyway. 'So I stayed to listen to the Coast FM bulletin.'

'And?'

'Nothing, thankfully.'

'So they're not dead,' Emmaline said thoughtfully. 'Sounds like you got away with it this time.'

'*This* time. But what about next time I slip up? I'm terrified, Em. It used to be such an effort to do any magic at all – now it's an effort *not* to. I can't control myself any more – electrical sparks, clouds of butterflies . . . Last night I made snow fall in the restaurant.'

The train drew up at that moment and there was a momentary scramble as we found seats and settled ourselves in a carriage. So close to Christmas there were few commuters and we managed to find a compartment to ourselves. I stowed our bags on the luggage rack and we drew out of the station to the sound of the guard's whistle.

Emmaline had obviously been thinking things over, because as soon as we were seated she said, 'Do you think you're taking the wrong tack?'

'What do you mean?'

'Over these . . . leakages, or whatever you want to call them.'

I snorted. 'Nice terminology! Shall I add incontinence pads to my Christmas list?'

Emmaline laughed.

'You know what I mean. I wonder if it's because you're trying too hard *not* to do any magic. So the power is building and building and it has to come out somehow, and it's escaping when you're concentrating on other things – moments of emotional stress or whatever. Small distraction, like, say, Mr Waters batting his lovely eyelashes at you, equals small leak; massive distraction, like, say, an attempted mugging, equals massive leak.'

I thought about her theory as the wintry countryside flashed past: dark wet fields, leafless trees, pools of morning mist in the hollows. The telegraph poles reflected the noise of the train like a human pulse.

'There could be something in that,' I said at last. 'So what's your solution?'

'Let it out, safely.'

'But what about—'

Emmaline didn't wait for me to finish, she didn't need to.

'Away from the outwith, so the Ealdwitan can't object. You could do worse than take up Mum's offer of lessons.'

She must have seen something in my face – dumb mutiny perhaps – because she leant forwards across the gap between the seats, suddenly serious, 'Look, I know you're doing some kind of normality kick, and I don't want to piss on your snowball, but you've *got* to get this under control. It's getting worse isn't it?' I nodded, tight-lipped. 'And your stress levels are only going to go up between now and A levels. What if something *really* serious happens and you totally crack?'

I looked away from her beseeching dark eyes, out of the window. Lessons. Witchcraft. Was I really ready to let go of my old life so completely? Did I have a choice?

'We could try,' I said at last. It was more to get her off my back than because I was convinced by her argument.

'OK. Good. Anyway, more importantly,' Emmaline changed the subject determinedly, 'what are we going to do in London?'

I made an effort to drag my mind back to pleasanter subjects.

'Well, Selfridges and then maybe Bond Street, I thought. Dad gave me some money for clothes and I'll probably find something there. And then Dad's asked me to get some stuff from Fortnum's for Christmas lunch, and I'm going to get him books, so we can nip to Hatchards. It's a bookshop,' I added in response to Em's single raised brow. 'What do you want to do?'

'I realize you're revelling in your role of sultry urbanista, but please try not to rub in the fact that I'm just a lowly provincial. All those sound good – I'm going to get Sienna clothes so Selfridges works for me, and Abe and Simon will get books so Hatchets sounds fine.'

'Hatchards,' I corrected automatically.

'Nobody likes a know-it-all, Anna. What are you getting Seth?'

'Oh, he's sorted. What about your mum?'

'I don't know . . . I thought something a bit different – an antique maybe. Is there anywhere, you know, kind of vintage, junk-shoppy?'

'Not on Piccadilly,' I said doubtfully. 'Unless you want to spend a couple of grand. But we could go to Portobello Market. It's right near where I used to live.'

We ended up wandering round Notting Hill, a mountain of shopping bags over each arm and hot bourek burning our hands in lieu of lunch.

'There's this bakery' – I spoke round a mouthful of scalding feta – 'that does these amazing little Portuguese custard tarts. It's just down this road. Shall we head there and we can have coffee and a tart for pudding?'

'You're so lucky,' Emmaline sighed, uncharacteristically soft with longing. 'Growing up round here, all these amazing shops, the cinemas, the nightclubs . . .'

'Not that I got much use out of the nightclubs at any rate,' I said regretfully. 'I left before they'd believe my false ID. Anyway, I'm not lucky any more; I'm just one of the lowly provincials too, remember?'

'But you'll go back, will you? For uni, I mean?'

'I don't know . . . maybe.' Ms Wright had pushed me into applying for Oxford, but I still wasn't sure – partly put off by the shady rumours of Ealdwitan involvement in some of the colleges, although I didn't want to admit that to Emmaline. But Dad had been up at Magdalen and I knew he'd burst with pride if I followed his footsteps. And then of course there was Seth, who wasn't likely to get into either Oxford or Cambridge with his results – and wouldn't have wanted to anyway. He planned to study Marine Biology and was applying to Plymouth, Bangor and UHI up in the far north of Scotland. Either way, I was unlikely to see much of him unless I was prepared to go to a coastal institute.

I looked around for something to change the subject and stopped dead in the street. We'd been wandering almost aimlessly towards the Portuguese bakery and I'd barely noticed where my feet had taken me.

'Emmaline – look! Look where we are!'

'What?' Emmaline looked up and down the road. 'It looks just like all the other streets. Is it famous?'

23

'It's *my* street – my street where Dad and I used to live.' I stopped outside number 31, gazing up at the long clean lines of the terraced house. 'And this is our house. I'm home!'

'This one?' Emmaline jerked her thumb at the dark-green door. 'This one right here was your house?'

I nodded.

'That's my room.' I pointed to the second floor; the little window still had a CND sticker on it from my passionate Green Party phase.

'Yuck.' Emmaline shuddered involuntarily and backed away into the road.

'What's with you?' I was suddenly deeply offended. This was the house where I was born, had grown up, where all my childhood memories were. I thought of me and Dad in the kitchen, baking my first fairy cakes, flat and burnt on top. I remembered climbing into his bed on Sunday mornings for hot milk and chocolate digestives, leaving chocolately handprints on his duvet and the *Sunday Times*. All the memories of my life before Winter, all bound up with this tall white house. It had been my home for more than seventeen years and, in some way, would always be home in a way that Winter never could. Every inch of me bristled at Emmaline's reaction.

'What on earth do you mean, yuck?'

'Anna, this place is just lousy with magic. Can't you feel it?'

With a great effort I took a step back from my nostalgia and looked at the house anew – as a witch.

She was right. A strange dead-feeling magical force was throbbing over the entire front of the house. I couldn't believe I'd never noticed it before – the stench of magic was like a physical slap in the face. Once I *had* noticed it, I couldn't suppress an echoing shudder of my own.

'What is it?'

'I've no idea, but it's coming from *there*.' Emmaline pointed distastefully at the front step of the house.

'Can't we find out what it is?' I asked.

'I think there must be something buried under there – it's too localized to be anything general. It must be a charm, I guess – no way of knowing without seeing it though.'

'So what are you saying – we need to dig it up?'

Emmaline nodded.

'But . . . but it's solid stone! And we haven't got so much as a spade!'

Emmaline rolled her eyes. 'Not with a spade, you divot. Have you forgotten your powers?'

'But . . . but *here*? In front of everyone?'

'Who's here?' Emmaline pointed out. 'Anyway I can shield us from any outwith who come past – it's not hard to do a deflecting spell.' She rapped on the door and listened for a moment. 'No one in the house, so that's good. Go on, you blast the step and I'll keep us hidden.'

She looked up and down the road and, as if on cue, an old lady's face peered curiously out of the window opposite. Emmaline pointed a finger at her imperiously; the lady's face went blank, and she turned back to her front room, suddenly quite uninterested.

'Go on!' Emmaline urged. 'This'll be a good test of my theory about your magical incontinence. Let a bit out and we'll see if you have any more leaks tonight.'

'Em, please, I don't want to.'

'For God's sake, why not?'

'Do you have to ask? After what happened last year?'

'Oh, come on! You haven't heard from the Ealdwitan in months. I don't believe it's anything to do with them; this is about you trying to pretend you're an outwith so you can be the perfect couple with Seth. Anyway, you didn't have any qualms about blasting them to shards last summer, did you?'

'That wasn't a choice, it was a necessity.'

'Well, try this for necessity,' Em said. 'I'm going to lift that step; if you value your continued liberty from the

Ealdwitan then give me a shield.' She pointed a finger at the step and raised an eyebrow.

'I don't know how!'

'Oh, of course you do, it's not hard. Just, you know, think blanketing thoughts. If anyone looks out, tell them that there's nothing to worry about. Ready?'

I stiffened, ready to shield us from any passers-by – but nothing happened. I could feel my power throbbing with painful intensity in the core of my body, but I couldn't access it. It was like being in the loo and desperately needing a pee, but hearing someone in the stall next door and being unable to let go.

Emmaline pointed her finger at the step and I yelped out, 'Stop!'

'What?'

'I can't do it!' I said desperately. 'I can't get it out. My magic, it's like it's trapped.'

'Don't be an idiot,' Em said shortly. 'You're just worried because of what happened last night. Don't force it – just relax.'

I shook myself, took a few deep breaths, and tried to let the magic flow. Nothing. Nothing. Nothing! What was happening?

'Anna, I'm warning you, I'm lifting that step in five . . . four . . . three . . .'

'I can't!' I gasped. 'I don't know what's wrong, but I just can't. Someone's going to see us.'

'Oh, for God's sake, do I have to do everything around here?' Emmaline snapped. Her shoulders tensed and I could see she was concentrating desperately on shielding, while still trying to maintain enough of her power to lift the step. There was a moment's internal struggle, and then a crack, and the earth erupted in a small quiet volcano, rich soil bubbling up through the snapped stonework. Emmaline gave a great sigh of relief and we both hurried forwards to examine the earth. There, in the middle, was a stained oilskin packet, caked in dirt and tied up with red string. It stank of magic so strongly I could hardly bear to touch it, but with a great effort I snatched it up and shoved it in a shopping bag. Then, with a glance up and down the street, Emmaline crushed the earth back down and smoothed the stone step back in place, and the house and its porch looked just as it'd always done for all the years I'd lived there.

At the Portuguese bakery we ordered custard tarts and coffee, although I really didn't need anything likely to make my hands shake any more, and then sat at a quiet table in the little back room. I was too preoccupied to drink. The packet felt like it was burning a hole in the plastic shopping bag.

'What are we going to do with . . . *it*?' I asked at last in a low voice.

'I don't know.' Emmaline bit her nail. 'I wish we knew what it was. It feels . . . bad. I think we have to open it.'

'What – here?' I said incredulously. 'But what if there's some kind of dreadful magic that leaks out – kills someone maybe?'

'I don't *think* it'll be anything harmful to the outwith – I mean, it's been under your step for a while, by the looks of things, and all your neighbours seem to be OK. If there's any danger I'd say it'd be to you or me. But what choices have we got – dump it here or take it home, basically, right?'

'We can't dump it here,' I said instantly. Emmaline nodded grimly.

'And I'm not letting you carry it back to Winter without checking it out. Besides, don't you want to know what's been hiding under your step all these years? Don't you want to see?'

I did. I did want to see. I lifted the bag on to the table and fished inside.

In spite of her encouragement Emmaline fell back at the reek of magic. So did I. The small packet throbbed with a bizarre numbing sensation that I'd never encountered before. I could hardly bring myself to bend closer, but I forced myself to pick at the knot of red string, and then peeled back the crusted oilskin, my eyes watering all the time.

'For goodness' sake.' Emmaline was leaning as far back in her chair as she could go, her face averted from the parcel. 'Get it over with. Just look and then get it back in the bag.'

Through my watery eyes I could see scraps of something – some kind of parchment. There seemed to be two pieces, and as I unfolded the first I saw writing on it – small spidery letters draggling across the page. But the characters swam in front of my eyes and I couldn't make out the words – in fact, they barely looked like letters at all.

'I can't read it, can you?' I pushed the paper towards Em and she recoiled hastily.

'Anna, please! Get that thing out of my face! No, I can't read it either. It looks like . . .' Mastering her disgust she peered closer, her eyes watering just as mine had with the effort of getting so near. 'It looks like Greek, or maybe Russian?' Then revulsion took over and she pushed it away. 'Put it back in the bag; I'm sorry I asked you to look. This is beyond me – I don't know what it is at all.

Just . . . just wrap it up. We'll take it home; maybe Mum will know what to do.'

I folded it up, wrapped it as securely as I could, and then tied it in the thickest plastic bag and shoved it to the bottom of my shopping bag. Emmaline shuddered and wiped her hands involuntarily on her denim miniskirt where she'd touched it. Then we downed our coffees, paid our bill and left, glad to be back in the fresh air at last.

CHAPTER THREE

'What in heaven's name is that *foul* magic?' Maya was at the door as we climbed the steps to the flat, weary in body and soul from the ceaseless stench of the packet battering at us all the way home.

'You may well ask,' Emmaline said dourly. 'A little souvenir from Anna's old house.'

I opened the carrier to show Maya the packet and she reeled back.

'Good grief, what possessed you to bring it here? What if it's dangerous?'

'We dug it up out of Anna's front step,' Em said. 'We could hardly dump it on the street.'

'No, but . . . oh, Lord.' Maya put her hand to her head as if warding off a headache. 'Why on earth did you dig it up? No – don't answer that. I can see that you needed to know . . . but what are we going to do?'

'We hoped you'd have an idea.' Emmaline's face crumpled and she looked suddenly frightened. 'It's written magic but in a foreign script – Russian, I think. We couldn't read it.'

'OK, OK, let's think. Simon maybe? It's his sort of thing – he might be able to read it, or failing that maybe he'll know how to safely dispose of it.'

'Fantastic idea,' Emmaline said gratefully. 'I'll ring him now.'

She went to the phone in the corner of the flat. While she dialled, Maya rolled up the carrier and put it on the windowsill outside the flat, closing the window and the curtains too. It did little to hide the reek but shutting out the sight was somehow comforting.

With the curtains drawn the place was suddenly dim and I watched Maya as she moved about lighting lamps and candles until the ramshackle cavern was filled with the gleam of light on copper pans, the glint of crystal and prism. Maya was holding a match to the last lamp when the screech of a boiling kettle split the air and we both jumped.

'I think we all need a hot drink,' Maya said. She poured water into the little earthen pot and the comforting smell of spices rose up. 'Here, drink this.'

She handed me a mug and we sat down at the corner

of the long table, listening to Emmaline's side of the conversation with Simon.

'So, aside from your little archaeological dig, how was your day?' Maya said as I drained the cup with a grateful sigh, feeling the spices do all kinds of good things for my weary muscles and strained nerves. I had my suspicions about Maya's tea, for all her edicts about not misusing magic.

'Good,' I answered slowly. 'Good shopping. It took my mind off last night, anyway.'

'Last night?' Maya asked. I told her about the night before, the men in the alley – staring deliberately into the depths of the mug, so that I wouldn't have to face her horrified expression.

'Oh, darling . . .' Maya put a hand on my shoulder as I finished. I felt magic flow out of her, tendrils of reassurance and calm burrowing into my skin and bone, a flow of power designed to soothe and gentle.

But I shrugged ungratefully and she took it away, a flicker of sadness crossing her face, though I could see she was trying not to be offended. For her, spelling out her love was no different to giving someone a hug to comfort them, and I sighed.

'I'm sorry, Maya. I didn't mean . . . I don't mean . . .'

'I know.' She put an arm around me. 'Is that better?'

I nodded and felt tears well up as her strong, slim arm hugged my shoulders.

'Emmaline thinks I'm incontinent,' I said, with an attempt at a laugh. Maya smiled back, cheering me in my attempt to be cheerful, but there was concern underneath.

'That's one way of looking at it, I suppose. But she's right, in that power will find a way. If you don't master it, it will master you. And that's a bad situation to find yourself in.'

'It won't master me,' I said fiercely. Maya looked at me, her face serious in the candlelight.

'Are you sure? Anna, in your head you may still be nine-tenths outwith, but your heart knows what you are. You're—'

She stopped as there was a pounding at the street door and Emmaline jumped up from the window seat, her nails in her mouth.

'Is that . . . ?' Maya looked startled. 'That was quick.'

Emmaline gave a nod.

'Yes. I caught him on his way home.'

The sound of feet on the stairs, and then Simon's long, serious face with its black beard and Roman nose peered round the door, wearing an uncharacteristically excited expression.

'Good evening, ladies. Well, no need to ask where that

parcel is.' He nodded at the window. 'From the reek coming from over there, I assume it's behind the curtains?'

'Outside the window actually.' Maya rose to open the sash and retrieved the carrier, holding it by the tips of her fingers.

'We're hoping you'll take it away and magically deodorize it or something,' Emmaline said.

'Well, I can't promise that but I'll do my best.' He began to unravel the carrier.

'Hi, Simon, how are you? How nice to see you. How's my sister? Yes, fine, thanks and you?' Emmaline said sarcastically.

'Sorry,' Simon said mildly. 'I realize I'm skipping the small talk here, but as you know, I rather like written charms so this is quite interesting. In fact the power is—' He stopped and choked as the bag fell away and the full force of the magic flowed into the room, 'Qu-quite beyond anything I've experienced. Good Lord, what *is* it?'

He was picking at the red threads I had loosely retied. As the parcel fell apart he peered at the scraps of parchment. It was a measure of his enthusiasm that he managed to examine them so closely.

'What's the writing?' Emmaline asked from the other side of the room.

'Russian. I know the characters but I'm not very

proficient in the language. It's something like: *Let the witch of the living* . . . No, hang on, *the witch dwelling here* . . . What's that word – *harmed*? No, wait. Let me read that again.'

He sat hunched over the page for what seemed like an age, occasionally tapping words into his phone and presumably getting online translations or something. At last he raised his head. His face was pink above his black beard and his eyes sparkled.

'Well, the first piece reads something like: *Let the witch who dwells herein be crippled in magic; let her be as those without magic for as long as she call this place home.* And the second piece is harder to translate but I'd stab at something like: *Let those who dwell herein be as twigs within a forest, as feathers in a mattress, as rain upon the sea. For bone and stone and stick, for plate and water and inner eye, let this be so.*'

There was a moment's silence and then Emmaline said wonderingly, 'What the hell does that mean?'

'The first bit is pretty clear, I'd say. You did say you found it under Anna's old house?' We both nodded. 'Well, it solves one riddle at any rate, doesn't it?'

'It doesn't solve anything!' Emmaline exclaimed. 'Who put it there? Why? When? Did they want to harm Anna? I can't see that it solves anything!'

'It solves the riddle of why Anna's powers manifested so strangely,' Maya said slowly. 'Isn't that what you mean, Simon?'

He nodded, looking at me. 'Yes, as long as you thought of home as London, this little charm was crippling your magic. When you moved to Winter and gradually stopped thinking of London as home, your powers recovered. The more at home you feel in Winter, the greater your powers become.'

'Of course . . .' I said slowly. 'And that was why I couldn't use my magic to break the step, back in London. For a moment I felt like I was home. I even said it – do you remember, Emmaline?'

Emmaline struck her hand on her forehead, 'Of course – I'm such a doofus. And that must be why you didn't notice it at first, or while you lived there. I couldn't work out how anyone could live within a hundred yards of that charm and not feel like a dying duck but, without magic, you wouldn't feel its effects.'

'Yes, it's quite a clever catch twenty-two,' Simon said. 'Without magic you can't detect it – and without detecting it you can't recover your magic. Even if you leave temporarily, as long as you think of the place as home it will work its magic. It's only the chance fact of your moving away for good, Anna, that saved you.'

Saved me? I would have laughed, if I hadn't felt so bitter. Had I really been *saved* from a life without magic? It wasn't the word I'd have chosen. But Simon obviously saw it quite differently – to him I'd been rescued by chance from . . . what? Obscurity? Normality?

Emmaline's voice broke into my thoughts. 'And what about the other one?'

For a moment I wasn't sure what she was speaking about, but then I remembered: the other parchment.

'Ah,' Simon said. 'Well, I'm guessing it's some kind of confusion charm, perhaps designed to give some protection from people scrying for your location. But I don't know what's been lost in translation. I'd need to get someone else to look at it. There may have been subtler implications in the original Russian.'

That last word recalled me to something that had been puzzling me from the first.

'Of course – they were written in *Russian*. Why would that be?'

'I don't know.' Simon was frowning now. 'But to me that seems one of the more worrying and puzzling aspects of the whole business.'

'Worrying?' I asked.

'I'm more concerned about the strength of the charm,' Maya said. Her eyes met Simon's and the anxiety in their faces made them a strange mirror, in spite of their dissimilarity.

'Yes,' Simon said. 'That is a poser, I must admit. This is power the likes of which I've rarely seen. I don't personally know of anyone who could perform a charm like this, even in teamwork. The kind of talent required to pull off something on this scale is *extremely* rare. But it's rumoured that there are certain . . . techniques.' I wondered at the uneasiness in his voice. 'Methods of increasing the power of individuals.'

He exchanged another look with Maya that made the back of my neck prickle with cold, and I didn't ask, but Maya must have seen my expression for she came and sat beside me on the sofa and put her arm comfortingly around my shoulders.

'Try not to worry too much, Anna. We don't know what's behind it, but whoever did it, they've been content to leave you alone for nearly eighteen years. Let's hope that continues.'

'And it's quite possible,' Simon put in, 'that it was directed at a previous inhabitant of the house – maybe your dad just stumbled on to it.'

'Maybe,' I said dubiously.

'You don't sound convinced?' Simon asked.

'Not really – it's just that I'm pretty sure Dad bought

the house while he was still with my mum, who *was* a witch, as far as I know. So it seems quite unlikely that she could have moved in and not noticed.'

'But you don't know for sure, do you?' Emmaline asked. I shook my head.

'No, I don't really know anything. Dad's never told me a thing about her.'

'Well . . .' Simon spread his hands. 'I don't think there's any point in fretting about this. If you all agree I'll take the parchments back to the university, see if there's anything else we can discover, try to contain the power somehow. Is that OK?'

'OK?' Emmaline raised one eyebrow. 'Simon, it's the main reason we invited you. Go, and take that thing with you.'

'Anna, is that all right?'

'Me?' I looked up, startled. 'What are you asking me for?'

'Well, it's yours, if it's anyone's, I guess.'

'Take it,' I shuddered. 'Do what you like. I never want to see it again.'

We waved him off down the stairs. The feeling of relief as the parcel disappeared down the road was like the passing of a thunderstorm. Emmaline wriggled her shoulders like someone shrugging off a heavy rucksack.

'Thank goodness for that; it's gone! Out of sight, out of mind.'

Out of sight maybe, I silently corrected, but not out of mind. In fact I thought of little else, as I cycled the long, dark miles back to Wicker House.

CHAPTER FOUR

Luckily I had plenty to keep my mind off the packet over the next couple of days, what with wrapping presents, cutting holly and ivy for the house, putting up the tree and helping Dad with preparations for Christmas lunch. Four of Dad's friends from London were coming down, so we were making a special effort.

I always felt, not jealous exactly, but a little wistful when friends had great tribes of relatives descending on them for huge family celebrations. Dad was an only child, like me, and his parents were both dead. As for my mother's side of the family, I didn't even know their surname, let alone if they were alive. Dad had never let a single piece of information about his dead wife pass his lips since the day she disappeared.

In between jobs I thought about asking Dad about the buried parchment, but I couldn't seem to start the conversation. It wasn't just his resolute silence about my mother – it was the practicalities of phrasing the question without sounding like I was off my trolley. I didn't think, 'Dad, did you ever see a witch digging under our front step?' would do the trick. Besides, any witch who could perform that charm could certainly deflect outwith eyes while they concealed the packet – it was highly unlikely Dad would have noticed anything, even if he was sitting in the front room at the time. Still, for a couple of days I toyed with the idea of asking – until our Christmas guests turned up, which put the conversation well and truly out of bounds.

James and his wife Lorna, and Rick and his partner Ben, arrived on Christmas Eve bearing a mountain of presents and two enormous boxes of food and drink – as if we didn't have enough already.

I was doing my homework in my room when I heard their cars draw up and by the time I came downstairs Ben was already unpacking a bulging Harrods bag on to the kitchen table.

'Dates, figs, chocolate-dipped orange peel, bag of walnuts – hope you've got nutcrackers, Tom – kumquats, cranberry preserve, Christmas tea – nasty stuff I think but Rick loves it – marmalade, er, what else have we got? Oh yes, here's the Fortnum's bag – that needs to go in the fridge, it's got the foie gras and the smoked salmon in it. Rick's bringing up the rear with the champagne.'

'Ben, you've got enough to feed an army,' Lorna protested.

'An army of gluttons,' Dad agreed.

'Well, glutton number one's here,' I said from the kitchen doorway.

'Anna, darling!' Ben kissed me exuberantly on each cheek. He was one of my favourite honorary uncles – Dad had known Ben and Rick since university and my childhood birthdays had been peppered with their wildly over-extravagant and fabulously unsuitable presents. My favourite had been a Dior handbag I'd received for my sixth birthday.

'Hello, Anna!' Lorna gave me an affectionate peck. 'How're you? How's the new school?'

'Great,' I said. 'Not so new any more, really. I feel quite at home.'

'Enjoying the civilizing influence of the male sex are you? Ho ho!' James guffawed. This was his idea of humour as my previous school in London had been an all-girls private school, while Winter High was a co-ed state school.

Dad smirked from the corner. 'Anna's got a boyfriend.'

'Dad!' I groaned.

'What? I was merely stating a fact.'

'I hope you've horse-whipped the presumptuous young fellow?' Ben wanted to know. 'Or are you leaving the kinky stuff to Anna?'

Dad chose to ignore the second part of his remark and merely said, 'Seth is a very nice young man, and I thoroughly approve. Perhaps he'll be over this Christmas and you can meet him. Anna, will we be seeing Seth?'

'Mmph,' I muttered crossly. Dad's enthusiasm for Seth bordered on the unseemly, in my opinion. I'd lost count of the number of times I'd come home to find Dad and Seth side by side on the sofa watching the cricket highlights and earnestly discussing England's hopes in the Ashes, or companionably tinkering with some piece of misbehaving plumbing. Wicker House was a work in progress – far from the wreck it had been when we moved in, but not nearly complete – and Dad was not above co-opting Seth as occasional chippy and plumber's mate. It was all deeply creepy. Surely fathers were supposed to hate their daughters' boyfriends? And Seth was equally to blame. It was all 'Tom said this' and 'Tom reckons that'.

'Is that "yes mmph" or "no mmph"?' Dad enquired.

'Maybe mmph. I'm seeing him tonight, if that's OK, but it depends what his mum's plans are for tomorrow.'

'Invite them over for a drink, why don't you?'

'Mmm . . .' I bit my lip. 'I'm not sure . . .'

'Why ever not?' Dad looked a touch offended. 'I'd like to see Elaine.'

'Oh, it's not Elaine,' I hastened to explain. 'It's Bran, Seth's grandfather. He's staying with them for Christmas and . . .' I trailed off, not sure how to say, 'And he doesn't approve of me because I'm a witch so I doubt he'll agree to cross our threshold.' I tried to think of a way of rephrasing Bran's vehement hatred – one that didn't make him sound senile.

'Darling,' Ben put a hand on my arm and lowered his voice a dramatic octave, 'don't tell me, is he . . . a *homophobe*?'

'Oh for God's sake.' Rick hit him with a baguette. 'Leave the poor girl alone. She doesn't want her dad's aged mates cramping her style and who can blame her?'

'No, it's not that, honestly,' I hastened, even though I knew they were both joking. 'It's just that Seth's grandfather . . . he doesn't approve of me. He doesn't think I'm the right girl for Seth. And since he's staying, I don't really want to cause a family argument at Christmas so I've agreed to see Seth tonight in the pub and then I might leave it at that. I'll just see how it goes, OK?'

'Anna!' Ben's silliness had gone as he wrapped me in a warm Gaultier-scented hug. 'Who could disapprove of you? In that case I positively decline to share even a single drop of Veuve Clicquot with the silly old goat. If he turns up we'll make him sit in the garden and drink rainwater.'

I squeezed him back. And then, as Ben pointed meaningfully at the ceiling where the mistletoe hung, swaying gently in the warm air from the Aga, I gave him a kiss on the cheek.

At eight p.m. I left Dad and the others comfortably ensconced in front of the roaring fire in the living room, arguing about whether Quorn was a valid word in Scrabble, and got on my ancient bike to cycle off to the Crown and Anchor, where Seth was helping behind the bar. I hadn't expected it to be particularly busy but, by some mysterious form of teenage ESP, it looked like most of the Winter High sixth form had congregated there in a spontaneous Christmas Eve 'my parents are driving me nuts' meet up.

I said hello to at least three people from school as I padlocked my bike to the beer garden fence and bumped into half a dozen more in the saloon bar. Sitting in an alcove by the fireplace were June, Prue and Liz, along with two boys I didn't know. June looked very pink and happy, her round face shining under her deep fringe.

Things had been a little funny with them since last

year – they'd been the first at Winter High to befriend me and then, from their perspective, I'd made off with the best-looking boy in the school and taken up with the aloof, sarcastic Emmaline Peller, leaving them without a backward glance. And the worst thing was, I could never explain. But when I gave a tentative wave, they smiled back, and June called, 'Anna, this is Philip – Philip Granger.'

Philip Granger? She looked as if she was about to burst with pride and, as I drew closer, I saw they were hand in hand. For a minute I felt a huge throb of resentment – it was June, with her sodding crush on Philip Granger, who'd persuaded us to try that stupid love spell in the first place. Of course, the charm had had no effect on him whatsoever since June wasn't a witch. And now she'd got it all anyway, without any of the horrors and guilt I'd had to suffer over Seth . . .

I sighed. There was no point in blaming June for my own mistakes. I had Seth. She had Philip. It was water under the bridge.

'Nice to meet you at last,' I said. And I meant it.

Then I saw Seth, signalling to me over the heads of the customers at the bar. I smiled goodbye and threaded my way through the throng of students to where Seth was handing out drinks and taking change.

'Sorry, Jack,' he was saying to one pink-faced lower sixth-former. 'You and me both know you're only seventeen. Please don't do this, mate. It's just embarrassing for us both.'

'Anna's only seventeen,' Jack grumbled. 'I don't see you throwing her out – or is it different rules for your girlfriends?'

'Well, Anna's not buying alcohol,' Seth said. I could see his temper was fraying. He hated having to refuse school friends. 'Come on, Jack. Just get a soft drink or go somewhere else.'

'Fine.' Jack stomped away from the bar and I elbowed into his place. Seth flashed me a relieved smile.

'Hello, gorgeous. Don't, whatever you do, show me a bad fake ID and claim to be twenty-four, will you?'

'I won't,' I promised. 'I'll just have a Coke.'

Seth poured me the Coke but wouldn't take any money. I made a mental note to stick it in the staff tips jar later.

'I've got your present.' I patted my shoulder bag. Seth smacked his forehead.

'Oh damn, I left yours upstairs.' He glanced up and down the heaving bar. 'I don't think I can knock off with the queue like this . . . Tell you what, wait until Tim comes back from his break and then we'll swap, how's that?'

'Fine. Come and find me when you're done.' I bent over the bar on tiptoes and brushed his lips. It was only intended to be a peck but he gripped the back of my head and gave me a full-on passionate kiss. There were wolf whistles from up and down the bar and a bloke shouted, 'I'll give you one of those, mate, if you'll serve me next!' A girl called out, 'I'll have whatever she ordered!'

I broke away, blushing crossly, and glared at Seth over the soda siphon. I was still not used to his triumphant happiness with our status as a couple and his willingness to advertise our togetherness to the whole of Winter. Certainly Seth's ex, Caroline, hadn't forgiven me, even six months on, and there were plenty of others who continued to resent me as the outsider from London, swanning in and pinching the school hottie. I fought the urge to look over my shoulder to check for hostility on people's faces or – even worse – the sight of snow, rain or some other magical disturbance breaking over the bar. Seth, however, had no such worries and grinned unrepentantly.

'See you shortly.'

Hmph. I retreated with my drink to a quiet corner. But I'd barely sat down when I heard a familiar voice.

'Well, well, well. If it isn't my favourite witch.'

'What?' I spun round, almost knocking over my Coke.

51

Simon's brother, Abe, stood behind me, his wild black hair even more unruly than usual, his mouth twisted into a wry half-smile.

'Abe!' I wasn't sure whether to laugh or hit him. 'Keep your voice down.'

'Oh, relax. None of these drunkards would know a witch if she hit them between the eyebrows with her broomstick. Although from what Emmaline tells me, it sounds like you're more prone to just fuse the lights or make it rain beer.'

'She told you, did she?'

'She said you were having a little bit of trouble. I think her exact words were, "Anna's suffering from incontinence" – or is that a separate problem?'

'Shut up!' I couldn't help laughing; he was so impossible. 'No, that's not a separate problem, thanks very much.'

'Oh good, so you can still laugh without crossing your legs? That must be a relief to all concerned. Mind if I sit down?' He indicated the bar stool next to me with his dripping pint and I waved a hand.

'Please, feel free. Make yourself at home.'

He sat and looked at me thoughtfully as he sipped his beer.

'So what's the plan? Tena Lady?'

'Emmaline thinks I need lessons. To help with the incontinence.'

'Lessons?' Abe snorted. 'From who – Maya?' I nodded and he took another pull of beer, shaking his head as he swallowed. 'There's nothing she can teach you.'

'Abe, that's rubbish, and you know it.'

'OK, let me rephrase that. There may be stuff that she can teach you, but I highly doubt that's the problem. Granted, you probably don't know a whole lot about the effect of St John's wort on sleeping charms, but so what? You've more natural ability in your little finger than most witches have in their whole body. You could control yourself, me, Emmaline, this whole room if you wanted to. But you don't. The question is, why not?'

'I promised . . .' I said in a low voice.

'Who?'

'The Ealdwitan, for a start.' I felt again that sickening jolt of fear in the alleyway when the hooded boys had come towards us; the nauseating terror before I'd realized they were nothing to do with the Ealdwitan, just outwith kids. There was no way I was risking their shadowy wrath again. The danger from my leaky powers was nothing compared to their fury if I started deliberately casting spells – I'd just have to try harder to keep myself in hand.

'Hmm.' Abe studied my face over the top of his glass

for a long minute, his black eyes disquieting, intense. Then he changed the subject. 'Where's loverboy then?'

'He's behind the bar.' I nodded towards Seth, pulling a pint with one hand and draining an optic with the other. Abe made a face.

'Great, so we'll be getting his company later? There's something to encourage me to drink up.'

I ignored his jibe and only said, 'He might join us, depends how busy it is. Where's Emmaline?'

'At the bar. No, I tell a lie; here she is.' He waved an arm as she turned from the bar with a frosted glass and a packet of crisps in one hand, 'Em, over here.'

'Hello, Anna.' Emmaline squeezed up to the tiny table. 'Merry Christmas.'

'Merry Christmas to you too. Thanks for telling Abe about my little problem.'

'Hey,' Emmaline bowed her head in mock seriousness, but there was an amused smile at the corner of her mouth, 'a problem shared is a problem halved, you know.'

'Well, thanks for being so caring.'

'Did you tell him about the parcel under your step?' Emmaline wanted to know.

Abe said, 'Already heard, from Simon. He's not happy.'

'Nobody's very happy, dur-brain, least of all Anna,

I imagine. It's just so weird. Why would anyone put it there?'

'As I see it there are three possibilities.' Abe raised three fingers to tick them off. 'One, to help you, Anna. Two, to harm you. Three, it's nothing to do with you and was there before you moved in.'

'But like Anna said – how could her mother have moved in without noticing a reek like that?' Emmaline asked. 'Someone *must* have put it there after her mother left, when Anna was small.'

I took a deep breath.

'About that. About my mother . . .'

'Yes?'

'I think . . . I think . . .'

'Oh my God,' Abe said slowly. His black eyes met mine, and I saw a kind of horrified understanding there.

'What? What about your mother?' Emmaline looked from his face to mine. 'Hang on – you don't think . . . your *mother* did this?'

'It seems like the most logical explanation,' I said. 'She left – and before she did, she buried a charm to hide us and . . .'

'And a charm to *cripple* you?' Emmaline finished incredulously. She was shaking her head, her face twisted with disgust. It was as if . . . as if I'd suggested that my mother had cut off one of my hands as a keepsake. 'The hiding charm, yes. That I can see; it might be to protect you in some way. But stunting your magic like that, deliberately? Why, *why*? It's such a hideous, horrible thing to do – what kind of mother would do that to her newborn baby?'

What kind of mother would run away and leave her newborn baby? That was what I wanted to say. But I bit my tongue and only shook my head.

'Did your dad know anything about it?' Emmaline asked. I shook my head again, more bitterly this time.

'I couldn't ask him . . . I know, I know.' I held up my hands. 'But, Emmaline, it's not like I haven't tried. I've asked and asked him about my mum. But it's like he *can't* tell me – he's just a brick wall. I don't know what to do.'

'You'll have to try again,' Em said flatly. 'If this – this *thing* is true . . .' She trailed off, shaking her head, and her expression confirmed what I'd already guessed; that charm was not a step anyone would take lightly, least of all a parent.

So, why? Why had she done it?

There was only one way to find the answer: start delving into the past. Find out the truth about my mother's life, and death, and what had set her running.

'Is there anyone else you could ask?' Abe put in.

I shook my head. 'My dad's lost contact with my mother's family – or severed it, I don't know which. And I can't trace them. I don't even know her maiden name.'

'It'd be on your birth certificate, wouldn't it?' Emmaline asked. I shook my head again.

'Not on the version I've seen – it's just a little thing with my name and date of birth and stuff.'

'That's the short version,' Abe said. 'There's a longer version, an A4 sheet with more information. You have to write off for it, I think. But depending on the surname I don't know that it'd get you much further – if you know she was Jane Smith then that doesn't help a whole lot. Is there really no one else you can ask?'

'No, well . . .' A thought suddenly struck me. James, Lorna, Ben and Rick had all known Dad for years. Could I . . . ? Did I dare? They were all leaving on Boxing Day – that gave me tomorrow, basically, to find out. 'There might be someone . . . I don't know. I'll have to think about it.'

The problem was they'd undoubtedly be worried about stepping on my dad's toes and telling me secrets that were not theirs to share. I'd have to be very tactful about who I approached, and how. Lorna perhaps? Could I pull some kind of fellow-female appeal, motherless girl, surrogate mum, schtick? But Lorna was pretty discreet, besides which I wasn't completely sure how far back she and Dad went. I couldn't bear the idea of screwing up my courage to ask, all for nothing.

Ben was probably the best bet. He'd been at Oxford with Dad so chances were, he must have met my mum. But would he know much? He'd lived in New York for several years after university. Perhaps that period covered my parents' brief marriage?

I was staring into space, only half listening to Emmaline and Abe's good-natured bickering, when a flash of red at the bar caught my eye and I saw a red-headed girl leaning confidentially over the bar to speak to Seth. It was the girl from the restaurant.

I bit my lip as she bent over, her breasts almost spilling out of her low-cut top. She was incredibly striking, with wide dark eyes made up with smoky eyeshadow so they looked even bigger and more soulful, and her flame-coloured hair spilt over her shoulders and back like a mane of fire. She was whispering something to Seth.

'What?' I saw him yell back irritably. 'Can you speak up? I can't hear you.'

She beckoned him over the bar and he leant forward. Then she grabbed his collar and pulled him towards her, her lips at his ear. I didn't quite see what happened next, but I could guess. Seth sprang back with a mixture of shock and astonishment in his face, wiping at his ear reflexively with a bar towel. There was a streak of her lipstick from his ear right across his cheekbone and the girl was laughing, her tongue caught provocatively between her teeth. I felt my cheeks flush scarlet with anger.

She said something else and I saw Seth shake his head and point to me, seated in the corner. Then he turned away to serve another customer. The girl shrugged and started to scribble something on a beer mat. Seth just ignored her. He stretched up to get a beer glass from the rack, his T-shirt riding up to expose a slice of tanned skin and an arrow of dark hair, and the girl leant across the bar and pushed the beer mat down the front of his jeans, behind the broad silver buckle of his belt. I gasped. Seth jumped convulsively and dropped the beer glass, sending shards of glass skittering across the floor.

Fury exploded inside me. How dare she? How *dare* she!

Out of nowhere came a terrible smell of scorching. Smoke filled the bar and the girl gave a scream, clutching at the back of her head.

'My hair! My hair's on fire!'

There was an immediate hubbub – someone threw a drink, someone else batted at the sparks with their hands.

The girl was weeping now, her hair drenched with beer, and her friends clustered around patting her back.

'Zoe, are you OK?'

'What happened?'

'It must have been someone with a cigarette – who's smoking in here?'

Seth just stood and watched with his mouth open and eventually leant across the bar to ask, 'Are you OK? Is there anything I can do?'

'She's fine.' One of the girl's friends put her arm around the heavily sobbing Zoe. 'She's had too much to drink. I'll take her outside.' She raised her voice. 'Whoever's smoking in here, I hope you're bloody proud of yourself. There's a reason it was banned, you know.'

She glared around the bar and then ushered the still-sobbing Zoe outside.

Emmaline looked at me. I had my hands to my face, covering my flaming cheeks.

'Anna?'

'Oh God, Emmaline. What's happening to me?'

Emmaline shook her head and her mouth compressed into a grim line. 'It's not working, Anna. All this pretending to be a normal person, whatever normal is. You're not. And your body knows you're not. Just admit what you are and stop pretending.'

She looked over my shoulder as she spoke and her expression changed, to something halfway between disgust and resignation.

'I've got to go anyway. Abe?'

Abe looked past me and nodded.

'I'll drop you. I'll be over the limit if I have another one anyway. See you later, Anna. Bah humbug and all that.'

I turned to see what had changed their mood. It was Seth.

'What sent them scurrying off so fast?' Seth asked as he slid in beside me. I shrugged, but in reality I knew. What made it worse, from their perspective, was that I was spilling not just my own secrets, but theirs too. Seth had seen too much, knew too much to be safe.

'Em's just tired,' I lied. Then my heart wrung as I saw how shattered he looked, the shadows under his dark eyes, his T-shirt drenched with sweat from working the bar all night. 'How are you?'

'Knackered.' He ran a hand through his hair, twisting the curls into a tousled, sweaty mess. 'Completely knackered. I spent all day trying to get this sodding Chemistry homework done and then all night working here. And then that stupid bloody girl! Sticking her tongue in my ear . . .' He shuddered. 'And how the hell did she get her hair set on fire?'

I put my head in my hands, unable even to begin to answer that. Seth saw my face and began to shake his head.

'No, no, you were nowhere near her! Anna, don't do this to yourself. You've got to stop thinking that everything bad that happens in a fifty-mile radius is to do with you.'

'She was flirting with you,' I said in a voice that sounded cold and hard even to my own ears.

'Anna, this is not you.' He took my face in his hands. 'You are a *good* person. I know you are.'

'What about those men in the alley?' I asked. 'What about *you*, six months ago? I don't remember you being so convinced of my goodness when I enchanted *you*. You said you hated me and never wanted to see me again.'

'I was wrong. And those men, you saved me from being stabbed, Anna. Would you be a better person if you'd stood by and let them gut me?'

'Maybe, I don't know.' I felt full of wretchedness, not sure how such a lovely night had turned so sour.

'Come on.' Seth stroked my hair, running his hands along the nape of my neck where the fine hairs tickled, curling his fingers around the tender skin behind my ear. 'Come on, sweetheart. It's Christmas Eve. Don't let's spoil it. Look.' He reached under the table. 'I've got your present.'

It was small and heavy in my palm, wrapped in gold paper.

'I've got yours,' I said, trying to smile. I reached for the bag. It was unguessable – I knew that. A square, anonymous box that might have been anything.

Seth rattled the parcel and looked intrigued.

'Is it fragile?'

'Not very. Don't hit it with a mallet.' I shook his parcel to me. It made no sound at all. 'Give me a clue.'

'Nope.' He grinned infuriatingly, happy to see me preoccupied with something other than magic. 'You'll have to wait until tomorrow like a good girl.' Then he stifled a huge yawn. 'Sorry, sorry. I'm whacked.'

'You need to get some sleep. I should go.'

'Don't go; come upstairs with me.' I hesitated and he pressed the point with a wickedly enticing smile. 'Go on; Mum's in the bar . . . There's enough din down here to cover any sounds from upstairs . . .'

'What about your grandad?' I hedged. 'I thought he was staying for Christmas?'

'He was asleep in front of the telly when I last checked, out like a light.'

I shook my head. If Bran was upstairs there was no

way I was risking a confrontation.

'Sorry, Seth, I don't think your grandad would be very pleased to see me.'

'But he won't see you! We'll creep past him. Please?' He was kissing my hands, one finger at a time. 'I could give you an early Christmas present?'

Desire coiled in the pit of my stomach like an unassuaged hunger, but I shook my head again, this time resolutely.

'No. Look, Seth, I make snow fall when we *kiss*. Don't you think that,' I looked around and lowered my voice, 'that doing anything *more*, particularly with your grandad in the house, would be a very, very bad idea?'

'You're worried the earth will move?' His smile was wicked, but I wasn't laughing.

'If you want to put it that way, yes.'

'Most girls worry that it won't,' he teased, but the laughter went out of his face when he saw my expression. 'Oh, Anna, Anna love. I'm sorry; I didn't mean to be an arse. I was only joking.'

He leant forward and kissed me gently, then wrapped me in his arms. I put my head on his chest, listening to the slow thud of his heart, and the hubbub of the bar seemed to drift away.

'Look, you don't want to,' he said softly, 'and that's

fine. That's completely, totally, utterly fine.'

I didn't say anything. How could I tell him that it wasn't because I didn't want to go upstairs with him, but because I *did*, so desperately, and that refusing him again and again made my heart crack a little more each time.

Just then the bell rang for last orders at the bar and Seth kissed the top of my head.

'Come on,' he said into the darkness of my hair. 'You're tired, let's get you home. I'll drive you.'

'I've got my bike.' I sat up awkwardly, trying to smile. 'It won't fit in your car. Don't worry. I'm totally fine; I'd rather ride.'

'Sure?' He looked at me closely. I tried for a more convincing smile and nodded firmly.

'Quite sure. The ride will clear my head.'

'OK. Give me a kiss.'

'Not . . .' I looked around the bar and he sighed.

'Outside then? Where it's quiet?'

'OK.'

We walked outside and he stood, arms wrapped around himself for warmth, and watched while I unchained my bike and clipped on the lights. Then he held out his arms.

'Come here.'

I don't know how long we stood there, entwined in the

65

frosty night air, my bike lights twinkling in the darkness beside us. I only felt his heart beating next to mine, his damp curls, his unshaven cheek harsh against my skin, and the heat of his lips against my throat.

When we broke apart we were both dizzy and gasping for breath, and it took a moment for me to focus – white swirling motes were drifting in the night air. Then suddenly I realized.

'Oh!' Panic rose inside me. I'd ruined this perfect moment, like so many others. 'Damn, damn, *damn!*'

'Anna . . .' Seth held me, and his face was alight with laughter and happiness. 'Didn't you see the forecast? It's *really* snowing; it's nothing to do with you. Anna, it's going to be a white Christmas.'

I cycled down the lane though the falling snow, my headlamp illuminating the flakes that swept past me in little eddies and flurries. My lips were still warm from Seth's kiss and my breath came in white gusts. The moon had a halo of ice around it and the landscape was heartbreakingly beautiful; Winter at its most lovely.

A single window was alight in one of the council houses dotted along the lane, the curtains open, making a golden river across the frosted grass. A figure was seated in the opening; a girl, her pale hair shining in the lamplight's glow. Her chin was resting on one hand and her face was turned towards the pub at the top of the lane. There was such soft wistfulness in her expression that I hardly recognized her, but when I did, the realization made me swerve and almost skid in the falling snow. The girl in the window was Caroline, Seth's ex-girlfriend, but I had never seen such naked yearning in her face before. I felt like a trespasser.

I put my foot to the pedal, ready to cycle away unnoticed, but my tyres slipped in the snow with a soft slushing sound and her gaze turned to me.

She frowned. She didn't recognize me, muffled up in the darkness. Part of me still wanted to hurry away, but now she'd seen me it felt cowardly, as if I'd been caught spying or something, as if I was ashamed. So I took off my helmet, shook out my hair, and raised a hand. I don't know what I expected – not for her to fall into my arms, that was for sure, but it *was* Christmas after all.

Whatever I expected, it wasn't what happened. She leapt up, so suddenly that I heard the crash as her chair fell to the floor, and her face twisted. For a moment she stared at me, her eyes burning through the darkness. Then she tore the curtain across with a sound like ripping fabric.

I bit my lip as I put my helmet back on, trying to get

my numb fingers to buckle the clip. Who was I kidding? I'd stolen her boyfriend, flooded her home, screwed up her life in pretty much every way you could imagine. She owed me nothing – certainly not forgiveness.

But before I could get the helmet fastened, a stream of light split the darkness and I turned to see Caroline standing barefoot in the snow, her hair a flaming halo against the bright doorway.

'Get out,' she said.

'I'm sorry.' I tried again to do up the clasp, but my cold fingers refused to cooperate. 'I'm going, honestly.'

'I said, get out. Isn't it enough that I have to put up with you draped all over Seth at school? Do I have to watch you simpering and grinning in my own front garden too?'

'I'm sorry,' I said again. I let the helmet clasps drop and put my foot to the pedal. 'I really am.'

'Sorry!' She gave a laugh, coming closer in the falling snow. She should have been shivering in her thin nightdress, her feet bare to the frosted path, but she didn't even seem to notice the cold. 'Sorry? You think you can ruin my life and then make it all go away with "sorry"?'

'I never meant to hurt you. Caroline, if you knew how bad I feel—'

'*You* feel bad?' She was inches from me now, looking

like an avenging angel in her white gown, her hair like an aura of fire. 'How d'you think *I* feel?'

'I'm sorry,' I said again. But I could hear the hopelessness in my own voice, the knowledge that I could never, never make this right.

'Shut up!' she spat.

And then she pushed me.

I staggered, but with the bike between my legs I couldn't right myself and I fell, heavily, the bike-frame crashing against my shin, ripping through jeans and skin. Caroline stood and watched me a for a moment as I struggled in the snow, and I felt hot blood start to seep through my jeans.

'If you think it's over, it's not,' she said. 'It'll never be over, not until you and Seth are finished.'

Then she turned towards the house. The door slammed behind her and I was left alone, in the dark and falling snow.

CHAPTER FIVE

I lay silently until she'd gone and then, when the house was quiet and I was pretty sure she wasn't coming back out, I wriggled painfully out from beneath the heavy bike and pulled up my jeans to examine my shin. There was a long bloody scrape down the front and a rip in my jeans. The cut looked ugly, but nothing I couldn't sort with some warm water and TCP.

But when I tried to haul myself upright, my crushed foot wouldn't bear my weight. Pain screeched up and down my leg, sending electric shocks of agony prickling right up to my thigh, and I collapsed back to the snowy grass, hot tears spurting from my eyes with the shock. I waited, biting the inside of my cheek to stop myself from crying, and the pain resolved itself into a dull throbbing ache in my ankle.

There was no way I was going to be able to cycle home.

I'd have to – what? Ring Dad? He'd finished his port and was just starting on the Laphroaig when I left; there was no way he'd be fit to drive. I looked up the lane towards the pub. It was a quarter of a mile away, too far to limp, and the windows were dark.

I shifted awkwardly, trying to reach the mobile in my jeans pocket without setting off the pain in my ankle again, and then I tried Seth's phone. It went straight to voicemail; he'd probably forgotten to charge it again. As I hung up I saw I had only one bar of battery left. Great.

Next I tried the pub phone, but they'd already flicked it over to the answerphone and all I got was Elaine's voice giving me their opening hours and telling me how to make a dinner reservation.

I left a message, but without much hope anyone would check it before tomorrow morning, and then I hung up and rang the flat landline.

It rang for several minutes. Was Seth in the shower? Still in the bar downstairs? The cold began to strike through my jeans as I listened to the insouciant, chirruping ring. My phone beeped, nagging me about the battery, and I was beginning to despair when there was a click and the receiver was picked up.

'Who's this?' The voice was gruff and slurred with

sleep. For a minute I was confused, then my stomach did a flip.

Bran.

'Hello,' I said. 'Hello, Bran, it's . . . it's me, Anna.'

No answer, just an ominous silence from the other end of the phone, overlaid with the faintest click and crackle of an old man's laboured breathing.

'C-could I speak to Seth, please? I'm sorry to call so late, but it's an emergency. I've hurt myself, fallen off my bike.'

Another wait.

'Hello?' I said, beginning to feel something close to desperation. 'Bran, please, I'm really . . . I can't walk. Is Seth there, Bran?'

'No,' the voice said harshly. 'There in't nobody here by that name. I know your kind, with your damn tricks, a plaguing respectable people at this time a'night. Leave us be, damn you.'

There was a deafening clap, as if the receiver had been slammed down, and the line went dead.

For a second I just sat and gaped at my mobile. Had I somehow dialled the wrong number? But, no, impossible – there it was on my last-number-dialled list: *Seth home*.

I stabbed at the redial button, my fingers shaking with

fury. God damn him, I would *make* Bran Fisher go and fetch Seth.

All I got for my trouble was the engaged signal. He'd taken the phone off the hook.

Damn Bran Fisher! Damn him for a bigoted old despot, with a soul eaten away by hate. For a second I felt like throwing my phone into the road and then stamping on it.

But I didn't. Instead I took a deep, shaking breath, trying to push down the rage, and scrolled down to Emmaline's number and pressed dial. It didn't even have time to ring. The screen flashed once and then the battery died.

This time, I didn't do anything. I just sat in the snow and, as the red-hot blaze of fury subsided, a feeling of anxiety bordering on panic began to steal over me. What was I going to do? What *could* I do? I couldn't just sit here all night waiting to freeze, could I?

At last I gritted my teeth and, with a horrible scrambling rush, I pulled myself upright using the bike as support. Then I stood, shaking with cold and pain, for a long sweating minute. Could I somehow hobble back up the road to the pub, using the bike as a crutch?

But as I took my first tentative step, the front wheel swung wide in the clogging snow, slithering off the pavement and into the road, and the bike fell again. I stumbled and fell with it, landing on my bad ankle with a pain so sharp it ripped a yelping scream from my throat. Then I just lay, half on the pavement and half in the slush-filled gutter, trying to choke back tears of agony.

Icy water was seeping slowly through my jeans and I shivered, a convulsive movement that made my wrenched ankle scream in protest. But as the pain in my ankle subsided, I realized I was cold. Very, very cold. And I had absolutely no way of warming myself up.

I didn't hear the car at first, but the dazzle of the lights made me turn. For a moment I was transfixed like a rabbit in the headlamps by the two blinding beams that cut through the falling snow. Then the driver spotted me sprawled in the road. The sudden blare of a horn split the night, followed by the shriek of brakes and a slushing grinding slide, as the tyres tried and failed to grip on the icy tarmac.

As the car slalomed across the road I squeezed my eyes shut, clenched my teeth, and put every ounce of magic I had into stopping the car. I opened them to find a number plate, stationary, just inches from my nose.

Then the driver's door creaked open.

'You total bloody . . .' A furious bellow cut through the silence. 'Are you drunk or were you just born stupid?' A tall shadowy figure was striding around the bonnet. 'What the hell are you doing lying in the—'

The figure stopped.

'Anna?'

I put a hand up, shading my eyes against the glare of the headlamps.

'Wh-who?'

'It's me.' Abe fell to his knees in the snow beside me. 'What in the name of Mike are you doing? Do you realize I could have killed you?'

'I stopped the car,' I said wearily.

'*I* stopped the car,' he snapped. Then he noticed the blood on the snow, my ripped jeans, the bike lying half across me. 'Jesus, Anna. What happened? Did you get hit?'

'Nothing so dramatic. I fell off.' I spared him the details about my spat with Caroline. Something told me that Abe would find the idea of two girls bitch-fighting over Seth less than enticing. 'What are you doing here?'

'On my way back from dropping Emmaline. Are you OK?' He was peeling away the wet, bloodstained denim as he spoke. His hands were gentle but when he touched my ankle I couldn't suppress a whimper and he shook his head. 'I'll take that for a no. Here . . .' He shifted the bike and then put an arm around me, supporting my weight.

'Come on, let's get you under a street lamp and we can take a look at the damage, see if it's an A&E job.'

He heaved me to my feet and I managed to stand, my teeth clenched against the pain, breathing hard. Abe looked at me quizzically for a moment, then he bent down, and swung me up into his arms.

'Abe,' I said. 'Abe! Put me down! I can walk, for heaven's sake.'

'Really?' He turned his head to look at me, his face strangely close now I was gripped against his chest. 'So all that screaming stuff when I touched your foot, that was just play-acting, was it? Look, if you've got an alternative suggestion, bring it on. Otherwise . . .'

'I'm too heavy . . .' I struggled half-heartedly as he began walking, but he only clamped me closer. 'Please, this feels weird, put me down.'

'You're not heavy, for God's sake. You're a teenage girl. Stop wriggling or I'll lose my footing in the snow and we'll both end up in A&E.'

I subsided, and a few minutes later we reached a street lamp and stopped beneath its pool of chilly light. Abe put me down in the snow and knelt beside me, pulling the blood-sodden denim up to my knee. What was underneath made me wince and Abe gave a low whistle.

'You don't do things by halves, woman. That's quite a

gash. And your ankle looks like you've got elephantiasis.'

'So what do you think – A&E after all?'

'Hmm . . . might not be necessary.' Abe put his hand to my ankle again, not prodding but just letting it rest there, cool against the swelling. I had the impression that he was feeling for something. 'If it was broken I'd say yes, we need a doctor, but . . .' He was silent for a moment and then shook his head. 'I'm pretty certain it's not. We can sort this.'

'What do you mean?'

'Heal it.'

'Heal it? How?'

'How do you think? Magically, of course. If it was broken I wouldn't mess with it – you don't want to cause a bone to set in the wrong position; that's worse than doing nothing. But this is just cuts and swelling, nothing your body can't sort, with a bit of help.'

'And you can do that?'

'Yep. Only . . .'

'Only . . . ?' I echoed.

'Only I'm not going to.'

'What? That's horrible! You're telling me you can fix this, but you're not going to?'

'No. *You're* going to.'

We stared at each other, hemmed together in the

intimate little circle of the lamplight. His black eyes reflected the cold glimmer of the snow.

'Well?' he asked at last.

'What will you do if I refuse? Leave me here in the snow?'

He was silent for a minute and then nodded, reluctantly. 'If that's what it takes, yes.'

'This is blackmail.' My voice cracked.

'I'm trying . . .' He swallowed and I saw his fist was clenched. 'I'm trying to help. Anna, you *have* to start doing magic. I know you don't want to, for some twisted moral agenda of your own, but you're going to end up hurting someone if you don't – probably yourself.'

'But I don't know how!' It was a sob of desperation in the still night air. 'Come on, Abe, I don't know the first thing about this – what do you expect me to do? I need a spell – something!'

'You don't need a spell,' Abe said impatiently. 'That's just bollocks, props, fiddling round the edges. Magic – real magic – comes from in here.' He banged his fist on his chest, his black brows drawn into a frown. The cold light glittered off his eyebrow ring.

'I need *something*,' I said. 'You're not being fair, Abe. Give me a chance – you've had years – and what have I had?'

'You've had enough time,' he said shortly. 'It's not time that's the problem – you're afraid.'

I wanted to snap back that I bloody wasn't afraid – and would prove it.

But he was right. I was afraid. Afraid of bringing the fury of the Ealdwitan down on myself and Seth again. Afraid of what might happen if I let go. And . . . afraid of myself.

'OK,' he said at last. 'Goodbye, Anna. Have fun freezing your arse off here.'

'No!'

But Abe just got up as if I hadn't spoken, brushing snow from his knees, and began to walk slowly back to where he'd left the car.

'No!' I shouted. 'Abe!'

He carried on walking, the crunch, crunch of his steps on the snow growing fainter as he disappeared into the night.

'Abe, Abe, you bastard, please!' Panic rose in my throat, choking me so that I could hardly breathe.

'OK!' I yelled at last. 'OK, OK – I'll do it. Please, please come back.'

The footsteps halted.

'I'll do it,' I repeated. 'Just please, please come back and help me.'

He came slowly back along the dark road and knelt beside me in the snow.

'Go on then.'

'But, what do I do?'

'You just have to want it. Spells, incantations, all that crap – it doesn't mean anything. None of that stuff has any real power. It's a way of concentrating the mind; that's why people use it. But it's just a crutch – and you can't rely on it. What counts is how much you want something, how much of yourself you're prepared to give to make it happen.'

'But for God's sake!' My teeth were clenched – with cold or fury, I wasn't sure which. 'For God's sake, Abe, of course I want my bloody ankle to be healed. If that were all it took I would've walked away from this situation before you even got here. Of *course*, I want it, but nothing's happening.'

'Want it harder,' Abe said shortly.

I sat there in the pool of cold light, feeling the pain from my ankle throb up and down my leg – and I willed it to heal. I wanted to be well, I told myself. I *wanted* it. I felt my power shift and flow, and tried to force it down into the damaged tissues of my leg, holding my breath with the effort of concentration. Abe just sat in silence and watched me, until at last I let out a great gasp of frustration, white on the night air.

'It's not working! It's not bloody working, Abe – I don't know what to *do*.'

Abe looked dispassionately at my ankle. It looked maybe a couple of millimetres less swollen, and a shade less red, but it was definitely not healed.

'You aren't trying, Anna. You want to be well – but you're not prepared to let go of your reservations about using magic. You want to be healed, but not if it means getting your hands dirty. Listen.' He crouched down beside me, his face so close to mine that I could feel the heat of his breath on my cheek. 'It's no good wanting it in a wishy-washy, "Oh, wouldn't it be simply super if I'd never bashed my leg" kind of way. You have to want it so much that you burn with it. You have to want it *specifically*. You have want each muscle and nerve and cell in your leg to heal. You have to want your blood to clot, your skin to knit, your white blood cells to kill infection. Here . . .'

Before I could protest, he gripped my cold numb hand in his and forced it roughly down on to the gash on my leg, so roughly that I yelped. Then he pressed my fingers into the wound, so that the nerve endings screamed in protest.

'Feel that? Feel where the pain is? That tells you what's wrong. It tells you what you need to do. Don't just stop it from hurting – that won't do anything but numb your leg and you'll walk on the wound and probably lame yourself for life. You've got to *want* to be healed, want to be *whole*.'

I lay in the snow, panting with pain, Abe's hand gripping mine, mine gripping my leg, and I made the power flow, hot and urgent through my body, down through my hand, into the flesh and bone and blood of my leg where the pain screamed and howled.

I wanted it. I *wanted* it. I wanted to be healed and healthy and not to be lying here in the snow unable to walk, unable to help myself. There was nothing else in my head apart from the overpowering need and the heat of Abe's hand on mine.

At last I collapsed. I crumpled sideways in the snow, still clutching my leg, and Abe caught me just before my head hit the pavement.

'I'm sorry,' I said hoarsely. 'I'm sorry, I can't. I can't do any more.'

'Look,' Abe said quietly, and he peeled back my hand from my leg. There was blood on my hand, blood on my jeans, blood on the snow. But my leg – my leg was whole. Abe wiped my skin gently with handful of snow, smoothing away the last traces of blood. A faint silver scar marked the skin. Abe traced the mark with his finger and I shivered.

'You see that?' he said. His face was set in lines almost like grief.

I nodded.

'That line, that marks the limit of witchcraft. Magic can help your body do what it can already do for itself, and it can help it do it better – but no more than that. You can help heal, you can fight infection, you can slow disease. But no one can regrow a limb. No one can take away a scar. You can't undo what's already done.'

'I see,' I said numbly. 'Thank you, Abe.'

'Don't thank me,' he said, suddenly cold. He hauled himself to his feet and then put out a hand to help me up. There was a twinge of stiffness as I put my weight to my ankle, but no more than that. 'You did it yourself.'

He walked me back to my bike and got into the car, revving the engine to help it warm up. Then he wound down the window and looked at me, his breath a cloud of frost as the engine growled.

'So long, Anna. See you around.'

'Abe—'

But he was gone.

I set my foot wearily to the pedal and began to cycle home in the still-falling snow.

CHAPTER SIX

When I awoke next morning even the slight stiffness in my ankle was gone. I lay for a moment, flexing my toes, and then I ran my fingers over the shallow ridge of the scar, pondering over what I'd done. What I'd done? Or what Abe had done? In spite of his parting words I still wasn't sure how much had been me, and how much he'd helped.

I didn't know whether to be grateful to him for helping me, or furious that he'd blackmailed me. Whatever Emmaline, Maya and Abe said, I still felt deeply uneasy about using magic. If I had to: yes. But not if there was any other way. Not just because I could. Not after what I'd done last year.

I'd lived without magic for seventeen years, quite safely. And since my decision, six months ago, to stop doing magic, I'd had six months of peace and happiness.

Peace from the Ealdwitan, happiness with Seth. Was it so impossible to carry on like that?

At last I braved the cold and climbed out of bed to pull back the curtains. The sun wasn't yet up, but there was a pre-dawn luminance in the sky, and the forest was white – a white so stark and beautiful it was almost unbearable. A perfect carpet of snow covered the meadow in front of the house, broken only by the footprints of birds and foxes, and behind it the black tangle of Wicker Wood was transformed into delicate frosted glory. As I watched, a group of birds took flight and wheeled up from the trees, sending a shower of snow to the carpet beneath with a soft pattering sound.

But in spite of the loveliness it was too cold to stay for long and I hopped back into bed. My toes bumped against the heavy, misshapen weight of a stocking and I slid my hand under my pillow, where Seth's parcel made a small, solid lump. As I drew it out I wondered again what the small box could be. It was heavy in my hand but not surprisingly heavy, just a satisfying weight for such a little thing. Like a watch, perhaps, or a paperweight, although the box was a little too small for either.

The gold paper peeled back and inside was a little wooden box, prettily carved. It was a lovely thing but still, I was slightly surprised at Seth's choice of present. What could I do with a tiny wooden box? Keep my earrings in it? It would barely fit one pair. Use it for pills? I didn't need any medication. Still, Seth had chosen it and given it to me, and that was enough.

It was almost as an afterthought that I opened it. Then I gasped.

Inside, padded with roughly scrunched-up linen, was a ring. No, not just a ring, but the most beautiful ring I'd ever seen. It was made of silver, twisted around an irregularly shaped stone of a strange, smoky dark amethyst-blue. It was heart-stoppingly lovely and I couldn't bear to think how much Seth had spent or how he'd obtained the money.

Grabbing my dressing gown I flew downstairs to the phone in the hallway and huddled in the stairwell, dialling Seth's mobile number with trembling fingers.

'Hey,' he answered sleepily. 'Merry Christmas, sweetheart.'

'Merry Christmas,' I said, my words tumbling over themselves. 'Oh, Seth, I opened your present; it's so, so lovely. But you shouldn't have – however did you afford it?'

'Don't worry.' There was a smile in his voice. 'I should have put in a note. It's not a gemstone, just a piece of seaglass I found one day. It reminded me of your eyes, so

I saved it and got a friend to set it in a ring. Like I say, it's only glass, so you'll have to be careful if you wear it; it's not as hard as a real gem.'

'I love it,' I said positively. The ring's humble origin did nothing to take away my delight. 'I really mean that; I love it more than I can say.'

'That's fitting then,' Seth said quietly.

For a moment I couldn't speak, I was so full of feeling, but then I managed to clear my throat and said huskily, 'Did you open mine yet?'

'Not yet. Mum's not up. Do you want me to? Hang on . . .' I heard creaking and rustlings and imagined him heaving himself out of bed, slinging on a towel and padding down the corridor to the living room. 'Where is it . . . ? Mum's moved everything around. OK, I've got it. God, you've done the tape tight. I'll have to put the phone down.' There was a clunk and I heard the sound of ripping paper and swearing as Seth tried to tear through the tough tape. I heard a gasp as he recognized the logo of the ship's chandler, and then the box tearing, and the phone was snatched up.

'Anna! Oh, Anna, you shouldn't have.'

'Do you like it?'

'Like it? I love it – it's so beautiful. How did you know?'

'How did I know?' I had to laugh. 'Seth, you've been

going on about needing a new ship's compass for weeks!'

'Yes but I never thought . . . the cost . . . Oh, Anna, sweetheart. I thought you'd get me some useless old shirt or something. This is . . . Oh, I love you.'

'Oh, Seth,' I shut my eyes, half faint with longing to hold him, kiss him. Instead I drew a breath. 'Anyway, it's completely selfish. This way, you'll always be able to find your way back to me.'

'I love you.' His voice shook. 'And you know, you know I'll always come back. No matter what.'

'I know. I love you too. Merry Christmas.'

I put down the phone and stood, looking down at the smoky depths of the stone. It was extraordinarily beautiful, filled with dark swirls of grey and deep amethyst, smoothed and misted by the rough sea. Then a voice behind me made me jump.

'Up already?'

'Morning, Dad. Merry Christmas.'

'Merry Christmas, sweetie. Come and huddle by the Aga. You can help toast the brioche for breakfast.'

'What a perfect Christmas.' Rick lay down on the hearth rug in front of the roaring log fire and stretched like a cat. 'Good food, good wine, good friends and snow to boot. What more could you ask?'

'Good food indeed.' Lorna groaned. 'That goose was divine, Tom. I think I may have done myself serious harm.'

'Well, for the last time, Merry Christmas, everyone.' Dad raised his glass around the group, a pleased, food-sated smile on his tired face. 'And now, if you don't mind, I think I might have a little snoozle.'

'I need to walk off some of that benighted bird.' Ben got up and stretched so hard his joints cracked. 'Anyone want to join me?'

There were groans and shakes of heads around the group. I was about to shake my head as well – then suddenly I realized: it was nearly six p.m. and they were leaving the next morning. This was it; this was my chance to ask him about my mum.

'Yes, I'll come,' I heard myself saying. 'Let me find my wellies and a torch.'

The sun had set long since and we stumbled through Wicker Wood with our torches always just failing to show up the side-swiping brambles, and then out on to the cliff road. Here it was quite different, the moon was nearly full, and the snow reflected every scrap of its light so that the landscape was eerily bright. We walked to the cliff edge through the shirring snow and looked out across the sea, the moon trailing a path of light across the slow, dark swell. And all the time I was trying to think up a way to bring up the subject of my mum – and failing.

'You're very lucky,' Ben said as we watched the moonlight shimmer on the dark waves. 'Living somewhere like this, I mean. Winter's beautiful.'

'Yes, it is. I am lucky.'

'Do you miss London?'

'Yes, in some ways. Horribly at first, but now . . . well, Winter's home, you know? I still miss all my London friends and everything, but it seems a long way away.'

'I can imagine,' Ben said quietly. 'It does seem a long way away, especially on a night like this.'

We watched as the lighthouse beam made a slow sweep of the bay, and I thought of Bran, and wondered how Seth was doing. By some telepathic link Ben added teasingly, 'And you've got your boy, of course . . .'

I smiled into the darkness. 'Yes, I've got my boy.'

'He sounds nice.'

'He is. He's lovely.'

'What did he get you for Christmas then? I notice you were very quiet about his present – I can only assume he either forgot or got you something too kinky for your old dad's heart to bear up?'

'No, he didn't forget and it wasn't kinky. Here.' I pulled off my glove and held out my hand. The seaglass ring was turned inwards to the palm on my right ring finger. Ben took my hand in his mitten, twisting the ring outwards, and gave a sigh.

'What a very lovely thing. What's the stone?'

'It's glass. Seaglass. Seth found it and had the ring set round it. He does a lot of sailing.'

'Hmm, I see. All the nice girls love a sailor, or so they say.' He held my hand, still looking down at the seaglass, which glowed with a quiet luminescence borrowed from the moonlight. 'Well, I may not have met the man, but based on his taste – by which I mean his choice of this ring and more importantly of *you*, dear little Anna – I'm prepared to like him.'

'You would like him, I think,' I said. Then I laughed. 'Well, you'd like the way he looks, if nothing else.'

'Oh really? Little Anna's snagged herself a looker, has she?' Ben laughed too.

'Yes, he's absolutely out of my league; I still have to pinch myself to believe that we're together.'

'Hey, hey.' Ben squeezed my hand. 'I won't have that sort of talk. There aren't many girls who can match up to you on a good day, missy.'

'Thank you, Ben.' I stood on tiptoes and kissed his

91

cheek. Then silence fell, a silence broken only by the pounding of the waves on the beach and the pounding of my heart as I tried to think of a way to bring the conversation round to my mum. How? How to bring up a subject dormant for nearly eighteen years?

'Ben . . .' I said hesitantly.

'Yes?'

'Ben, I . . .' I stopped, my stomach sick with indecision. I felt as if I were standing on the edge of a cliff, trying to screw up the courage to dive. Ben turned me to face him, studying my expression in the moonlight.

'What is it? Come on, spit it out. There's been something on the tip of your tongue since we left the house, hasn't there? Whatever it is, it can't be that bad. Let's see . . . Pregnant? STI? Secret piercing in an embarrassing location that's going to set off the metal detectors on your next holiday?'

'No, you idiot!' I was laughing now, in spite of myself. 'None of those. No it's . . .' I steeled myself for the plunge. 'Ben, did you know my mum?'

'Oh.' He looked down at his mittens, flexing and unflexing the fingers inside the sheepskin. 'Do you know, I've been waiting for that question for a few years now. Yes, I knew her. But you know, you have to ask your dad the things you really want to know.'

'I *have* asked him, Ben! I've asked and asked, and nothing. Don't you think I have a right to know about her?'

'Yes, I do.' He stopped and bit his lip, his brow furrowed in indecision. Then he took a deep breath and looked out to the quiet sea. 'But your dad has a right to his reasons too.'

'What are they? Can you tell me that at least?'

'What are any of our reasons? Love, cowardice, a reluctance to probe where it hurts, a desire to protect . . .'

'Protect who? My mum? She's gone, Ben! Himself?'

'Himself, maybe. But mostly you, I think, Anna.'

'Me? Protect . . . me?'

Ben nodded, his face troubled.

'Yes. Perhaps he's waiting until you're ready.'

'Ready for what? And when will that be? For God's sake, Ben, this is killing me. I need to know; I *deserve* to know.'

'Look, there are some things I can't . . . I won't tread on Tom's toes. But maybe – well, ask me your questions and if I can answer them I'll tell you.'

I gulped. So. This was it. What did I really want to know? Why did she leave? Did she ever love us? Was she a bad person? All of those. Most importantly, was she the person who took away my magic, and if so why, what did she fear about me? But I couldn't ask Ben that – and anyway, perhaps it was better to ask something I could bear to hear.

'What did she look like?'

'Oh!' Ben laughed as if he'd been expecting something more difficult. 'Lovely. Very lovely. A lot like you. Dark hair, intense eyes, skin like cream and cochineal. Yes, Isla was lovely.'

'Like me?' I whispered. He nodded, his eyes full of compassion.

'Yes, sweetie, a lot like you.'

'And . . . what was she like?'

'Very clever, very opinionated, very funny. Very lovely too. Even . . . even at the end, when things were worst.'

'What things?' I asked, hardly daring to breathe. 'Ben? What was so bad?'

'Anna . . .' He took a step forward and took my hand. 'Isla was ill, you have to remember that. She—'

'Ben!' A furious roar made us both jump and turn towards where the darkness of the wood was suddenly pierced by the beam of a torch. A shadowy figure was coming towards us, stamping across the snow.

'Tom . . .' Ben held up his hands placatingly. 'Tom, I wasn't saying anything . . .'

'Really? What was that I just heard then? Figment of

my imagination? Voices in my head, or hadn't you got that far?' Dad was spittingly angry. I had never seen him so furious.

'Tom, I hadn't said anything about that.'

'Good, because it's *none of your damn business*,' Dad hissed.

'No, but it's Anna's business.'

'Anna's business is my business.'

'She needs to know sooner or later.'

'And I will tell her – but when *I* decide, not when some drunken arsehole blurts it all out.'

'Tom, please. Be reasonable. She's seventeen!'

'She's too young.'

'She's old enough to understand.'

'Understand? I'm not sure *I* understand, even after all these years. And I'm sure as hell that *you* don't understand, you interfering tosser. Anna's a child, how can a child—?'

Suddenly I'd had enough. Rage boiled up inside me.

'I am *here*, you know!'

Both of them turned to look at me, their faces blank with surprise. I truly think they'd both forgotten.

'Anna . . .' Dad put out a hand.

'Get off me!' I took a step back. 'I'm sick of being treated like a kid. I'm not a child. If you knew what I'd had to deal with this past year . . .' I stopped, too full of anger to form the words. Fury choked me at the thought of it all and I couldn't speak.

'I know,' Dad said. 'I know it's been hard.' His face twisted with pain.

'You *don't* know. You don't know anything about me – but you know what's worse? *I* don't know anything about me, because *you* won't tell me. Who am I? Mum is half of me – I need to know who I am!'

'Please, Anna, *please* don't do this.' Dad's face looked like a man on the rack, deep lines of pain etched into his face.

'Tell me,' I said, and I put all my power behind the words. Dad groaned, a sound of physical pain.

'I c-can't.'

'*Tell me!*'

'No . . . Oh God . . .' Dad moaned, and he fell to his knees in the snow, forced down by the strength of my witchcraft.

Suddenly I was horrified. What was I doing? Breaking and battering my dad like a ragdoll? Was this what my mum would have wanted?

I put my hands to my mouth and dropped to my knees beside Dad.

'Dad, oh, Dad, I'm so sorry. Are you OK?'

He was shaking his head dully, like a man with water

in his ears. Then he straightened painfully and put a hand on my shoulder, trying to stand.

'I'm OK . . . funny turn . . . too much goose maybe.' He gave a hoarse, shaky laugh. I looked at him and, suddenly, in the lines of pain in his face I saw . . . something. A flicker. Nothing more. But it was there. Enchantment. So deeply buried it was barely perceptible, but the magic was strong. Now I'd noticed it I could see it more clearly, woven through and through, weft and warp, until it was a part of the very fabric of his soul. Something was binding him, binding his will, and had done for so long that it had grown to be a part of his psyche.

'I can't tell you, Anna,' he said. 'Not yet. But I will, I promise. Just – just give me a little time, will you?'

'OK.' I was too stunned by the realization of Dad's enchantment to argue much more. Who'd done this to him – my mother? How? *Why?* The ground seemed to shift beneath my feet. 'OK. I won't ask again. But please, Dad, soon.'

'Soon.' He nodded and took my warm hand in his cold one, putting them both in his coat pocket together, as he used to when I was little and my hands were the cold ones.

'Ready for some mulled wine, Anna?' Dad asked. I nodded and Dad turned to Ben with a rueful, half-apologetic smile. 'Ben? I think we could both use a drink.'

'Yes. Quite.' Ben smiled too and the awkward moment was over.

Dad turned back to the house. He put his free arm around Ben's shoulders and we began to walk, Dad's pace still slow. He was getting old, I realized. No longer the giant who'd carried me for miles on his shoulders when I was little. The realization made my heart give a painful clutch and I let my glove fall to the ground.

As I retrieved it they drew a pace or two ahead and I watched them lean on one another. Two old friends, no longer in their prime, their heads drawn together in companionable reminiscence. I could only hear snatches of their conversation, but I knew they were discussing old times, old friends, and yet always skirting painfully around the subject closest to my dad's heart.

CHAPTER SEVEN

'The scraper's in the door, Lorna.' James was heaving suitcases into the boot of the car. 'No, the *other* door.'

'Oh for heaven's sakes, James. Why can't we use de-icer like normal people? Honestly, men, Anna. Don't ever get married.'

'Bye, Tom.' Ben gave Dad a crushing man-hug and then turned to muffle me in his thick greatcoat. I hugged him back, breathing in his particular scent; the smell, I realized suddenly, of London. He smelt of expensive cologne, dry-cleaned wool, and the sooty tube-air I had almost forgotten. My heart throbbed for a moment with something that was not quite homesickness – for my home was here now – but was close.

'Goodbye, little Anna.' Ben kissed the top of my head and spoke quietly, next to my ear. 'Come and see us sometime.'

'Thanks, Ben. I'd love to.' I meant it.

'We're only a train ride away.' Rick stuck his head out of the car window. 'And you've always got a bed at ours if you need it. Well, a sofa bed.'

He grinned through the window and James honked the horn, penned in behind their convertible. Ben stuck up two fingers and then lowered himself behind the wheel, and they bumped off up the rutted lane, the ice crackling beneath their tyres.

Dad put his arm round me and we stood watching for the glimpse of their cars as they crested the hill. Then they were gone, and the stillness of the forest settled around the house again.

We were just turning back to the house when I stopped.

'What is it?' Dad asked. 'Did they forget something?'

'No . . .' I said slowly. I put out a hand, pointing.

There were footsteps, boot-marks, in the snow, all around the house.

Two sets of prints, maybe more, traced a wavering path, right around the outside. In places they led so close to the house the walkers must have almost brushed the walls. In other places the tracks wavered out a few feet as if the walkers had wanted a better view of the building. Dad stared at them for a moment, as puzzled as me.

'Huh. How odd.'

'Whose are they?' I asked.

'Not mine,' Dad said. We peered closer. The prints were much bigger than my size sixes, closer to Dad's size tens. Then Dad seemed to shrug it off.

'Probably Rick or James. James was saying last night he wished he'd had more time to explore the countryside. Maybe he came out this morning for a poke around.'

'What and just walked round the house? Twice?'

'Why not?' Dad shrugged. 'I can't see what else it could be, can you? Who'd come out here just to walk round the house?'

'I guess . . .' I trailed off. I couldn't put my finger on it, but something about the wavering yet purposeful tracks creeped me out. It just didn't seem like something James would do. Why would he walk steadily twice round the outside of the house, so close he could peer in each window? If he'd come outside to explore he would have gone round the outbuildings, up the lane, into the woods.

But Dad was right, of course. Who on earth would come all the way out here, just to walk around our house? Granted there wasn't much to do in Winter, but the kids weren't *that* bored.

'So what now?' Dad asked as we made our way back to the house. He'd clearly dismissed the matter from

101

his mind. 'Toast? Telly? Fancy giving me a hand with the tiling?'

'Dad,' I blurted, 'why don't you ever talk about Mum?'

His face got that agonized, shuttered look I knew so well and I realized that for years – ever since I could talk, basically – I'd backed away from causing my dad pain. I'd shielded him from discussing my mum, even helping him to skirt around the conversation when it came up with other people. Now, as I saw the expression in his eyes, every instinct was shouting at me to stop pushing, stop hurting him.

Except this time, I didn't stop.

'Please, Dad. I'm starting to realize, there's so much about myself I don't know.'

Like, why one of the most powerful groups of witches in England wanted to recruit me. Why my own mother had wanted to hide my existence. Why she'd tried to stifle my magic, prevent even the chance of me becoming a witch. What was *wrong* with me?

'Dad . . .' I begged.

I could see the ripples of pain coursing through him as I spoke, see the way the spell ran through him, controlling his every word. I ought to stop hurting my dad – but . . . but wouldn't the right thing be to set him free?

I pushed against the enchantment with my power, feeling its subtlety and steely strength.

'Dad . . .' I said again, and I took his hand, reaching into him. I could feel it woven through and through his mind, twined so closely into his own desires that it was impossible to tell where Dad's own reticence ended and the spell began. This was no crude charm, slapped on top of his psyche like a gag. This had been done by someone who *knew* Dad, knew exactly how he worked, what he himself wanted. It *had* to have been my mother – it had to have been.

It was also way beyond me, I could tell that immediately. I had a strong suspicion it was probably beyond Maya too, maybe even beyond *anyone's* power to remove without slicing through Dad's psyche, ripping his mind into useless shreds. It had grown into Dad, grown to be part of him as much as his blood and his bones.

I sagged into a kitchen chair, overwhelmed by the strength of my mother's opposition, her strength of will reaching back over the years to thwart me even now.

Dad looked at me, misunderstanding my frustration, and his face was full of compassion.

'I will tell you, sweetie. I promise I will, just, please, trust me.'

Trust you? Or trust her? How could I trust her?

'Never mind,' I said tiredly. 'I think I'll go upstairs; I've got English coursework to do.'

'All right, sweetie. Oh wait, hang on. I nearly forgot. Seth rang.'

'What? Why didn't you wake me?'

'He said not to. Asked me to pass on a message.' Dad led the way into the hall and passed me the message pad by the phone.

Seth rang, it said in Dad's handwriting, *to let you know his grandad had a funny turn. Bran's in hospital. Elaine's there. Seth'll be down at the harbour for the rest of the morning if you want to see him.*

Oh no.

The cold sea air was searing against my face as I strode along the cliff road, my face turned unseeingly towards the channel. Please, *please* let this have nothing to do with me. Please let Bran be OK. Please let it all be all right.

Then Seth's voice, urgent, furious, came into my head. *Anna, don't. You've got to stop thinking that everything bad that happens in a fifty-mile radius is to do with you.*

I was totally engrossed in my thoughts, so that when the voice in my head called, 'Anna. Hey, Anna!' I jumped and almost tripped.

'Seth!' I hadn't noticed I'd reached the harbour. I hadn't noticed the small yacht drawn up by the quayside. I hadn't even registered Seth, standing on the deck and waving, until he called my name. 'Seth, sorry, I was completely . . . I was thinking about something. How are you? Are you OK?'

'I'm all right. Come aboard and I'll tell you about it.'

'Who does it belong to?' I asked, looking bemusedly at the sleek lines and tall mast. I knew every boat in Winter harbour by now, at least at this time of year, and this was not one I'd seen before. It was run-down though, even I could see that. Peeling varnish, cracked woodwork . . . The name *Charley's Angel* was painted on the stern.

'Belongs to a customer at the pub – Charles Armitage. We got chatting – he needs it doing up and said he'd pay me. Come on, I'll show you round.'

He held out his hand and I fought down the nausea that immediately clutched my stomach. I'd never felt the same about the sea, not since the fight with the Ealdwitan. Every time there was a storm I listened to the crash and roar of the waves and saw, in my mind's eye, the waters rising, the foul sightless things of the deep ocean invading Winter's streets again.

I hadn't swum, or paddled, or been to the beach since. But sailing was another matter. Sailing was life itself to Seth and there was no way to love him without loving his boat.

So I shut the terrifying images away in the part of my mind that I kept for my nightmares, and leapt, with my heart in my mouth, across the narrow sliver of oily water between the boat and the quay.

Seth caught me safely and steadied me, and then I followed him down into the small cabin, ducking my head and blinking as my eyes adjusted to a blinding combination of orange corduroy wallpaper and purple flowered curtains.

'Wow.'

'You said it. Last refurbished around the time of *Charlie's Angels*, the original.'

'That wallpaper! Those light fittings!'

'I'm more worried about the engine and the state of the hull.'

'Seth, can you do it?'

'I think so. I can take it to the chandlers if there's anything really wrong and charge it back. Basically Charles just doesn't want to have to bother with it himself. He's only got a holiday cottage down here; most of the time he lives in Surrey so it's just a pain for him to have to supervise. But of course the more work I can do myself, the more money it means for me. And God knows, anything I can save will come in handy next year.' He looked sober. We were both worried about funding university.

'Anyway . . .' He seemed to shake himself. 'It's got a little generator so we can boil a kettle. Would you like a cuppa?'

'I'd love one.' I sat down on the nylon bunk cushions and bit my thumbnail. 'Listen, how's your grandad? I was so sorry . . .'

Seth grimaced.

'Not half as sorry as I am. I mean, of course I want the old bugger to get better for his own sake, but this is going to make life bloody difficult for you and me.'

'He's still . . . ?' I trailed off. Seth nodded grimly. 'Have you tried talking to him, or your mum?'

Seth bit his lip and looked out of the porthole, not meeting my eyes. At last he sighed.

'I wasn't going to tell you this but . . . well, maybe it's better just to spit it out.' He stopped and I was suddenly worried, worried by his unhappy stance and refusal to meet my eyes.

'Seth, what is it? You're frightening me. Is Bran OK?'

'Well . . . not really. Look, I didn't want to tell you because I thought it would make you feel bad. But I did talk to Mum and I asked her to talk to Grandad. I said that it was my house, mine and Mum's, I mean, and that I wanted to have you over, as my girlfriend, during Christmas. I said I was fed up of tiptoeing round Grandad's feelings. I said I wanted to have you over to dinner with Grandad there and put an end to this. And I wanted Grandad to be nice to you. Anyway Mum thought it was perfectly reasonable, though she was a bit doubtful about bringing Grandad round to the dinner idea, but she said at the least it was completely reasonable for me to want to see my own girlfriend in my own house. So she talked to Grandad – we both did – and . . .' He trailed off.

'It didn't go well?'

'Worse than that.' Seth ran his hand through his hair, tousling it into wild curls. 'He went into a rage; I've never seen anything like it. Mum simply couldn't get a word in edgeways. He just bellowed at us both for about ten minutes without drawing breath and, then, when Mum tried to reason with him, he had a kind of . . . a kind of fit.'

'His funny turn,' I whispered, suddenly cold with the realization. Seth nodded.

'Yes. It was like, I don't know, some kind of seizure, almost like a heart attack. His face went grey and he couldn't speak. Mum had to take him to hospital in the end and he's still there. But it looks like he's never going home, or at least not home to Castle Spit. He's too ill to live in such an isolated place.'

'Because of me.'

'*No*,' Seth said forcefully. 'Not because of you. Because he's a stupid, prejudiced old man. Because he's never been crossed in his damn life and can't cope with it now. Because he's so full of rage that he can actually induce a seizure to get his own way. This is *his* fault, not yours.'

'He hates me that much.' It was a statement, not a question.

'I don't think . . .' Seth's brow furrowed, trying to explain it. 'I don't think he hates *you*, exactly. That's the weird thing. He just doesn't want you to be with *me*. It's his bloody obsession with oil and water, oil and water. He kept muttering about it in hospital. They thought he was cracked, and no wonder.'

'He doesn't want you to be with a witch,' I said flatly. A wrench of pain crossed Seth's face. I knew he wanted to deny it. But he couldn't. There it was.

'I'm sorry,' he said, and I knew he didn't just mean about Bran, but about the whole situation, the whole fact of us being on opposite sides of a chasm-wide divide.

The kettle came to the boil, screaming its shrill whistle into the silence that had fallen between us. Seth got up and took it off the ring and then came to sit beside me, putting his arm around me.

'Anna, it'll be fine.'

'It won't be fine,' I said. 'It won't. I can't see how it'll ever be fine.' I almost wanted to revel in the awfulness of it all. This at least was a concrete problem you could sum up in ten words – not a shifting, nebulous enigma like my past, my mother, my growing power.

Instead of trying to persuade me, Seth kissed me. Perhaps it was to make me feel better, perhaps to shut me up; I didn't care. He twisted one hand in my hair to bring me to him and I felt his lips, his tongue, his hands, hot, intense and full of love. I melted under his warmth, melted into him, feeling my limbs grow soft and heavy with desire. Seth leant me gently back and we lay together on the narrow bench, rocking with the waves that rocked the boat, pressed against each other so that all I could hear was the crash of waves and the roar of my own breath and blood, harsh and urgent.

Except I couldn't let go. I couldn't let go, just in case . . .

'Emmaline thinks I need to do magic.' I tried to keep my head above the rising tide of desire. 'You know, so it doesn't come . . . the wrong time . . . Seth . . . I . . . she says . . .' The words tangled on my lips, losing themselves between gasps. I couldn't think, couldn't speak . . .

'I don't care about Emmaline,' he said, very low. His lips were against my collarbone and I felt the words, breathed hot against my skin, as much as I heard them. 'I don't want to talk about Emmaline. I don't want to think about Emmaline. I want *you* . . .'

It was almost dark by the time I tore myself away. I didn't want to leave, but it was getting late and I knew Dad would start worrying soon.

'I'll walk you,' Seth said as I pulled on my shoes and buttoned up my coat.

'It's too far. You don't need to, I'll be fine.'

'I want to,' Seth said firmly. He took his sou'wester off the peg. 'I need the walk. I don't want to go home.'

Home. To sit in the empty flat above the pub while his mum kept a quiet vigil at Bran's hospital bed.

'OK,' I said. Seth zipped up his jacket and I opened the cabin door, bracing myself for the achingly cold air outside. For a minute everything was dim as my eyes adjusted to the twilight. Then the black gleam of the harbour and the glinting lights from the pubs along the quayside swam into focus – and so did the shape of the man standing on the quayside watching the boat. Something about his stance told me that he wasn't just admiring the view of the bay.

'Seth,' I said in an undertone, then louder, 'Seth.' His head appeared out of the cabin door behind me, then he sighed.

'Hello, Greg.'

'Flemish your damn line,' the man growled.

'What the hell d'you mean?' Seth vaulted easily over the boat rail on to the quay and examined the mooring rope twisted round a bollard. It looked fine to me, but Seth picked up the loose end snaking across the icy footpath with a disgusted expression. 'What the . . . ? Look, Greg, you know I didn't leave it like this.'

'Unravel itself, did it? Someone'll break their leg on that.'

'I'll put it right,' Seth said shortly, coiling the rope into a neat pile. Greg only stood and watched, his arms folded. Then Seth straightened, helped me flounder across the narrow gap to the quay, and put his arm around my shoulders, turning us towards home, Greg's eyes on our backs.

'Night,' Greg said, and there was something mocking in his tone.

'Night,' Seth snapped. His pace was uncomfortably brisk as we walked along the quay, feeling Greg's silent gaze following us, until the darkness of the cliff road swallowed us up.

'Seth,' I said at last as he forged up the hill, his arm around me painfully tight, 'Seth, slow down. It's not a race.' I tried not to pant.

'Sorry.' Seth slowed to a more normal pace and dropped his furious hold on my shoulders. 'Sorry, I was just . . . you know. Greg pissed me off back there.'

'So that was him? *The* Greg?' The Greg who goaded Seth into a fight years back, I meant. A fight which left Seth facing police questions and Greg in hospital.

'Yes,' Seth said, and his mouth set into a grim line that stopped me asking any more questions.

Instead I took his hand and we began to walk again in silence, just the sound of the waves crashing against the foot of the cliffs and the crunch-stamp of Seth's boots on the snow. As we climbed I felt his mood begin to lift a little. His hand relaxed in mine and I heard him sigh, wriggling his shoulders inside the sou'wester as if shrugging off a weight.

At last, as we passed the castle ruins, he spoke, his breath drifting white in the night air.

'Where do you think we're heading, Anna? You know, in the future.'

'Where? I don't know. I can't see past A levels at the moment. Uni, I guess. Maybe a year out. Why?'

'No, I meant us. As a couple.'

'I don't know.' I thought of Bran's implacable opposition to our relationship, and Emmaline and Abe's quiet hostility.

'It's just . . . I was wondering. I mean . . .' I heard him swallow in the night air. 'I was wondering what's next. For us. Do you think . . . the next step . . . I mean, are you ready?'

'Ready?' I echoed foolishly.

'Oh, Jesus.' He stopped under a spreading oak and ran his hands through his hair so that it stuck out in all directions. His face in the moonlight was a cold, chiselled sculpture of light and shadows. I wanted, almost, to close my eyes to his beauty, hardly able to bear the constant reminder of how lucky I was to be with him. But I couldn't tear my gaze away.

He swallowed again; I saw the muscles in his throat move. Then he took my hand. We stood in the shadowy moonlight, hand in hand, and Seth rubbed his thumb over the seaglass ring.

'Anna, I don't want to pressurize you. I know it's different for you. After all, you're . . .' He stopped.

'I'm what?' I asked, completely confused. A witch?

'A virgin.'

Oh! *Oh* . . . Heat suddenly flooded through me, a spreading wave pulsing outwards from my heart until it reached my cheeks.

'And I want it to be right. I want it to be special. But do you think . . . ?'

'I want . . .' My voice trailed away, my throat too tight to speak. What did I want? I wanted Seth. I *wanted* him, completely and utterly, so much that it hurt. But something was stopping me. It wasn't the strength of my feeling for him – because I knew that I loved him. I had no doubts about my feelings for him, no fears that they would change. So what was holding me back?

'I want . . .' I swallowed.

'Yes?' He looked at me, his eyes smoke-dark in the winter dusk and so hungry they tore at my heart.

'I want . . .'

I want you, I thought.

But instead I heard myself say, 'I – I just want a bit more time. I'm sorry, Seth. You know I love you, it's not that. And I do want to, but just – just not yet. Is that OK?'

'Of course.' If he was disappointed he hid it well. 'Of course, I understand completely. Anyway, you're only seventeen. Not even legal in some places! You'd be jailbait in California.'

I laughed.

'Well, it's my birthday in January, don't forget. So

you're safe after that, no matter where I choose to seduce you.'

'So, Californian holiday in February?' he teased. I smiled and then hugged him, burying my face in his warm neck.

'Oh, Seth, thank you for being so lovely. I'm sorry, I just feel . . .'

'Anna . . .' His arms around me were firm and his lips moved against the top of my head. 'Don't be stupid. You've got nothing to apologize for. We don't need to rush anything – God knows my first time was pretty crap; I wish *I'd* waited. I don't want to be the person you regret for the next ten years.'

'I would never regret you,' I whispered, my lips against his shoulder. 'I would never regret anything we did together.'

We stood, locked together in the gathering dusk, my head against his shoulder, his cheek warm against the top of my head. The wood was full of soft shiftings and patterings as the snow slipped from leaves and branches on to the forest floor. Apart from that the only sound was our breath, making clouds of white in the darkness. I was as close to completely happy as it was possible to get, and I felt light and drained of magic. The hollow space it occupied in the middle of my ribs was filled up with love and contentment.

'I wish we could stay here for ever,' I whispered, a catch in my throat.

'Oh, love.' Seth kissed the top of my head, his breath warm in my hair. 'It'll be OK.' I don't know what he meant – Bran, exams, magic, us; it could have been any of them. But it didn't matter. Just for a moment I believed him.

CHAPTER EIGHT

I awoke on the sixth of January with a feeling of foreboding. It was Twelfth Night – the end of Christmas and the first day back at school.

I hadn't finished my coursework essays and I hadn't revised for the January exams. But, as it turned out, they weren't the only problems.

'Bloody vandals,' I heard. 'Bloody kids. You should call the police, Tom.'

Oh no. My stomach lurched. Please tell me I hadn't done something awful in my sleep. I stumbled out of bed and stuck my sleep-draggled head out of the window. The cold hit me like a slap and my eyes took a moment to adjust to the searing light off the snow. Dad and the farmer who owned the stableyard up the lane were standing on the snow-covered drive, looking at one of the outbuildings round the corner of the house.

'Anna!' Dad called up, hearing the sound of my window. 'Know anything about this?'

'About what?' I croaked.

'Come down. I'll show you.'

I pulled a fleece on over my pyjamas and stumped downstairs, wondering what time it was. The kitchen door stood wide, letting a blast of cold like a freezer into the house, and I stuck my bare feet into my wellies, shuddering at the collection of twigs and grit in the toes, and made my way blinkingly into the snowy morning.

Dad and Miles Garroway were both looking at the outbuilding that served as our garage.

DEUT 18 10-12 MM

It was painted in crimson letters a foot high across the side of the barn, and below it was a crude drawing of something that looked like a pick, or perhaps a hammer of some kind. The red paint had dripped to the ground and stained the snow like blood.

'Graffiti!' I said, surprised. I don't know what I'd expected, but not this – whatever it was. My first feeling was of relief – relief that it was nothing to do with me. My second feeling was a fear that perhaps it was.

'What on earth does it mean?' Dad said wonderingly. 'It's bloody odd graffiti. Whatever happened to *Sharon 4*

Trevor 4 Eva or *Fred Woz Ere*? Have you seen anything like it before, Miles?'

'It's anti-capitalists,' Mr Garroway said grimly. 'Look at that hammer. Dead ringer for the Soviets.'

'But what anti-capitalist in their right mind would come all the way out here to daub on a fallen-down barn?'

'If you ask me, most of them aren't in their right minds. You used to work in the City, didn't you?'

'Used to!' Dad protested. 'I was sacked! Hardly makes me one of the blood-sucking classes.'

'Animal rights then,' Miles said. 'Christ knows we've had enough trouble with that up at the stables. Even though it's all bloody drag hunts now anyway.'

'But we don't own any animals,' Dad said, baffled. 'I haven't even bought the chickens I've been banging on about.' He turned to me. 'Anna? There isn't anyone local I've offended, is there?'

'No, Dad.' That was true enough. There was no one *Dad* had offended.

I managed to hold myself together while Dad said polite goodbyes to Miles, but as soon as he crunched off up the snowy lane I ran back inside, up to my room, and googled *DEUT 18 10-12 MM*.

Link after link came up, all pointing towards the same thing. By now I knew, or at least guessed, what the text would say – but I couldn't stop myself clicking on the first link, wanting to know for sure, to see it in black and white before me.

DEUTERONOMY 18

10 There shall not be found among you any one that maketh his son or his daughter to pass through the fire, or that useth divination, or an observer of times, or an enchanter, or a witch.

11 Or a charmer, or a consulter with familiar spirits, or a wizard, or a necromancer.

12 For all that do these things are an abomination unto the LORD: and because of these abominations the LORD thy God doth drive them out from before thee.

I sat for a long time, staring at the screen, until the words shimmered in front of my eyes, burning into my retinas. Cold fear coiled in my stomach and trickled down the back of my neck. At last I erased my internet history, closed down the browser and shut down the machine.

It didn't erase the words from my mind though.

Witch. Abomination. And, in dripping blood-red letters on the side of our barn, the letters MM. What did it mean?

* * *

'I need to talk to you.' I grabbed Emmaline during break and pulled her into a cloakroom. There were two first-years there and I tried not to show my impatience as they slowly washed their hands, chatting all the while. 'Where were you? I tried to phone you all morning.'

'Oh, sorry.' Emmaline took the clip out of her hair and started rearranging it in the mirror. 'My phone's out of credit. Do you have a brush?'

'No.'

'Do you have a brush?' she asked the littlest first-year. The girl blushed pink and nodded, holding out a sparkly brush with a *High School Musical* sticker on the handle. Emmaline started dragging it through her hair, her clip in her mouth. 'What d'you want anyway?' she asked indistinctly. I made a face and nodded at the two girls. 'What?' Em said unsubtly, frowning over her glasses. 'Cat got your tongue?'

'No,' I said crossly. 'It's, you know. Private.'

'Oh.' She handed the brush back to the little girl. 'Cheers for the brush. Now trot along, you two. Bell's due in a sec.' They fluttered out, full of excitement, and Emmaline turned to me with an air of long-suffering calm. 'Come on then, spit it out. What's the drama?'

'Someone knows,' I said through my teeth. 'About me.'

'Knows? What do you mean?'

'What do you think I mean? They came in the middle of the night, while we were all asleep. They painted a Bible reference on the wall of the barn; Deuteronomy 18: 10–12.'

Emmaline didn't need me to tell her the rest. Her expression remained impassive, but she stood stock-still for a moment. Then she kicked open the cubicle doors to check we were absolutely alone and wedged her Philosophy textbook under the door into the corridor, jamming it shut.

'OK. First things first.' Her face was pale but her voice was grimly calm. 'Were there any other letters? Any signs?'

'Yes, there was a kind of hammer and the letters MM. What do they mean?'

'Nothing good.'

'Really? I'd never have figured that out by myself. Cheers, Em.' My fear was making me cross. 'Would you like to be more specific?'

'MM means Malleus Maleficorum. Do you know what that is?'

'Malleus . . . what did you say?' It sounded familiar. I racked my brains and a memory came. 'It's a book, isn't it? About . . .'

'About witch-hunting and witch trials. Yes. *Malleus Maleficarum*, Also known as *Der Hexenhammer* or *The*

Hammer of the Witches. It was written in the fifteenth century by two German nutters who saw witches hiding under every bale of hay and thought every woman who wasn't a good German hausfrau was shagging the devil and hexing cattle. It's full of crap and was responsible for the deaths of a lot of people, mostly women, and very few of them actually possessing any magical power. So far, so dumb, but unfortunately it's also an organization. Spelt with an O. Also full of crap but rather more immediately worrying. If you thought the Ealdwitan was scary, think again. *They've* ultimately got our society's best interests at heart, even if they have a funny way of showing it. The Malleus would like nothing better than to see us all dead.'

'Nice.'

'Quite.'

'So—' I began, but at that moment the bell rang, loud and shrill, and I jumped and bit my tongue. Emmaline looked at her watch and we stood, indecisive for a moment.

'Want to ditch?' Emmaline asked at last. I bit my thumbnail. There was nothing I would have liked more than to ditch Classics at that precise moment, but our coursework was due in. My absence would definitely be noted.

'I can't,' I said at last. 'I really can't. Damn, damn, damn. Lunch, then?'

'Won't Seth want to reprise your eternal tryst?' Em said sarcastically, referring to the fact that Seth and I usually ate lunch together, a fact that had not ceased to piss her off in the six months I'd been going out with him.

'He'll deal with it,' I said shortly. The second bell rang and I shouldered my bag. 'Meet you . . . where? South gate?'

'South gate.'

We walked off in opposite directions to our lessons, and I spent the next period giving wrong answers to easy questions and fretting over the half-story I'd got from Emmaline. I couldn't quite see what a bunch of superstitious dead Germans had to do with me, but just the fact that the name had stopped Emmaline in her tracks was enough to get me worried. And, undeniably, dead or not, someone had painted those words on my dad's barn. On the other hand, from what Emmaline had said, it sounded like these were just ordinary people, outwith. That had to be good, right? My experience with the Ealdwitan had taught me that a nutter armed with magical power was a force to be reckoned with. Surely in comparison a nutter armed with nothing more deadly than a pitchfork had to be preferable?

*　*　*

At twelve forty I was standing at the South gate, shivering and looking at my watch. The snow had finally melted and the playing fields were a lake of icy mud, blasted by the salt sea wind. Just as I was about to get cross I saw Em flying across the quad, her long dark hair whipping behind her in the wind.

'Sorry, sorry, got held up. Shall we walk into town and get a sandwich on the way?'

'I'm not hungry,' I said.

'Well, I am. And getting into a size eight won't impress the Malleus, you know.'

'Em, this isn't funny.'

'Yes, thank you, Ms Winterson. I am aware of that. Probably even more than you.' Her face was grim and I was reminded of her family's constant obsession with secrecy, fitting in, camouflage. I'd violated every rule in their book – cast spells on the outwith, shared my secrets with Seth, let magic spill out at the most inopportune times and places. I'd brought the Ealdwitan's wrath down on their heads and endangered the fragile peace they'd constructed in Winter. And yet here Emmaline still was, walking beside me, protecting me, giving me the information I needed to survive in this strange new world.

'We've not got long,' she said, 'so I'll talk quick. Stop

me if you don't understand something, otherwise I'll just assume you know what I mean – I can never remember what I've explained to you before. OK, so where were we when the bell went off?'

'The Malleus Maleficorum.'

'OK. Well, you probably know the basics about the history of witch-burning, don't you?'

'The basics, I guess – as far as I understand it, everyone tolerated the village crone for centuries, and then it all goes a bit haywire in the sixteenth and seventeenth centuries. Lots of poor old women get tortured into mad confessions and burnt; the whole craziness dies down in the Age of Reason. Does that cover it?'

'Pretty much. Wasn't humanity's finest hour, but to be honest the outwith suffered a lot more than we ever did. Our kind suffered too, though. The young and stupid, the old and senile. It's pretty hard to perform strong magic when you're sleep deprived, half drowned and being tortured. It was men like Heinrich Kramer and Jacob Sprenger who did the torturing.

'They wrote a treatise, the *Malleus Maleficarum*, explaining how to get poor deluded people, usually women, to confess to lying with the devil, wishing ill on their neighbours and consorting with familiars. Since their favourite methods were pretty grim, not surprisingly huge numbers of women did confess. They were imprisoned, executed or burnt.'

I shivered and Emmaline cast me a sidelong look. We were walking into the wind and her long black hair was flapping behind her, giving her a particularly witchy appearance. I would not have been surprised to see her leap astride a broom and swoop, cackling, into the iron-grey winter sky. But I said nothing and, wrapping her scarf more securely around her throat against the biting wind, Emmaline continued.

'Eventually the Ealdwitan got their act together and got control of the situation; the Witchcraft Act of 1735 was passed and, without the law behind them, the witch-burners were out in the cold. Because this new act didn't cover real magic at all, the only thing it made illegal was *claiming* to be able to invoke spirits and cast spells. Even if you were found guilty you were just treated as a con-artist. Eventually the burning stopped and we were back in the shadows, out of harm's way.'

It was strange and uncomfortable to hear about this benign, protective side of the Ealdwitan but I shrugged that off and only asked, 'So, what happened next?'

We'd reached the harbour and Emmaline sat on a bench facing the sea. I sat silently beside her, waiting for her to marshal her thoughts and continue. When she did, her face had a new grimness of expression.

'So far, so good. But, like always when the law changes, there were some people who preferred things the way they were before. When America banned slavery, the Ku Klux Klan sprang up. When our government stopped burning witches, the Malleus Maleficorum was born. They see themselves as continuing Sprenger and Kramer's legacy, only this time, outside the law.'

'So, who are they?' My fingers felt like blocks of ice in my gloves. Emmaline shrugged.

'I have no idea; we steer very well clear of them. They seem to be organized on a cell basis, with local chapters of varying intelligence. Often they're not much better than Boy Scout troops – one or two families of nutters who like patrolling around in black hoods and painting sinister slogans. If we're lucky, this is just a pack of local loonies and they're acting on suspicion rather than knowledge.'

'Oh.' I felt completely blank. Last year the witches wanted to kill me, now it was the outwith. I felt like I should make a joke: *Was it something I said?* But Emmaline's expression told me that having a group of masked crazies on my trail wasn't a joking matter.

'But they're only outwith, right?' I said at last.

'Yes,' Em admitted, 'they're only outwith – and consequently pretty dim and pretty helpless if it comes down to direct combat with one of us.'

'Exactly,' I said. Em had put her finger on what was bothering me. 'Direct combat with one of us; *I* can take care of myself, Em. But what about Dad? What about Seth?'

'They won't hurt their fellow outwith,' Emmaline said confidently. 'It's you they're after. They've got no beef with your dad.'

I hoped she was right. Her comparison to the Ku Klux Klan stuck in my head. As I recalled, the KKK weren't too keen on their fellow whites aiding and abetting freed slaves. What if the Malleus saw Dad and Seth as traitors to their kind?

Damn, damn, *damn*. I felt a cold, fierce fury against these outwith nutjobs and most of all with myself, with my witchcraft, for putting Seth and Dad in danger all over again.

'Anna . . .' Emmaline said, breaking in on my thoughts. Then, more urgency, 'Anna, Anna . . .'

I looked up. Ice was spreading out from the puddles under our feet, across the quay and down into the sea. The choppy waves were turning to frozen slush and coalescing into crystal shards around the quayside and along the ropes of tethered boats. Icicles hung from the anchor chains and frost crept over the floating buoys.

I swore and caught myself back, reining in the power that had seeped out with my bleak, icy anger. In a matter of seconds I'd drawn the cold back inside me and the harbour was free of ice once more, the puddles liquid and sloshing around our feet. Emmaline said nothing, but she shook her head.

It began to rain as we walked back to school and I realized as we got to the gate that we'd forgotten about lunch. Apparently neither of us was very hungry now.

CHAPTER NINE

It continued to rain all afternoon, the grey trickling windows matching my mood. I sat in English and my problems ran a rat's maze around my head – the Malleus, Dad, the tendrils of my mother's fierce purpose reaching out of the past to thwart me at every turn . . . Why had she run? Why had she hidden me?

The need to know the truth was so strong it burnt, like acid, in my gut. But without Dad's memories, how could I find out the truth about my past, my powers, myself? If I didn't know, I would always be running, always afraid – afraid of the Ealdwitan coming for me again, afraid of the monsters in the shadows, and afraid of the worst monster of all: the monster inside myself.

But it seemed everywhere I turned my mother was blocking me, and her will was so much stronger than mine; Dad, me, our house – nothing was sacred, nothing was too precious to be bent and warped to her purpose.

I thought again of Abe's words in the falling snow: *What counts is how much you want something, how much of yourself you're prepared to give to make it happen . . .*

I thought of the steely strength I'd sensed when I pushed against the spell on Dad's memories, and I shivered.

My mother had given everything. Not just herself, she'd fed everything she loved to the flames. But . . . for what?

'Good lord!' Dad looked up as I squelched slowly into the warm, steamy kitchen, my wet hair leaving a little trail of raindrops on the flags. He was sitting at the kitchen table drinking a glass of red wine and holding something in his hands, but he put it down as I came in and hurried across with a tea towel.

'Thanks.' I wiped my face, peeled off my soaking coat, and sank into a kitchen chair while Dad draped my dripping jacket over the airer above the Aga. 'Ugh, it's been a thoroughly crappy day really.'

'Oh dear.' Dad slid back into his seat opposite me at the table and picked up the piece of paper he'd been fiddling with when I came in. 'What a shame. Especially today.'

'Especially today? Why today?'

'Well . . .' He looked up at me, with a funny little smile. 'You'll think this is a bit bonkers, sweetie.'

'Why?'

'Well, today . . .' He stopped and looked . . . What? I couldn't place it. Shifty? Embarrassed?

'Today . . .' I prompted impatiently.

'Today is really your birthday.'

OK. I wasn't expecting that. I stared at Dad blankly and he gave a sort of sheepish laugh.

'Sounds a bit bizarre, doesn't it?'

'Too right it sounds bizarre! What on earth do you mean? My birthday's not for another ten days.'

'Well, yes and no. This will sound a bit funny but there was a mistake when we registered your birth. Actually it was your mother.'

My mother.

The two words hit me like twin punches to the stomach and strangled whatever I might have said. I could only sit, gaping at Dad like a fool.

Did he even realize that this was the first time I'd heard those words pass his lips in – well – ever?

I reached out blindly with my mind, feeling for the spell – but it was gone. Gone! And Dad was continuing as if nothing had happened.

'There was some kind of typo when she registered the birth – they mis-transcribed the date on the notification. It should have been the sixth of Jan, and instead they put down the sixteenth of Jan. We only noticed later.'

I gasped and managed, 'And . . . you didn't think to change it?'

'It seemed . . .' He flapped his hands helplessly. 'It was just . . . well, Isla thought it was easier just to let it lie. And you know, I didn't want to upset her. She was . . . There were more important things to worry about. It was only ten days – it didn't seem important.'

'Not important! You mean I've been putting a false birth date on every piece of paperwork I've ever signed?'

'Well, not really. I mean, you've been putting the date of birth on your birth certificate – which is what this is. Some people don't know their date of birth, you know; people who immigrate to the UK and so on. They just pick an official one that looks about right. This is really no different.'

'It is different! It's massively different!'

'I know but your mother – she just wanted to let it lie. She was very persuasive.'

'But – but . . .' I stammered.

I wanted to ask, how could you do this? How could you let your wife persuade you into such a bonkers course

135

of action? A fake birth date, for the love of Mike! But of course I didn't need to ask. There was much about my mother I didn't know, but I had no doubt that she'd had enough power to convince Dad, the registrar and anyone else that this was the right thing to do. The only question was *why*? And I was pretty sure Dad would have no idea of the answer to that.

'I'm sorry, sweetie.' Dad looked suddenly grey and weary. 'I should have known it would upset you. I was in two minds about whether to tell you. But you see, there's this.'

He looked down at the piece of paper he was holding and then laid it on the table between us. I don't know why, but my heart suddenly started to hammer with painful intensity. It was an ordinary cream envelope, but it looked . . . old. Used. As if it had been carried around for a long time. The corners were bent and creased, and the glue that sealed the flap had begun to yellow.

There was something written, in faded bluish ink, a single word, *Anna*, and then below it a date. Today's date. My . . . my eighteenth birthday.

I reached towards it, but before I could touch it Dad spoke.

'Wait.'

I paused, my hand hovering over the envelope, my

fingers itching with the desire to rip it open. I had the strong feeling that the envelope contained something momentous, something I *needed* to know. But Dad's words, hanging in the air, held me back. I waited and he continued, his voice oddly hesitant.

'I . . . I know I haven't . . . Oh dear. How can I put this?' He stopped and looked into the inky depths of his red wine, swirling it around his glass. I let my hand fall to the table and waited. When he finally spoke it was more to himself than to me. 'Heaven knows, I've had long enough to prepare myself for this. And I still don't know what to say.' He took a deep breath and I found myself holding mine, willing him on, willing him past whatever barrier was holding him back.

'You mustn't think . . .' he said at last, so softly I had to strain to hear. 'You mustn't think that because I haven't mentioned your mother all these years, it was because I'd forgotten her, or didn't love her. I loved her very much, too much perhaps. But somehow . . . somehow I could never find the words. And I didn't think . . . I didn't know . . .'

He stopped and then began again.

'There are some things a child would find difficult to understand. And some things they shouldn't *have* to understand. Do you know what I mean?' He looked at me

137

with an intensity that almost frightened me. Then he shook his head. 'No, of course you don't. But I – I didn't want to hurt you; I didn't want all that hanging over you. And – this will sound strange – but at times it was as if I literally *couldn't* mention her name, as if there was something holding me back. Can you understand that?'

'*Yes*,' I said fervently. I tried to put into my tone exactly how much I understood that, at least. 'Yes, I understand. But now . . . ?'

He shrugged.

'You're eighteen now; you have a right to know. And, of course, there's this.' He tapped the letter, very lightly, and sighed. 'I just wish I knew what it said – not that I think she would write anything to hurt you. Not deliberately. She was so lovely, so beautiful. She looked like you, actually.' To my horror a tear coursed over his cheek. He seemed hardly to notice it. 'And very kind, always. Even at the end, when she was at her most unwell . . .'

'Unwell?' This was not what I'd expected to hear. 'Did she die? But I thought she ran away?'

He sighed and shut his eyes, rubbing beneath his glasses with his fingertips as if very tired.

'She was . . . Oh, there's no easy way to put this, I

138

suppose. She became mentally ill. Depressed. There's an illness called post-natal depression; do you know what that means?'

'When people have a baby and become depressed?'

'Yes, basically. But in some women it's much more serious than what you'd normally think of as depression. It's rare to have it so seriously, but in some cases people hear voices, they become paranoid, they think people are trying to harm their baby. It's a kind of psychosis really.'

'And my mum . . . ?' I couldn't finish. Dad nodded.

'She became very . . . odd, I suppose, towards the end of her pregnancy. She became paranoid about everything, but particularly about the safety of the baby – about you, I mean. And she thought there were people chasing her, out to get her. In the end she ran away when she was almost due. We managed to track her down and . . . well, unfortunately she was sectioned.'

Sectioned. Another punch to the stomach. I could hardly breathe.

'But . . . but she got better?' I choked.

'For a while, yes. But then after the birth it got worse. First of all she thought that everyone was trying to steal you or harm you – she wouldn't accept any visitors; she wouldn't go out. She'd cut ties with her family a long time before that – but she refused to let them know about the birth, even. And then it changed and she started to behave as if *she* was the risk. She became very odd. She disappeared for long stretches, did strange things. And then . . . then she disappeared for good.'

He had, I thought, almost forgotten that he was speaking to me. He was talking softly, almost to himself, letting the accumulated weight of eighteen years' silence roll off his shoulders.

'The shock of her absence was dreadful . . . brutal. I was half crazy with worry and trying to look after a newborn – you were only six weeks old. But in a horrible way I was almost glad, can you believe that? She had been *so* deranged, so convinced that her presence was harmful to you, that I'd almost started to believe it myself. Now, of course . . . well, I've read a lot, over the years. I think I understand a lot better what she was going through. And I think I failed her, just when she needed me most.' He blinked and the tears ran down his cheeks again. 'She had no one, you see. Her family had cut her off when she married me. Only me. And I failed her.'

'Dad . . .' My voice cracked. I didn't know what to say, how to comfort him. I reached across the table and took his hand. He squeezed it, smiled, then took off his glasses and busily wiped away the moisture, coughing to try to cover his emotion.

'She left a note,' he continued, clearing his throat again, 'saying that she loved us both but this was the only way she could think of to protect us, and that she hoped I could forgive her. She asked me not to tell you too much, not to haunt you with her devils, was how she put it. "Let her have her childhood innocence" she wrote. I think she was right.' He smiled at me and patted my hand. Then he drained his wine glass with businesslike determination and refilled it.

I just sat in silence, reeling with all the new information Dad had given me, trying to fit this with the picture I'd built in my head so far. The clock above the dresser ticked and Dad gulped down his wine like a man just back from the desert. At last I cleared my throat and pointed to the envelope with my name on it.

'And . . . this?' I managed.

'Her note asked me to give this to you on your eighteenth birthday,' Dad said. 'I don't know what's in it.' He stopped and rubbed under his glasses again in that nervous gesture of strain. 'She wrote it just before she left. She may not have been . . .' He broke off, then said, 'What I mean is, that's why I wanted to tell you about her illness. Before you opened it. In case . . . in case the letter's not . . .'

'Not sane,' I said dully.

'I'm sorry,' Dad said. 'But I had to warn you.'

'I understand.' I looked down at the envelope and drew a breath. 'Dad, please don't be offended, but would you mind if I opened this by myself?'

Dad looked surprised for a minute, but then he recovered himself and nodded. 'Of course. Of course. I understand.'

'I know she was your wife,' I tried to explain, 'but it's just—'

'Anna, don't be silly,' Dad said firmly. 'This is your letter. Heaven knows, there's little enough else I've been able to give you from your mother. You deserve to have this to yourself. Go on.' He pushed the envelope across the table to me and I took it. My hands shook as I put it in my pocket, but whether with fear or excitement, I couldn't have said.

Then I stood up.

'Thank you, Dad,' I said. 'For, you know. This. Everything.'

'Thank *you*, Anna.' Dad pushed his chair back with a screech of wood on stone and kissed my forehead. 'I know I'm a maudlin old man who's drunk too much wine, but I need to get this off my chest. You've been the best daughter an old dad could have. No –' as I shook my head uncomfortably, blinking against my suddenly swimming eyes '– no, I mean it. Every day I've been thankful that if Isla had to be taken from me, she left someone so wonderful in her place.'

'Oh, Dad!'

He folded me in his arms and I smelt his familiar comforting smell: aftershave, perspiration, woodsmoke. For a minute I rested against his shoulder and the years melted away, the moment melding into all the other hundreds and thousands of times Dad had comforted me against his shoulder. Then I straightened and wiped my eyes. Dad laughed and blew his nose, pretending that he hadn't been crying.

'Dear, dear. That's what happens if you get through the best part of a bottle of merlot before supper. Let that be a lesson to you, my dear; red wine will turn you boring and sentimental.'

'Quite,' I said, managing a shaky laugh. 'And senile too, if you're not careful.'

'Go on.' He thwacked at my legs with the tea towel. 'Get away, you cheeky whippersnapper. I've got important drinking to do.'

Up in my room I turned on my side-lamp and took the envelope out of my pocket. My heart was thumping painfully. So. This was it.

I ripped along the top edge, tearing back eighteen years of past in a moment. A single sheet fell out into my lap and I picked it up.

It was folded in half and, just for a moment, I almost couldn't bear to open it. Then I drew a deep breath, and smoothed out the sheet.

My dearest, it read.

I wish I could stay, but I can't.

I love you so very much, but this is the only answer. It's better this way.

All my love, always.

~~*Is*~~ *Mum*

And then, underneath that, a poem that I half recognized.

> *Death is nothing at all*
> *I have only slipped away into the next room*
> *I am waiting for you for an interval*
> *Somewhere very near*
> *Just around the corner*
> *On the other side.*
> *All is well.*

For a minute I just sat and stared at the sheet, my chest rising and falling with strange, heaving breaths that hurt my ribs. There was a hard, painful knot near my heart.

This was it? Eighteen years – eighteen years I'd waited; eighteen years Dad had guarded this envelope, waiting faithfully for the prescribed day, and this was *it*? A four-line note and a poem cribbed off the internet?

Some huge bitter emotion rose up in my chest, making it hard to breathe.

I felt . . . betrayed. Betrayed by that moment of optimism I'd had downstairs – that this letter would explain everything, give me the answers I needed.

Betrayed because the letter hadn't given me anything – instead it had taken something away, extinguished a tiny spark of hope I'd never knew existed, until now. If you'd asked me that morning whether my mum was coming back, I would have answered an emphatic 'no'. But now, to see the word 'death' in her own writing, and next to it the glib cliché about 'slipping into the next room', as if the act was nothing at all, when it was everything, *everything* . . .

I crushed the envelope in my fist, wishing I could blister it into cinders and ashes – but something made me stop. There was something else in the envelope, something hard, like a little square of cardboard.

I uncrumpled the envelope, turned it upside down, and out fell a little passport-sized photo of a woman, just a few years older than me. She had my smudgy grey-blue eyes, my pale skin. But her long dark hair fell in ripples down her shoulders, where mine rioted in tangled curls. Her face was a china oval, her lips curved in a smile. She was young, happy, carefree. She looked infinitely familiar and yet I had never seen her before. I knew, without anyone to tell me, that this was my mother.

I held the photo in shaking hands, hardly able to see through my falling tears. What had happened? What had she been running from? Her face shimmered and rippled through my tears and, suddenly, out of the corner of my eye, I seemed to see a faint writing going diagonally across the portrait, the letters painstakingly small. It was just a shadow, like the indent of a pen transferred through from another page, but it was there.

Blinking back my tears I held the photo closer and looked more carefully. Nothing. I couldn't even see the ghost of a letter. I was just about to put it down when something, some instinct, made me look again, *really* look, as a witch. I narrowed my eyes, sent all my power flowing out towards the little photo. It trembled in my hand as if swept by a strong wind – and suddenly the words sprang out, traced so clearly I couldn't believe I hadn't seen them before.

Anna, I'd so hoped that you would take after Tom's kind and not mine. If you can read this, that hope was false. I'm so sorry. Be careful who you trust. Be careful who you love.

I let the papers flutter to the floor and sat in the growing darkness.

When Dad's call to supper echoed up the stairs, I pulled myself together and got up to switch on the light. For a moment the shocked ghost of a girl stared fearfully at me, white face and shadowed hair black in the darkness. Then I flicked the switch and it was just my reflection in the mirror, blinking at me in the sudden flood of yellow light.

'Anna!' Dad bellowed again.

'Coming!' I called back, trying to make my voice as normal as possible. And I clattered down the stairs to pretend I was just a normal girl, eating curry on a normal school night. Not a reluctant witch, choking down food on her secret, concealed birthday, trying to piece together the fractured shards of her past.

I ate in near silence, forcing out the odd reply to Dad's chatty monologue, then we did the washing up side by side, Dad washing and me drying and putting away. I was just putting the last dish in the cupboard when the hall clock struck ten and Dad yawned.

'Right, up the stairs to Bedfordshire for me. I spent all day shovelling snow and it doesn't half take it out of you. And tomorrow I'd better whitewash the barn.'

He was about to leave the kitchen when he remembered something and turned back.

'I'd almost forgotten.' He put his hand in his pocket. 'We'll do your birthday properly next week, like usual, but I didn't want the day to go unmarked so . . .' He held out a small box with a smile.

'Is this a present?' I asked uncertainly.

'Sort of. Open it, why don't you.'

I looked down at the little worn cardboard box in Dad's palm, feeling an odd reluctance. So many secrets in sealed packets; could I stand any more revelations tonight? But Dad was waiting, so I picked it up and took off the lid.

Inside were two earrings, small silver droplets like drops of rain, quicksilver tears.

'They were Isla's,' he said softly. 'The one thing of hers I have left to give you.'

My throat was suddenly tight and to cover my emotion I moved to the hall mirror, trying to insert the earrings with fumbling fingers.

'What do you think?' I turned around with an effort at a smile and Dad smiled back, his eyes unnaturally bright.

'They look lovely on you.' He framed my face with his big, work-roughened hands and looked at me, his eyes liquid and shining. 'You know, tonight, in those earrings, in this light, you could almost *be* Isla. The likeness really is extraordinary.' He coughed and dashed at his eyes and then kissed my forehead. 'Happy birthday, darling, and goodnight. Sleep well and remember it's school tomorrow, so don't stay up too late.'

I watched him as he climbed the stairs, emotions churning inside me. His words should have brought a glow to me, but instead they made me shiver. Did I really want to be like her, my doomed, beautiful, hunted mother? At that moment I felt her fear had reached across the years and infected me.

Be careful who you love.

Oh, Dad, you should have listened to that.

CHAPTER TEN

I couldn't sleep. I lay in the darkness and listened to the sounds of Dad huffing and turning in bed, and then the faint sounds of snores coming down the landing.

Thoughts, words and feelings were scrabbling around inside my head, scrapping and fighting for dominance. I should have been stressing about exams, coursework, social life – but they were the last things on my mind.

What had driven my mother away? Was she mad or sane? Had she been right about the demons hunting her, or was it just paranoia? What about the letters on the barn, were they connected to my birthday, or just a horrible coincidence?

The questions battered at the inside of my skull until I felt like screaming, but instead I ground my fists into my tired, scratchy eyes and tried to think rationally, concentrating on what I knew, or thought I knew.

I was now completely certain that my mother had left the charm under our step. It fitted with Dad's account of her paranoia, her fears for me. And, as I'd suspected, she must have been the person to put the spell of silence on my father – the date on the letter coincided with the lifting of the spell; that couldn't be mere chance. She'd crippled my magic, changed my birth date, sealed Dad's tongue, and then left. But why? *Why?* I felt as if the answer were there, but hovering just out of my grasp.

There must be *something* about me – something that made it necessary for me to be hidden. Was it the same something that had set the Ealdwitan on my track last year? Was it connected to the Malleus's sudden interest? But whatever it was, why couldn't she just tell me? What was so unspeakable that my mother couldn't bear to put the facts on paper, not even in the secret witch-message she'd left for me, written on the photograph?

As I lay in the darkness, unspoken fears hardened inside me, suspicions that had been festering and growing for days, weeks even, coalescing into a dark shadow that seemed to swallow up my past and future. What if . . . What if there was something . . . bad about me?

Maya and Emmaline had always talked as if there must be something desirable about my powers that the Ealdwitan wanted to use, for their own ends. But my mother, my own mother, had left a charm in our house to cripple my magic for as long as I lived there.

I began to think about everything I'd done with my witchcraft since we moved to Winter. I'd smashed up our house and cracked the seawall protecting the town. I had summoned up demons and watched powerless as they ravaged Winter. I'd set fires, destroyed property, hurt people, hurt myself.

I'd hurt Seth. I'd obliterated his love for Caroline with a single spell and made him love me for ever more, with a love so passionate and steadfast that it scared me sometimes.

I couldn't think of a single good thing I had ever done. Was this what my mother had known? Was there such a thing as a truly evil power, independent of whatever the owner wanted to do with it; a witch with a limitless potential for harm?

Lying motionless in the darkness was suddenly intolerable. I switched on the bedside light and got out the photograph, as if my mother's gaze could somehow tell me what she'd feared for me.

But there was nothing in the photograph to help. She looked back at me from the paper, laughing, fearless. A feeling of intense warmth and love washed out towards me, and I suddenly knew from her open happiness that the photographer must have been a friend. If only I knew who it had been . . .

Narrowing my eyes, I looked more closely at the background of the photo. It looked like she was in a shop, a bookshop; there were stands of books to her left, fuzzy and out of focus. Behind her was the shop window and I could see letters etched on the glass, but they looked strange, unfamiliar.

It took a moment for me to realize why. It was mirror writing – designed to be read from the street. I was seeing it reversed, as it would look to customers inside the shop.

My hands shook as I held the photo up to the mirror beside my bed, so much that for a minute the reflection was completely unreadable, just a trembling mess of lines and images. I bit my lip, forcing myself to be still, and the letters swam into focus. *Truelove Books*, *Soho*, I read, and then something underneath in letters too small to read with the naked eye.

But before I could try to remember where I'd last seen Dad's big magnifying glass, there came a sound that sent my heart racing; a crack. Then a stealthy scrabble from outside.

I thought of the red letters, of men in hoods creeping round our house, of Dad lying unprotected just yards from me. Power began to build inside – and just as I was about to snap, there came a knock at the window and Seth's low voice saying, 'Anna, Anna, it's me.'

'Seth!' I flew to the window and let him in on a gust of cold, wet air. 'What are you *doing*? You nearly gave me a heart attack.' It wasn't the first time he'd climbed up to my window, but each time scared me afresh.

'Sorry.' He rubbed his chilly feet, bare for climbing the creviced brickwork. 'Christ, it's brass monkeys out there.'

'What are you doing here?'

'I wanted to see you. I had a hideous night – bar full of braying tossers, and Mum's staying overnight at the hospital with Grandad so I'm all alone.'

'Is he bad?'

'Yes. They said she probably shouldn't go home, you know . . . in case.' His voice cracked on the last word.

'Oh, Seth . . .' I bit my lip. I had no idea what to say. I had no family except Dad so I could only try to imagine Seth's feelings. It must be made all the worse for him by the memories of his own dad, who'd died of cancer in that same hospital four, nearly five years ago. I put my arm around him. Seth tried to shrug but I could feel the stiffness in his shoulders.

There was nothing I could say, so instead I took his hand and pulled him to the warmth of my bed and we curled together. He was damp and chilled to the bone, even his clothes struck cold through my thin pyjamas, and my teeth were chattering with sympathy as we drew the duvet up. I tried to wrap my warm feet around his ice-cold ones and gradually we both stopped shivering as my body-heat communicated itself to Seth. I felt his muscles begin to thaw and his clenched limbs unfurl, twining with mine.

'You can't stay, you know. Not long, anyway,' I said feebly, as he nuzzled into my neck, trailing chilly hands down my spine. His touch set me trembling again, but now it was from desire, rather than cold.

'Mmmm. Why not?'

'Be-because . . .' It was hard to think with Seth's hands running over my waist, caressing the ticklish dint above my pyjama bottoms. 'Because . . . Dad . . . Stuff . . .'

'OK. But just a little while?'

'Just a while.'

He reached out and turned out the light and we pressed together in the darkness, tracing each other's features with blind fingers and lips and tongues, licking, nipping, biting.

'Anna . . .' He spoke into my collarbone.

'What?' It came out as a gasp.

He kissed me again and I let my hands explore beneath his T-shirt, feeling the flex and strength of his muscles and the ridges of his ribs, the curve of his spine, the tender, hard nape of his neck. It was hot beneath the duvet now, both of us pressed together and breathing hard, and when Seth flung the cover aside I didn't complain.

It felt like desire was burning me up from inside, radiating out through my skin. Seth sat up and tore off his T-shirt and then bent and ran his tongue across my belly. The cool air on his saliva left a path of ice. I gasped and arched and he kissed my mouth hard, stifling the too-loud sounds with his lips, and then trailing down my throat.

'Seth . . .' I don't know what I wanted to say, I just wanted to hear his name, gasp it in a whisper. 'Seth . . .'

He made a sound, halfway between a whisper and a groan, his lips at the hollow of my throat, and I wrapped my arms around him, my desire so fierce and tender that I could hardly contain it. I thought my heart might burst with love.

'Anna . . .' And then more urgently, '*Anna!*'

He was tearing at my arms, pushing me away as if he hated me, as if he couldn't stand to feel my touch a second longer. He staggered back from the bed, gasping and whimpering, and I could only scramble to my knees on the tumbled sheets, my outstretched arms bereft.

'Seth!' I reached for him in the darkness, hating the neediness in my voice but unable to contain it. 'What's wrong?'

'Don't touch me!' His voice was sharp with pain and there was a strange smell in the air. 'Where's the damn light?'

'Seth, what's wrong?' I stumbled out of bed and he backed away.

'No, Anna, don't touch me!'

His fumbling fingers found the switch, and light flooded the room. But it wasn't the brightness that made me flinch.

Seth stood in the middle of the room, his naked torso golden in the lamplight. But where my hands had gripped him were great crimson welts. Shiny scarlet burns striped his ribs. A fat blister welled in the small of his back. There were charred dark patches on the sheets of the bed and the acrid smell of burnt hair hung in the air.

I covered my mouth. I wanted to shut my eyes, but it seemed like the coward's way out.

'Oh God. Oh God. Oh, Seth, what have I done?'

'It's OK – you didn't mean it. You didn't mean it.' He reached out to me and I recoiled.

'Don't! How can you bear . . . After that . . .' I looked away. There was a long silence and then I heard a hiss and turned to see Seth emptying a glass of water on my smouldering mattress.

'Sorry.' He gave me a sideways smile and a half-shrug. 'Looks like you'll be sleeping in the damp patch after all.'

I didn't laugh at his pathetic joke. I wanted to rage, scream, punish myself. How *could* I? In spite of all the stupid, dangerous things I'd done recently, it had never entered my head that I could *really* hurt Seth. Not physically.

Seth saw my face and tried to take my arm but I flinched away, cowering from him against the wall.

'Don't touch me.'

'Anna,' he said quietly, and then, as I refused to look at him, more angrily, '*Anna*. Stop being so bloody stupid. It was a lapse, a second's lapse. Stop beating yourself up.'

'Stop beating myself up? Seth, have you *looked* at yourself?' I ripped open my wardrobe, pointed to his reflection in the mirror inside the door. It was horrific. 'Look,' I said brutally, watching him take in the scarlet welts. '*Look*. You look like I've branded you with a hot iron. How can I live with that?'

'It was an accident.'

'It doesn't *matter*.'

'It *does* matter. Would you be treating me like this if I'd . . . if I'd accidentally dropped a lit fag on the bed?'

158

'Don't try to argue this away, Seth. Look at what I've done – look at *you*. How . . .' My voice cracked and I couldn't continue.

'Stop it.' He grabbed me, stifling my rising sobs with his hand. I'd rarely seen him so angry. '*Stop* it.'

'Let go!'

'I will not! Your skin's cool now, stop being so bloody melodramatic—'

'Melodramatic!' I could hear the edge of hysteria in my voice. 'Seth, I *burnt* you! I'm a horrible, horrible person. No wonder—'

'Shut up!' He gripped my arms so that I couldn't turn away and his voice was almost brutal. 'I won't go through this again, do you understand? I won't. All your self-hatred, self-blame, all this sodding renouncing me because you think it's the heroic thing to do. I'm fed up of it. I'm a *person*, Anna. I can make my own decisions. If I decide that being with you isn't worth the price, I'll walk away, but that's *my* decision to make, understand? So don't try to make it for me.'

'You can't ask me to put you through this.'

'I *can* ask you to give me a bit of bloody credit, Anna. Listen to me: if *you* want to walk away, do it. That's your choice. But if you do, I'll refuse to believe any of this crap about your higher motives. If you walk away from me, do it for one reason and one reason only – because you don't love me any more. Not because of what you *think* I want, or what you *think* is best for me. Until you can look me in the eye and tell me that you don't love me, I don't want to hear about it. *Then* you can leave.'

'How dare . . .' I began. And stopped.

Without realizing it our voices had risen to shouts and now from down the corridor I heard Dad's door open and his sleepy voice call, 'Anna, are you OK? I heard yelling.'

'Shit.' Seth looked around the room and then slipped behind the curtain. It was pretty lame – you could see his bare feet – but if Dad wasn't wearing his glasses . . . I turned down the lamp and flicked on the radio, just in time for Dad's bleary-eyed head to come round my door.

'You all right?'

'Sorry, Dad . . . I . . . I couldn't sleep. I was listening to the radio, a play – that was the shouting. I didn't realize it was so loud.' The story sounded weak even to my ears but Dad was preoccupied with something else.

'Can you smell that? Is that . . . something burning? Oh Lord, I didn't leave the kettle on the Aga, did I?'

'No it was me – sorry, Dad. I had . . .' I racked my brains, feeling the desperation rise. I'd always been a pretty rubbish liar and I could hear Seth's stifled breathing from behind the curtain, adding to my stress. Inspiration came. 'I was kind of dozing and I must have knocked my light over on to my bed. It scorched the sheet. Look . . .' I showed him one of the scorch marks on the bed and he frowned perplexedly.

'Blimey, I thought those energy-saving bulbs were meant to be low-heat. Terrifying they'd make a mark like that – are you all right?'

I nodded and he shrugged.

'Never mind then. No harm done, I suppose – just be a bit more careful in future.'

'Yes, Dad.' I breathed a sigh of relief that he'd bought my pathetic line.

'Night, love. Put your radio off and get some sleep now, hey?'

'Yes, Dad.'

'And for goodness' sake, turn the light out this time!' He kissed my forehead and shuffled off down the corridor, and from behind the curtain I heard Seth's shaky exhalation of breath. As Dad's door clunked shut, Seth stepped out.

'Nice lying there, Anna,' he whispered.

'Are you being sarcastic?' I hissed back.

'Er, yes! That was the lamest story I've ever heard!'

'Look, you try coming up with a cast-iron fib at two in the morning, while your boyfriend heavy-breathes from behind your bedroom curtain.'

'I'd have come up with a better one than that, even if my boyfriend was heavy breathing underneath my dressing gown.' We stood, glaring at each other, and then simultaneously broke into sheepish smiles. Seth held out his arms and I walked warily towards him. I held my breath – but there was no stifled exclamation of pain, no hiss of burning flesh. Seth gripped me painfully tight and kissed the top of my head, his breath warm in my hair.

'Sorry,' I said, my face muffled by his chest.

'No, I'm sorry. I was being a jerk before. It's lovely that you worry about me; I just wish . . .'

'Yes?' I looked up into his cloud-coloured eyes.

'I just wish that your worries didn't always take the form of pushing me away. It breaks my heart.'

I couldn't think of a reply to that; his words were dangerously close to breaking *my* heart. I only held him tighter, hoping he didn't see the tear that ran down the bare golden skin of his chest.

At last he sighed and stroked a hand down my hair.

'I should go,' he said. I nodded, but made no move to release him, and at last he prised my fingers from his ribs and kissed my forehead. 'Come on, only a few minutes ago you were kicking me out . . .'

'*It is the nightingale and not the lark . . .*'

162

'You know I got a D in English, sweetheart.' He pulled his T-shirt over his head and added, his voice muffled by the fabric, 'It's Shakespeare, right? I barely even know how that one ends.'

Not well, I thought, but I didn't say it. Instead I sighed and said, 'OK, go. Be careful, Seth.'

'I'll be careful. I always am.'

Not where I'm concerned, I thought.

I watched as he lowered himself out of the window, with a muffled volley of swearwords as his skin scraped the cold, wet bricks. There was a cautious, scrabbling rush and a thud as he hit the ground, and then with a whispered 'Bye, love . . .' he was gone, loping off towards the main road in the stark moonlight.

I climbed back into bed and switched off the light and then lay in the darkness, my mind running back across our argument. I didn't know whether to be glad or sorry that Dad had interrupted us. I knew that if he hadn't I would have blurted out the truth – that what I still feared was that Seth *didn't* have the power to walk away from me. That in spite of everything, he was still bound by that long-ago spell, unable to stop loving me, his heart enslaved no matter what.

CHAPTER ELEVEN

'Caradoc Truelove . . .' Emmaline bit the finger of one gloved hand, her breath making a white cloud as she pondered. 'Never heard of him. Where did you get the name from?'

I explained about the photo.

'So I looked at it under Dad's big magnifying glass, and you could just make out "Proprietor Caradoc Truelove" underneath the shop name.'

'What makes you think it was him taking the photo though?'

'Because when I looked at it under the glass, I could see the sign on the door was turned to "closed". If my mother was in the shop, it must have been with the owner, don't you think?'

'Could be the shop assistant.'

'I guess, but do you think it's likely the shop assistant

would be entertaining his mates after hours?'

'I suppose it's worth a try anyway – even if this Caradoc Truelove isn't the goods, he may know the right person. Do you want me to ask Mum?'

'Don't worry, I'll goog—' I was interrupted by roar of the crowd as the ball ricocheted off the Winter defender's hand and the ref's whistle blew, awarding a penalty to West Riding.

To say I wasn't the biggest football fan in the world would be putting it mildly, but this was a big game for Winter, and Seth was playing as striker. Unfortunately we were seventy minutes in and Winter was two–one down, so unless things looked up, we'd be losing the trophy. The Winter boys on the pitch moved into position for the penalty and stood waiting with tense muscles. The ref's whistle blew and the West Riding striker ran in and belted the ball. It sailed through the air in a perfect arc, heading for the far corner of the goal – and the Winter keeper flung himself sideways in a miraculous, suicidal save, crashing into the sea of mud with the football clasped in his arms.

'YEEEEEEEEEEEEEEEESS!' Em shrieked beside me, waving her arms in the air like crazy.

'I didn't know you liked football,' I said as she sat back down. She shrugged and gave me a sidelong smile.

'Sweaty, mud-covered, panting men wearing shorts –
what's not to like?'

'I see your point. There's definitely an impressive
amount of eye candy down there.' The sheer amount of
rain-drenched, mud-streaked male skin on display made
the game magnetic whether or not you cared about the
result. I saw Seth pounding down the field, his hair
slicked close to his skull, and watched as he tackled a
defender for the ball, weaving in and out of West
Riding players to take it back up the pitch. Then, with a
brutality that made me flinch, another player cut in to
tackle Seth and he tripped and pitched headlong into
the mud with a wet smack that was audible even up
in the stands.

'Yowch!' Even Em looked taken aback, but Seth was
up and running again in an instant. He flashed a quick
smile up towards the crowd, searching for me, and gave
me a little wave before plunging back into the action.

'Anyone in particular catch your eye, then?' I said
curiously to Em. She'd never shown any interest in the
boys at school – in fact I'd sometimes wondered if her
inclinations lay elsewhere.

'What, seriously, you mean?' She glanced over at me
to see if I was joking and then shook her head firmly.
'No, no way.'

'Why not? Seth's friend Matt, say.'

'Who's he?'

'The tall guy in goal.' I pointed at Matt, his sun-streaked hair turned dark gold with sweat and rain. 'You know, he's the one who's always bunking off to go surfing. He's lovely.'

'Huh.' Em snorted derisively.

'You don't even know him,' I said mildly.

'I don't need to. He's just an—'

She stopped and I looked at her, half cross and half amused.

'Just what? Just an outwith, that's what you were going to say, wasn't it?'

'Well . . .' She had the grace to look a bit embarrassed but I could see she wasn't really repentant. 'He is.'

'So's Seth. So's my dad. What are you trying to say?'

'Nothing. I'm not trying to say anything. I just don't think it ever works out.'

'How would you know?' I was getting cross now and the words came out more hotly than I'd intended. 'I'm half-outwith, you know.'

'No you're not.' Em shook her head dismissively.

'What – are you saying my dad's not my dad?' I was furious now, my voice rising above the roar of the crowd.

'Keep your voice down – and your knickers on. No,

I'm not saying that at all. I'm saying if you've got magic, that's it. If you haven't, you're an outwith. There's no such thing as half-outwith. If it comes to that, *I'm* half-outwith.'

'*What?*'

'My dad, he was just some random outwith, you know.'

'Some *random* outwith?' Her dismissive tone made me reel back. I wasn't sure if I was shocked, or disgusted, or pitying. 'And you've never wanted to meet him – to know him?'

'Not really.'

'What about Sienna?'

'No, her dad was one of us, but he died. I think that's what made my mum turn . . . outwards. She wanted a relationship without . . . without complications. Getting knocked up wasn't part of the plan, as far as I know. I don't think she let him hang around long enough to find out.'

'So he was just . . . just stud services?'

'More or less.' Emmaline looked slightly defensive, but she wasn't backing down. 'Look, it would never have worked. She didn't have anything in common with him – neither would I, if I ever met him. It just doesn't *work*.'

'Oil and water,' I said under my breath, my words swallowed by the roar of the spectators.

'What did you say?'

'Doesn't matter. But Em, how can you be so sure it'd never have worked – that you'd have nothing in common with your dad? You never gave him a chance.'

'Look.' Em's face was hard. 'You may not like it, and I'm sorry if this pisses you off, but it's true. It doesn't *work*.'

'What about me, what about *my* dad?'

'Yeah, and look how well that turned out with your mum,' Emmaline snapped back.

I don't know what reaction showed in my face – it felt like a stiff mask of cold. But Em looked stricken. 'Anna, I'm sorry, I shouldn't have said that.'

'Why not?' My voice sounded hard in my own ears. 'It's true.'

I turned back to the match and we sat side by side in silence, watching the boys running up and down in a weird, futile dance that suddenly made no sense to me at all.

'Go, Seth!' someone screamed behind me and I leant forward and saw that Seth had the ball and was tearing down the pitch towards the goal. A huge defender blocked his path but he feinted left, swerved right to avoid a second, and then paused for a microsecond, weighing up the closing gap between the sidelines and the defenders thundering towards him. He could go for it – but it would be a slim chance and there was another Winter player, Ahmid, waiting to his right.

'Shoot!' the crowd screamed, but the defenders were closing in. Seth passed to Ahmid and Ahmid took the shot and levelled the score to screams of adulation from the crowd. Seth clapped Ahmid on the back – and if he was frustrated at losing the shot you wouldn't have known it.

There were only a few minutes left now and the game was sliding towards a draw in a sea of mud. Five minutes, by my watch. Four. Three. And then there was a scuffle on the pitch, players down, grappling with each other in the mud. The shrill whistle blasted out and the ref called a penalty against West Riding.

The Winter team conferred for a minute and then Seth stepped forwards to take the penalty.

The crowd held its collective breath as Seth walked out in front of the goal and bowed his wet, seal-slick head. Then he ran his hands through his hair in the characteristic gesture I loved and ran towards the ball, as if he were a matador charging down a bull. His foot connected with a smack that echoed round the silent pitch and then the crowd erupted with screams of joy as the ball slammed into the corner of the net and the ref's whistle blew.

* * *

The crowd's celebrations were finally dying down, and I was shouldering my bag and ignoring Emmaline, when I felt a slippery, muscular arm snake round my neck and a hot, wet cheek press against mine.

'Do I get a kiss for the winning goal?'

'Seth!' I swung round and flung my arms around him, mud and all. 'Well done.'

'Photo finish, eh?'

'You did really well.'

'Well, I'm off for a shower. Are you coming to the pub to celebrate?'

I hesitated. Oil and water. Caradoc Truelove. Questions, answers, possibilities battering at my brain.

'Would you . . . Would you mind if I didn't? I'm just . . . I'm really tired. You won't miss me with all the team there.'

'Of course I'll miss you.' He kissed my cheek. 'But don't be silly – you go on home. Have a good night's sleep. Shall I see you tomorrow instead?'

'Actually . . . maybe not.'

'Not? What d'you mean?'

'I think . . . I think I might be going to London.'

Truelove Books returned far too many hits and *Caradoc Truelove* in quotes returned none, so I tried *Truelove Books*

Soho and *Truelove Books London*. There was nothing on the first two or three pages that looked remotely like a shop – almost all Amazon listings for authors called Something Truelove. None of them were Caradoc.

OK, yell.com maybe. There were no results for *Truelove Books* but when I widened the search, *Truelove & Fox* popped up on screen. Their listing described them as *Sellers and Dealers of Antiquarian Books and Curiosities*. I clicked to show it on a map. Not Soho, but Cecil Court – a little alley off Charing Cross Road. Close enough. Could this be it? Well, it was possible that he'd taken on a partner, I supposed. The other possibility, it suddenly occurred to me, was that he'd retired, or died.

I thought about ringing – for about two seconds. What could I say? 'Er, hello, could I speak to someone who might have known my possibly crazy, possibly deceased mother slightly more than eighteen years ago, possibly under her maiden name which I don't know? Oh, and did I mention the witchcraft?'

No. There was only one way to do this.

I wrote down the address of the bookshop and the times of the London trains tomorrow, and was just about to close down the computer when my email pinged. It was Em.

Hey. Sorry I was a bitch. I guess we both struck a nerve with each other – but that doesn't excuse me being a heinous tit.

I heard what you said to Seth. London, I mean. I'll understand if not, but if you want me to come, just say.

Em. x

I sat and stared at the screen for a long time. Then I pressed reply and wrote:

Hey. Me too. Etc.

Winter station, 10.05 tomorrow. No worries if you can't make it.

See you there. Or not.

A x

'We're going the wrong way,' Em said again. 'Surely it should be off the top end of Charing Cross Road – we're practically at the National Gallery.'

'It's this way; I'm telling you.' I looked down again at the A–Z and up at Charing Cross Road. But I had to admit, it didn't look promising. Then a small gap opened up between the towering buildings to our left and a little alleyway appeared between. It was full of narrow, Victorian shops, each stuffed full of books and maps. As we passed I examined the names painted on the discreet, understated signs and etched on the glass doors. *Goldsboro Books . . . David Drummond . . . Marchpane's . . .* I wanted to stop at all of them, rummage through musty stacks and ruffle crisp new hardbacks. But Emmaline was pointing to the farthest corner, where the littlest shop of all displayed a modest grey sign which proclaimed, in white letters, *Truelove & Fox.*

Suddenly my courage failed. If Em hadn't been there I would have turned back, fled to the Underground. But she saw me waver.

'Come on.' Her voice was low. 'Do you want to be always wondering?'

No. No, I wanted to know.

I pushed on the door and jumped as a small brass bell rang out in the silent, empty shop.

'Hello?' Emmaline called. There was no one behind the counter so we turned to look around. Dusty shelves rose up on every side, full from floor to ceiling with crumbling leather-bound books with gilt spines and marbled endpapers. Emmaline began walking along the shelves, her head tilted to one side to read the spines. I was more interested in the small glass case on the counter which displayed a small, heavy volume with a gilt lock.

'The *Grimoire of Honorius*,' I read from the ticket. 'Seventeenth-century kid-bound edition.'

'There's a lot of occult stuff here,' Emmaline said, 'but it's all well-known public stuff, if you know what I mean. I wonder—'

'Can I help you, ladies?'

We both jumped and turned to see that a man had come in silently from behind the counter and was surveying us over rimless glasses. He was tall and blond, with a neat goatee and a discreet gold stud in one ear. If he knew my mother eighteen years ago it must have been at primary school – there was no way this man was Caradoc Truelove.

I coughed and wished I'd rehearsed this with Emmaline on the train instead of deciding to wing it.

'Ah, yes. Er, can you tell me, we were looking for a Caradoc Truelove, who owned Truelove Books in Soho some years ago.'

'Yes?' said the man unhelpfully. Damn.

'Well, we just wondered; Truelove & Fox – is there any connection?'

'Yes.' His face was blank and unreadable.

'So, Mr Truelove – is he . . . ?' Arse. This was harder than I'd thought. I couldn't just blurt out, '*Is he dead?*'

I ground to a halt.

'Is he available?' Em put in, taking pity on my floundering. 'We were hoping to meet him. We think he knew my friend's mother.'

'Really?' Goatee-man looked slightly more interested. 'And who might you be?'

'My name is Anna Winterson. My mother was Isla Winterson. She died when I was a small child but I think Mr Truelove knew her before that.'

'I'm sorry, I've never heard of that name,' Goatee-man said firmly.

'Well, could we speak to Mr Truelove and ask him?' Em asked. There was impatience in her voice now. I could see she was tired of all this pussy-footing around.

Goatee-man thinned his lips.

'Mr Truelove is semi-retired. He works with our special collection and only sees certain clients.'

'Special meaning *what*?' Em jerked her head at the *Grimoire*. 'More special than that?'

'If you like to put it that way, yes.'

'We're not outwith,' Em stated baldly. I winced, as did the young man.

'I'm delighted to hear it,' he said rather tersely. 'Unfortunately, I can't take your word on that.'

'I see. Any particular hoops you want us to jump through?' Em nodded at the counter and a pile of invoices burst into flame.

'Stop that at *once*!' yelped the young man, his face ashen.

'Sure.' Emmaline shrugged and the fire died away, leaving the invoices untouched. 'Now, are you ready to let us see Mr Truelove?'

The young man was pale as clay and he glanced nervously out of the window at the shops opposite, but he shook his head.

'It's policy not to open up the special collection to anyone. Customers who cannot find the door do not get entry.'

'Find the door, eh?' Emmaline's eyes kindled and she began looking around her, at the shelves, behind the counter. Goatee-man shook his head.

'No, if she wants to see Caradoc –' he jerked his head at me '– *she* needs to open the door.'

'Oh no,' I said reflexively. Goatee-man only folded his arms, and a small spark of anger flared inside me.

I took a deep breath. I'd come this far; I wasn't going to be defeated by a bloody door. Here I was, surrounded by spells in every form, but all I could hear was Abe's voice nagging inside my head. How much did I want this? How much did I want the truth about myself, my powers?

I clenched my fists.

'Open,' I whispered. Then louder. 'Open.'

Nothing happened.

'Open, please.' I let my powers trickle out, terrified of

what might happen, but pushing in spite of my fears. The shop door flew open and a gust of wind began to scatter the invoices all round the room.

Goatee-man crossed his arms and his lips thinned.

'OPEN!' I shouted and I stamped my foot. A pile of books on the counter all flung open, the topmost ones crashing to the floor with a sound like muted thunder. The cash register jangled as the drawer shot out and the lock on the *Grimoire of Honorious* burst open, the cover flapping against the glass of the display case like a bird in a too-small cage.

'Please avoid damaging the stock any further,' Goatee-man said, furiously slamming shut the cash register, 'or I will have to ask you to leave.'

Oh God.

'Caradoc Truelove,' I said, and there was an edge in my voice that sounded like someone begging, 'please, please, wherever you are, open up, let me in.'

There was a creak.

We all froze and Em and I watched in amazement as an inky crack opened up in the centre of the shop, like a door opening out of nothingness.

Inside it was dark, but I could see something moving in the thin slice of shadow.

'I am Caradoc Truelove.' The voice was rich, croaky

and American, like Louis Armstrong on his tenth cigar. 'Who is asking for me?'

The crack opened wider; a doorway yawned impossibly out of the thin air. Inside, a dimly lit staircase led down into the solid floor. And a man was climbing the stairs, stepping into the room. He looked from Em to me, and as his eyes met mine he seemed to stagger. Goatee-man reached out an arm but Caradoc ignored it and stepped forward, his eyes fixed on mine.

'Oh my dear. My dear Isabella.'

CHAPTER TWELVE

He was nothing like I'd imagined. I'm not sure what I'd pictured – but not the elderly gentleman standing before us. He was very old – much older than I'd expected – and very black, with a white beard and inky black eyes so dark his pupils and irises merged into one. He was wearing gold-rimmed spectacles, a tweed jacket and a neckerchief of white silk, and as I stood, gaping, he fumbled with a silk handkerchief and then held out his hand to me. I shook it, feeling the papery old skin and the fragile veins beneath my fingers, and he blinked.

'You surely do look like Isabella, my dear.'

'Isabella?' I said, confused. 'My name is Anna.' I suddenly wondered if Mr Truelove was older than he looked. Mr Truelove looked annoyed with himself and tutted.

'I'm so sorry, one forgets as one gets older. Of course

you would only know her by the name she used after marrying your father. Isla, isn't that right?'

'That's right,' I whispered. False date of birth, false name . . . what else had my mother done to throw dust over her tracks?

'And you are Isabella's daughter.' His face creased into a sudden, charming grin that made him look twenty years younger. 'Come downstairs and you can tell me all about yourself. Are you happy to mind the shop, Jonathan dear, while I entertain our guests?'

'Of course, Caradoc.' Goatee-man gave a thin smile and then shot an appraising look at Emmaline and me that made me slightly nervous. It was clear he didn't quite trust us and didn't like not knowing what was going on.

Then Mr Truelove opened the inky-black crack in the centre of the room until it gaped, and beckoned us into the shadows.

'This is our inner sanctum,' Mr Truelove said as he led the way down rickety wooden steps. 'It is where we house all our more *curious* tomes. Entry is by invitation only; browsers are not encouraged.' He shot us both a look. 'As you will have discovered.'

As we reached the bottom of the steps I looked around, amazed to see a huge vaulted room stretching out metres in each direction. The shop above could not have been more than six or eight square metres – this basement was five, ten, twenty times larger than that: a shadowy cavern criss-crossed with stacks of shelves, each filled with hundreds upon thousands of books.

They varied from the very old to the brand new, from huge things like family Bibles to slim stapled pamphlets, but they all had one thing in common – I did not recognize a single title or publisher's name. Emmaline evidently did, and within moments she was walking along the shelves, reading titles and suppressing a moan of envy every few feet.

'Oh! Mum would kill for a copy of this.' She tapped a copy of a small hardback with a design of lavender on the spine. Caradoc adjusted his glasses and looked over her shoulder.

'Ah! *Herbs for Help-meets*. A classic. Is your mother interested in the subject?'

'Very.'

'Well then, you must allow me . . .' Caradoc pulled down the little tome and pressed it into Emmaline's hands.

'I really doubt I can afford it,' Em said, but there was longing in her voice.

'Please.' Caradoc inclined his head courteously. 'It is the bookseller's *raison d'etre* to find the perfect owner for a book. I am lucky enough to have arrived at a position where profit need not always be a barrier to that satisfaction.'

'Thank you,' Emmaline said, and she smiled at him – her rare disarming true smile. 'So you're . . . something of a specialist bookshop then?'

'Yes, indeed. Obviously our upper floor is open to all and we frequently welcome browsers and tourists – there's quite a market for grimoires and spellbooks among the outwith; dear Jonathan's province. But as you can see, this floor is quite separate; my own special domain, open only to the cognoscenti. Enough of all this, however.' He drew up two stools to the impressive roll-top desk that stood in the corner of the room and flicked a switch on an electric kettle. 'That's not what you're really here for, is it, Anna?'

His liquid black eyes felt like they were reading my soul.

'No. I'm here to find out about my mother.'

'So what can I tell you?'

I shut my eyes, pressing my hands into my closed lids until I saw stars. Then I drew a breath.

'Everything. What happened . . . Why was she so afraid? Why did she have to leave?'

'And what do you know?'

'Nothing.' My voice cracked at the truth of that statement.

Caradoc Truelove looked at me very directly for a moment, his eyes fathomless. Then to my shock his voice spoke, quite quietly and distinctly in my head.

Do you trust this girl you're with – Emmaline? Do you trust her absolutely?

His voice in my head was grave, with an urgent emphasis on *absolutely*, but I nodded.

Are you quite sure? I can make an excuse, we can speak some other time. Are you sure you want me to continue?

I nodded again, decisively. Emmaline had helped me every step of the way since I'd discovered my witchcraft; there was nothing I could hide from her. Caradoc returned my nod and spoke aloud.

'Very well then.' He poured water into a coffee pot and we all watched as steam blossomed and the good smell filled the air. 'Let me tell you about Isla – or, as she was then, Isabella Rokewood.'

A shiver ran through me at the sound of the name. I'd thought my mother was Isla Winterson; that name was all I'd had for so long – that name and an echo of her face in mine. Now even her name had proved a fragile illusion, splintering into shards under the weight of the truth. It seemed like the more I tried to find out, the less I knew.

Even the facts I thought I had were disintegrating in my hands. Would I have anything left at the end?

Caradoc poured three cups and handed one to Emmaline and one to me. Then he drew a long draught of the scalding black brew and drew a deep breath.

'Isabella was the only child of two of my very good friends, Henry and Elizabeth Rokewood. She was a charming child and a very accomplished sorceress, as you would expect for one of her lineage. She was also headstrong and beautiful, and became more so as she grew. Eventually she went up to Magdalen to read History and met your father, Tom. He was an outwith and your grandparents were against the match from the start. Not only did they naturally dislike the idea of bringing an outsider into their family, but there was the question of grandchildren. Isabella was the last of the Rokewoods – a very ancient family – and they were relying on her to continue the family line. As you know, our women can interbreed with outwith men – but it is a very uncertain business. A high number of pregnancies fail and the outcome – magically – is very uncertain for the child. Some of our greatest practitioners were sired by outwith fathers – but it's not uncommon for the child to be born without magic, or to be born an uneasy hybrid, endowed with magic but unable to control it perhaps.'

I flinched, but if Caradoc noticed, he didn't show it.

'You are trying to mix two distinct elements,' he continued, 'witch and outwith, and they resist always. The outcome is always uncertain and frequently surprising. And, too, there is the strain on the child, growing up in a family ripped in two halves, hiding their nature from their father for ever.'

I cleared my throat, deliberately avoiding Emmaline's eyes. 'S-so what happened?'

'Henry and Elizabeth put up with the relationship for a while, but when it became clear that Isabella intended to marry Tom, they put their foot down. They said they would never agree to the match and that Isabella had to choose between her community and her lover. If she chose Tom, their door would be closed to her for ever – they never wanted to see her or hear from her again.'

Caradoc paused, took a gulp of his coffee, and wiped his forehead with his silk handkerchief.

'Well, my dear, you know how it turned out. She chose Tom. She came to see me before she left – they were going to America, she said, to start a new life. I know something about being forced to choose between one's community and one's love.' He cast a glance at a small black-and-white picture on his desk. It showed two laughing young men in sharp fifties suits, one black with liquid dark eyes, the other white and golden, with their arms around each other's shoulders. 'Perhaps that's why she chose to say goodbye, I don't know.

' "I love him," she said when she came to see me. "There's nothing either of us can do about that. There are stronger forces in the world than magic, Caradoc. And I can't tear my heart in half just to please my parents."

' "What about children?" I asked, and she shrugged.

' "I'm not a brood mare for my parents' breeding programme. Perhaps there won't be any children, perhaps they'll be outwith themselves. And if not, well, we'll have twelve or thirteen years to work out how to cope."

' "And you could love them?" I asked. "You could love an outwith baby just as much?"

' "Why not?" she asked simply. "I love Tom."

'I didn't see her after that for a few years, although she wrote quite often, telling me about their travels in America, Tom's work, the thesis she was working on. Her research topic was something to do with the history of witchcraft – prophesies, I believe – but that was the only reference she made to magic in her letters. They might have been written by an outwith. It was as if she was determined to cut the magic right out of herself, excise it from her soul.'

I could feel Emmaline watching me and I knew what she was thinking. I kept my gaze fixed on Caradoc instead.

He sighed and sipped again at his coffee, his glasses misting with steam.

'And then, out of the blue, she turned up at my flat above my old shop in Soho one night. She was wild-eyed, heavily pregnant, completely beside herself, and asking for a bed. I didn't question her; I took her in and made up a bed for her in my study. My first thought was the relationship with Tom had soured, for she was in such distress, and fearful of people following her. But soon I realized that it was not Tom she feared, but someone else, someone in our community.

' "Don't tell *anyone*," she beseeched me as she fell asleep that night, holding my hand in an iron grip. "They're after me, Caradoc; they're scrying even now. I've thrown up all the veils I can think of, but it won't last long. You mustn't tell anyone; I'll be gone tomorrow, I promise. I've found someone who will protect her."

'I sat and nodded and soothed her, and thought about what best to do in the morning – whether to try to contact Tom, though I had no number for him, whether I should consult her parents, or just try to elucidate what was troubling her. For the moment I just sat and watched as she fell into a troubled sleep, plagued by nightmares and fears of people pursuing her, harming her, harming her baby. It was very late before she fell into a calmer sleep and I dared withdraw my hand from her grip and creep to my own bed. Perhaps that explains why I slept so deeply and so long. I will never forgive myself for that, for when I awoke, she was gone.'

He sighed again, the tremulous sigh of an old man struggling with the painful burden of the past.

'I never saw her again. I tried to write to her at the last address I had – my letters were returned as "gone away". I looked for her name in all the directories I could think of but there was no listing for Isabella Rokewood. I didn't know if she was in England or America. I didn't even know your father's full name; she had always referred to him only as Tom.

'At first I expected to hear from her daily.' Caradoc took another sip of coffee and sighed heavily. 'But the days stretched into months, and the months into years. And I came to believe that either she was dead or – forgive me, my dear – that she had done something terrible to herself, in the name of love.'

'Terrible?' I said, not quite wanting to hear the answer. Caradoc looked down into his mug, and when he looked up his lined old face was troubled.

'I began to wonder, you see . . . Her letters had so determinedly excised the magic from her life. It was almost as if she wanted to *be* an outwith.'

'Can you do that?' I asked wonderingly. Both Caradoc and Emmaline flinched, an identical expression of revulsion and fear on their faces.

'It is . . . There are procedures,' Emmaline said, half under her breath. 'It's illegal and very dangerous – even fatal. But it has been . . . attempted, so they say . . .' She trailed away and her eyes met Caradoc's.

'You are not to know, my child,' Caradoc said quietly. 'You who have grown up with the outwith, almost as one of them. But could you cut out your heart, your identity, make yourself other than what you are, even if it was your dearest wish?' He looked once again at the photograph on his desk and an expression of regret and longing crossed his lined face.

'So . . .' I tried to gather my thoughts. 'You never heard from her again?'

He shook his head. 'Nor you, I take it, since you told Jonathan that she was dead?'

'No. I don't remember her at all. And my father doesn't talk about her – or rather, didn't. I think she bewitched him to keep silent until I was eighteen.'

'Interesting.' Caradoc's brow furrowed. 'With what aim, do you think?'

'To hide Anna.' Emmaline spoke unexpectedly. 'She put a charm on their former house to cripple Anna's magic. One presumes, because she didn't want her discovered.'

'So her delusion persisted . . .' Caradoc said slowly.

'Was it a delusion?' Emmaline asked pointedly.

'A good question. But one we cannot answer at this moment.' He thought for a while and then turned to me. 'I never asked, what brought you to me?'

'This.' I showed him the photo of my mother, the witch-letters flickering faintly in the lamplight.

Caradoc studied each side of it and then handed it back to me, tears in his eyes.

'Forgive me,' he said huskily, and wiped at his eyes with his pristine handkerchief. 'She was so lovely, so very happy in the days before the shadows came for her.'

The shadows – just the word made me shiver.

'Do you think she was mad?' I said in a small voice. Caradoc looked at me with sympathy, but shook his head again.

'I don't know, my dear. I'm not a doctor or a psychiatrist. She was not herself, that night she came to see me. But people can be transformed by great fear or great stress. You need not be mad to be driven to desperation.'

'Like they say,' Emmaline put in drily, 'it's not paranoia if everyone really *is* out to get you.'

'And what about the person who was supposed to

191

keep us safe – the one she mentioned when she came to you?'

'Again, I don't know. I'm sorry, my dear. But I can only think that whoever it was, they failed her.'

So many questions – and no answers. But in the end, only one that really mattered.

'Do you . . . do you think she could be still alive?'

Cardoc sighed – a deep, tremulous breath. And I knew at once that I was not going to like his answer.

'Frankly, my dear, I do not. I'm very sorry. But I find it impossible to believe that she could stay away so long and that a talent as great as hers could remain hidden. She was a remarkable woman. She would have made her mark wherever she ended up; she could not have failed to do so, even *in camera*. The only way she could have rendered herself so completely invisible, to my mind at any rate, is death.'

I closed my eyes. After my mother's letter it was nothing more than I'd been expecting, but . . .

Caradoc's old dry hand clasped mine, frail as paper, firm as wood.

'But, my dear, you should not take my word for it. If you're seeking to trace her, your grandparents would be the best people to advise. At least, your grandmother would. Your grandfather is dead.' His grip tightened on my hand. 'I'm sorry to tell you so abruptly. They were both desperate after your mother disappeared, you know. They tried every method they could think of – magical and mundane – and if there was the least trace of her, alive or dead, they will have found it, I'm sure. I think they never got over the guilt they felt about disowning her. It was a fine, dramatic gesture at the time, but I don't suppose they ever thought it would be for ever. I know that Henry regretted it until the day he died.'

'My grandmother. Could I . . . Could you . . . ?'

'Contact her? I can do it now if you like.' He put his hand towards an old-fashioned Bakelite telephone on the desk. 'Do you want me to?'

I sat quite still. Did I want him to? Was I ready to meet her? To meet my grandmother; the woman who'd disowned my mother, forced her to choose between her family and her love and to split her two identities down the middle and cleave her soul.

I hesitated – but I knew the answer already. I had to meet her. I might never know the truth about my mother, but perhaps my grandmother could lead me closer to that truth.

'Yes, I want you to.'

He put his gnarled finger into the holes in the dial and swiftly dialled a London number, one he knew by heart. Someone answered, and he spoke in a courteous, old-fashioned manner.

'Good morning, might I speak with Elizabeth Rokewood, please? Thank you, I'll wait.' There was a long pause – at least, it felt long to me – and then he spoke again. 'Elizabeth, hello, my dear. Well – and you? Thank you, thank you. Now, I have something rather curious to tell you – a surprise. A young woman has arrived at my shop; she would like to meet you if at all possible . . . Yes. Yes, her name is Anna. She is Isabella's daughter.'

There was a long pause and I could hear the voice on the other end speaking quickly and crisply, asking swift questions to which Caradoc replied with affirmatives and short explanations. More talk, while I tried to remember to breathe and swallow. Then, 'I'm sure that will be fine. Thank you, Elizabeth, I will pass on the message. Would you like me to attend? Very well. If you're sure. Goodbye, my dear. Look after yourself.'

He put the receiver down gently and then turned to me.

'She would very much like to meet you. She suggests tea at the Dorchester at three – would that be convenient?'

'Yes,' I said. My heart began to race. I was going to meet my grandmother.

* * *

194

I sat in The Promenade at the Dorchester and wished I'd worn something else – Dad had taken Lauren and me to the Dorchester for champagne tea after we passed our GCSEs, but I'd been wearing heels and a skirt then. Now I was wearing walking boots suitable for the rutted muddy track up to Wicker House, worn jeans that showed my hip bones, and a loose open-neck shirt belonging to Seth. I had to laugh though, when I looked down at my lap and saw that my ankles and hands were crossed in the demure posture favoured by my old headteacher. I still remembered her barking, 'A lady never sits with her knees apart!' at girls in assembly.

It was a good job Emmaline wasn't here. She would have been thoroughly impatient with it all – the hushed atmosphere, the deferential waiters. We'd conferred at the tube station and eventually she'd decided to leave me to it.

'Look, it's your first meeting with your long-lost family,' she said, when I told her she was welcome to come. 'I expect they'll want to clasp you to their bosom – and I've had my fair share of whiskery granny kisses, thanks. Besides, it's the bloody Dorchester. What if your grandma turns out to be an old skinflint and refuses to pay my share of the bill? I'm not taking a chance of getting stuck with a forty-quid cream tea, Anna Winterson.'

She was joking, of course – but there was enough of a seed of truth in the joke to make me laugh, and I still had a smile on my lips from the memory of her fake indignation when a small dark woman with snapping black eyes, streaked black hair swept into a chignon, and a heavy gold necklace around her throat stopped in front of my table.

'Are you . . . ?' Her voice was throaty; it sounded older than she looked. The hand she extended was veined and fine-boned, weighted down by a thick gold bracelet and three heavy rings set with stones. I stood, suddenly sick with nerves.

'I'm Anna. Are you . . . ?'

She closed her eyes and, for a moment, I thought she was going to faint, have a heart attack here in the Dorchester. A vein stood out on her forehead and her fingers gripped her handbag with fierce desperation. Then she opened deep, hooded eyes and nodded.

'Yes.'

This was it. This was my grandmother – the one living link to my mother.

'Gra-grandmother?' I stammered. She took my hand in hers, her grip strong and dry, the rings biting into my hand with surprising strength.

'My dear. I have waited so long.'

* * *

Some time later we were seated with a pot of China tea between us and an untouched plate of wafer-thin sandwiches. I was awkward with nerves and too jumpy to eat, and Elizabeth – I could not yet quite think of her as my grandmother – though glacially calm, was whippet-thin and looked as if she existed off melba toast and celery.

I had told her about my upbringing – my mother's disappearance, the decision to declare her dead when I was young. She said nothing, but her rings flashed a trembling fire as she reached for the teapot.

'And tell me about yourself, my dear,' she said, pouring herself a thin stream of golden liquid and adding a slice of lemon.

'I'm not sure what there is to tell.' I bit my lip.

'Well, you have power, I can see as much.'

'Yes.'

'How did you cope with that, growing up? Did you find any of our people to help you?'

'My mother left a charm that, um . . . kind of neutralized my abilities while I lived in Notting Hill,' I found myself explaining. 'So nothing showed until we moved to Winter. And then . . . well . . . there were a few problems but a local family helped me.'

'So you lived in Notting Hill?' Elizabeth gave a slightly bitter laugh. 'Our London house is very close – Kensington. To think that we were scrying and searching and paying private detectives in America and all the time round the corner . . .' She let her voice trail off and sighed. 'We did you a great wrong when we disowned your mother, though we did not know it at the time. Poor Isabella.'

'Tell me about her,' I said, surprising myself with the urgency in my voice.

'You never knew her?'

I shook my head.

'What a tragedy.' Elizabeth sighed again, more heavily, and passed her ringed hand over her eyes. 'She was a lovely child – lovely. And a lovely girl. But very wilful. I suppose our fault was in controlling her life too tightly – we thought, you see, that we knew her. Knew everything about her. We thought – we all thought – that her affection was engaged by a family friend, Gabriel, but of course we were wrong, as it turned out. Heaven only knows if her relationship with your father would have run its course eventually, but our absurd overreaction ensured that it did not. I see now of course that if we had *wanted* to push her into your father's arms we could scarcely have gone about it more effectively. But –' she made a dismissive gesture with one slim hand '– it is water under the bridge. We did what we did, for the reasons we did. Your mother did what she did for her own. She's gone. But now we have you, and a second chance to be better and wiser people.' She smiled at me and put her hand against my cheek. Her skin was very cool, the gold rings cold against my skin; the room was hot and the chill of her touch was strange, but not unwelcome.

'Would you like to meet my father?' I asked, but I regretted it as soon as I'd said the words – I knew what the answer would be. Even before I'd finished the sentence she was shaking her head regretfully.

'No. I am sorry, my dear, but I think no good could come of it. I am sure that we wronged him, and that he is a good man and a kind one, and he has clearly brought you up with love and honour and intelligence. But he is outwith, and our kinds are oil and water. No good can come of mixing the two – and in any case, he must feel resentment towards us; no one but a saint could not. It would be awkward and, worse than awkward, painful. No, it is better left.'

'Then what shall I tell him?'

'Whatever you like, my dear. You have sufficient power to deal with the eventualities, I can see that.'

It took me a moment to realize what she was saying –

and when I understood her meaning I shuddered, filled with horror at the idea of enchanting my father to get my own way. That would make me . . . it would make me no better than my *mother*. I shook my head vehemently.

'No! Never. I made a promise—' I stopped.

'Yes?' she prompted.

'I promised myself I would never do that,' I finished. It was not what I'd been going to say, but it was true. My grandmother shrugged.

'As you like.' Then she looked at the gold watch on her left wrist and made a small tutting sound. 'Anna, I am so sorry, the time has gone quicker than I had thought. I have a meeting. I wish I could have postponed it but Caradoc's call came so late. Let me think . . . Could you meet me in two hours perhaps? For dinner?'

I thought. It would mean ringing Dad but he wouldn't mind; he'd assume I was staying up with Emmaline. At least, he would if I didn't correct him.

'Yes, if I can be at Victoria at five to nine. The last train for Winter leaves at five past.'

'I think that can be arranged. Now, let me give you directions to my office.' She pulled a business card out of her purse. It was made of very stiff cream card, embossed with the name *ROKEWOOD* and a small emblem, a black rook, I thought. It looked familiar, and I furrowed my brow as she scribbled on the card, trying to think where I'd seen it before. Elizabeth saw me looking and said briefly, 'The etymology of our name is from Rook Wood, hence our family symbol, and our motto: *corvus fugit.*'

She capped her fountain pen with a snap and handed me the card, now covered with sloping black copperplate, written with the finest nib I'd ever seen.

'Take a cab to Vauxhall Bridge and follow these directions,' she said. Then she bent and, with surprising tenderness, kissed my cheek. 'Goodbye, my dear. I am so very pleased you have found us. I only hope we can make a fresh start. Heaven knows I was not a perfect mother, but perhaps I can be a better grandmother.'

And then she was gone, leaving only a trace of a curiously bitter perfume, which hung like incense in the air, and the lipstick stain on her bone-china teacup.

For a moment I just stood, foolishly, and then I began to pick up my bags and find my way out. The mâitre d'hôtel approached me as I made my way through the tables and a sudden, dreadful thought struck me – Emmaline's remark about being stuck with the bill rose up in my head and I had to repress the urge to giggle hysterically. What would I do? I had no money. I did have my cash card but would they let me out to go to an ATM?

'I'm so sorry,' I began nervously. 'My grandmother

just left and – you'll think this is so silly – but I've just discovered I don't have enough cash to pay the bill and—'

'Please don't concern yourself, Miss Winterson,' the man interrupted. 'It has been added to Mrs Rokewood's account. I merely wished to enquire whether you would like to rest in the ladies' lounge, or whether I can arrange for a taxi to take you anywhere. The expenses will be charged to your grandmother's account, naturally,' he added, as he saw me looking doubtful.

I was tempted, very tempted. I'd been walking round London all day and I was tired and footsore. But it seemed too strange to start spending my grandmother's money and I shook my head.

'No, no thank you. But if you could show me somewhere I could make a phone call . . .'

'Certainly.' He ushered me through a lobby and into a small drawing room, furnished with a desk, a fireplace and a row of bookshelves. 'Please, remain here for as long as you need to. I will ensure you are not disturbed. The telephone is on the desk.'

He shut the door behind him. It closed with an expensive-sounding clunk and I was alone.

I looked at the phone – a faux-antique gold thing with a turn dial – but I wasn't sure whether it would need a charge card, or how to get an outside line, and in the end I just pulled my mobile out of my pocket and dialled the house number.

It rang and rang, and I tapped my foot, waiting for Dad to hear the ringer and pick up. He was probably closeted in the kitchen cooking supper, but still . . . He often said he was going deaf in his old age. Maybe it was true. At last the answerphone kicked in.

'Uh . . . Hi, Dad. Are you there? Pick up if you're there. OK, well, I'm stopping in London for supper so don't worry about cooking for me. I'll catch the nine o'clock train so . . . well, don't wait up. I'll get a cab from the station, don't worry.'

Then I tried his mobile in case he was out and about. It went straight to answerphone but that wasn't surprising; there was no reception at the house. I left another message, just in case, and hung up. Then I went out into the cool London twilight, twinkling with the yellow lights of shops and cars.

When I got off the tube at Pimlico it was quite, quite dark. I clip-clopped my way down Vauxhall Bridge Road in the new pair of shoes I'd bought from Topshop in an effort to make my jeans look like something more than Saturday slob-wear. I couldn't afford a whole new outfit, but the heels at least made me feel like I was smart from the ankles down. I'd have to change back into my walking boots on the train home though, or risk breaking a leg on the walk back.

At Vauxhall Bridge I stopped, fished in my pocket and found Elizabeth's card. It was cold on the bridge, the winter wind howling along the Thames and straight through my thin anorak. My hair whipped around my face, obscuring my vision as I tried to read the spidery black writing on the little card.

'Go to the centre of the bridge,' I read. 'Stand above the second pier, downstream, statue of Fine Arts. When bridge . . .'

The last few words were in even smaller writing, cramped into the corner where she had run out of room. I couldn't read it in the dim light, but there was a streetlamp halfway along the bridge so I began to make my way along until I stood by the second pier, under the lamp. I leant over the edge, trying to ignore the black water greasily swirling around the foot of the pier, and saw that I was standing above a black iron statue – of what, I couldn't quite tell, but I was quite prepared to believe that it represented Fine Arts. I angled the card to the light again and the lamp flashed off the little embossed bird. Again it reminded me of something hovering just at the edge of my memory – but whatever it was eluded me and I peered instead at the narrow slanting letters cramped into the corner of the card. *When bridge . . . empties?* Yes, that looked right. The next word was even smaller, just three or four letters. *When bridge empties, jump.*

No, that couldn't be right. I angled the card again and then had an idea and got my mobile out of my pocket. I turned on the screen and shone it at the card. The word leapt out, clear and bold and unmistakable. *Jump.*

What was this – some kind of joke? A test? What would I find down there? I looked down at the black waters, sucking and eddying at the grimy concrete, and shuddered. I was pretty sure what I'd find down there; used needles, condoms, shopping trolleys, various dysenteric bacterium. Yum.

I could turn back – I could go back to Winter and leave my grandmother waiting, and my questions unanswered, and my yearning for a family and a link with my mother unassuaged. Yes, I could turn back.

But that would make me a coward.

The parapet was curiously low, with no real safety barrier. There was even, improbably, a little ledge to help you climb up. I put one foot on the ledge and the other on the parapet, and looked up and down the bridge. It was empty of traffic, not a pedestrian in sight on this chilly winter's night. The office windows reflected back at me blankly and the black waters swirled beneath.

I took a deep breath – and jumped.

CHAPTER THIRTEEN

I hit the river with a smack that knocked the breath out of me – and then the swirling grey-green waters closed over my head. The current seized me straight away, turning and buffeting and dragging me until I had no idea which way was up, whether I was swimming or falling, or drifting or diving, or whether I would ever surface again. My lungs protested and my eyes filled with scratching silt and murk – but just as I was beginning to wonder if this had all been a huge mistake, I saw concrete steps shimmer out of the murk and a steel door lit by a bare, unshaded lightbulb that swung in the current.

My feet in their stupid heels hit something hard and, as I stumbled, I was half aware of the swirling waters, but also of tumbling painfully down a short concrete staircase and hitting the floor at the bottom with a thump that ripped my jeans and took the skin off one knee.

I stood up painfully and looked about me. I was at the foot of a flight of concrete steps, in a subterranean corridor. It might have been the underground car park of an office block. There was a smell of damp and the sound of water dripping somewhere far off – but my clothes and hair were dry. The only sign of the river was a piece of weed stuck to my shoe.

I shook it off and turned to the door. There was no handle and no lock, only an intercom grille with a button. I glanced behind me, back up the stairs, but they disappeared into nothing – the way back cut off by a slab of concrete. There was nothing for it. I pressed the buzzer.

'May I help you?' The disembodied voice that came from the intercom was crisply polite.

'Er, yes . . . um, Anna Winterson. I'm here to see Elizabeth Rokewood.'

'Come in please, miss. Push the door when the buzzer sounds.' There was a click and the intercom went silent. Then the buzzer sounded, horribly jarring in the silent corridor, and I pushed and entered.

I was in a softly lit entry hall, lined with walnut panels that reflected the lamps set in sconces around the walls. A tall, grave man dressed in an undertaker's suit was standing behind a little desk and looked up as I entered.

'Miss Winterson?'

'Yes.'

'Sign in, please, and then take a seat.' He pushed a huge leatherbound tome over the desk and a pen, and I signed my name in the column marked *Name* and wrote 'Elizabeth Rokewood' in the column headed *Visiting*.

The tall man showed me to a bench against the wall and I sat and waited, resisting the urge to bite my nails nervously and trying to ignore the pain in my skinned knee. The building was very hushed, but not quiet – people moved purposefully up and down the hallway, their feet whispering on the soft, thick carpet. Office doors opened and closed, punctuated by the occasional deferential knock. So far, it could have been just a particularly luxurious department of the Civil Service, but the longer I sat, the more I noticed the extravagant magic underpinning everything.

There seemed to be no electricity, for instance. Heat came from fireplaces in every room, yet the flickering light in the sconces around the walls was not electric light or candlelight, but a white witchlight that burnt with a perpetual, smokeless flame. When an office junior dropped a cup of coffee with an exclamation of annoyance, the stain simply vanished into the thick carpet, which moments later was just as clean and dry as before.

The more I looked, the more I saw. Trolleys moving

silently under their own steam, tropical plants thriving in a sunless room. A panelled door which opened once, to reveal a small coat closet, and then a second time, to show a glimpse of endless rows of books shimmering into darkness. I thought of Maya and how disgusted she would be at this profligate waste of magic – part of me was shocked myself, but I was impressed too, at the huge pulsing flow of power running so quietly around us.

I was so caught up that I jumped when a woman in a smart grey suit halted in front of me, smiling.

'Anna?'

'Yes.' My voice was croaky with nerves and I coughed and repeated, 'Yes.'

'I'm Miss Vane. Your grandmother has been slightly delayed. She's asked me to show you to her office while you wait – I expect you'd like to wash and change your clothes if you've been travelling all day.' I stood up, wondering how to mention that changing my clothes wasn't exactly an option – unless she meant putting my walking boots back on. But she was already starting down the corridor and I had to trot to keep up.

'Library,' she announced crisply as we passed a set of tall double doors. 'Dining room . . . conservatory . . . speaker's chamber . . . and here is your grandmother's office.' She knocked perfunctorily and then opened the door to a comfortable room furnished with an oak desk and a selection of chairs. There was a Chesterfield sofa in front of a low fire, and Persian rugs on the floor. The walls were hung with delicate watercolours of landscapes and flowers, except for one painting in oils above the desk. It showed a man I'd never seen with a hawklike nose and a shock of dark hair. *Henry Rokewood* read the plaque beneath. Well, well. Hi, Grandad.

To my surprise, a pile of clothes lay spread out on the coffee table in front of the fire. They looked quite out of place and I was just wondering what they were doing there when Miss Vane picked up a hanger and held it up appraisingly.

'Your grandmother of course realized that you weren't prepared for formal dining when you came up to London, so she asked me to pick up some suitable clothes. I had to guess your size – and your taste, of course – but I hope you'll find something that suits, and please feel free to discard any that don't appeal. I'll leave you to change,' she added, and slipped out of the door, closing it with a click behind her.

After she was gone I stared around the office for a moment and then shook myself and began to leaf through the pile of clothes. They were all labels I recognized – the Winter newsagent stocked *Vogue* just to mock us – but I'd never imagined wearing any of them. I had a horrible feeling that each garment probably cost more than the entirety of my wardrobe.

The idea of taking off my clothes in this plushy office was frankly weird, but I shoved a chair under the door handle and peeled off my jeans and Seth's shirt as quickly and modestly as possible. The first dress I tried on was a sooty cashmere sheath that made me look like an extra from a Bond movie and the next was a slinky rose satin number that displayed an alarming amount of my non-existent cleavage.

Then I found a grey silk shift dress, cut on the bias. It was incredibly simple – just a tunic really – but it gave me curves I'd never seen before and the fabric flowed seductively over my hips like cool water. It was utterly, utterly lovely. I loosed my hair and let it fall around my shoulders, and wished that Seth could see me – in this dress I could almost do him justice.

A sudden knock at the door made me jump and I pulled away the chair and opened it to find Miss Vane outside.

'Are you ready, Anna?'

I stuffed my clothes into the Topshop bag and left it in the corner of the sofa, then picked up my handbag.

'Yes, quite ready, thank you.'

My grandmother was waiting in the dining room when we entered and she stood up from her seat with a smile.

'Anna, dear. You look lovely. Thank you, Miss Vane, that will be all tonight.'

'Goodnight then, ma'am.' Miss Vane inclined her head, not quite a curtsey but not far off. 'Anna.'

I sat nervously in the chair that my grandmother indicated and spread a napkin on my immaculate grey silk lap. The room was filled with small tables of twos and threes, eating and drinking and talking in low voices. A waiter came up and my grandmother glanced at a small card on the table.

'Hmm . . . Let me see, Wilson. I think we'll have watercress soup, followed by the lemon sole. With . . . *pommes boulangères* and wilted cavolo nero. Does that sound all right, Anna dear?'

I nodded, too overawed to speak.

'And a half bottle of the Gosset Grand Reserve. Do you like champagne, Anna?'

'Yes, thank you,' I murmured.

'Very good, ma'am.' The waiter gave a half-bow and retreated and my grandmother put her chin in her hands and looked at me over the flickering candle between us.

'Oh, my dear . . . you look astonishingly like your

mother in this light. Her eyes were just as beautiful. How old are you?'

'Seventeen,' I said automatically, and then realized that wasn't true. It seemed too complicated to explain.

'I bitterly reproach myself for all the years you were lost to me, to us. I was wrong, I realize that now, in my approach. But I never guessed how mortally offended Isabella would be, the lengths she would go to.' She sighed and I fought the urge to reach across the table and touch her gnarled, bejewelled hand.

'Well, we can't undo the past, heaven knows.' She seemed to shake herself out of her introspection. 'Tell me about yourself, Anna. What are your interests?'

'Well, I like reading,' I said nervously. 'Um, I'm hoping to go to university and study English. I'm doing English, Maths, French and Classics for A level. Er, that's kind of it really. I'm not very sporty – I don't do much in the way of extra-curricular stuff.'

'That's very nice,' my grandmother said, and I saw that she was suppressing a smile. 'But I meant magically. What are your strengths?'

'Oh! I have no idea.'

'No idea? You mean, you're not studying?'

'No.' I shook my head.

'But that's abominable! I can see from a glance the

214

power you have! Show me something – something simple. Let me see . . . This glass of water.' She held up a crystal glass. 'Can you turn it to ice?'

'What – here?' I looked around the crowded room in shock. Again her lips thinned in a smile.

'My dear, we are all the same here. You need not hide your power among friends.'

'Oh!' Of course. It was obvious when you thought of it. But still, I was reluctant.

'I don't know – I'm not very . . . very practised.'

'Please.' She tapped the glass with a finger, her ring making it chime like a bell. 'Please try. For me.'

I bit my lip, but there was no way out without seeming rude – and a part of me did want to show her that I had some power. And here, at least, I would be safe. I could let my magic bubble out, unworried about exposing myself or hurting passing outwith. 'Oh . . . all right,' I said at last. 'I'll try.'

I set the glass on the table and let my power flow out towards it, thinking of cold, of ice, of snow and hail and winter and . . .

It was coming – it was coming too fast, too forcefully. I tried to pull back, but too late – the glass shattered with a noise like a gunshot, shards of crystal splintering away from the frozen chunk of water. There were echoing cracks and crashes all around the room. Cries of alarm, shouts of pain – plates shattering, glasses cracking, as the cold flowed unstoppably out, turning everything to ice: the wine in the glasses, the vases of flowers on the mantle, the huge tureen of soup on the sideboard. I whimpered and strove to control it. I had it reined in within seconds, but seconds was all it had taken to devastate the room.

'Stop! Stop!' My grandmother cried.

'I'm so sorry!' I cowered in my chair, holding myself as if to stop the power escaping any further. 'I'm so, so sorry, I didn't mean . . . It's all my fault. I can't . . .' I wanted to sink through the floor with shame and horror. What had I done?

'Goodness me!' My grandmother brushed shattered glass off her lap. 'Well, you can't say I didn't ask for that.'

I couldn't meet her eyes, but when she said, 'Darling, look at me when I'm speaking to you,' I could hardly refuse. And when I looked up, her face was unconcerned, even amused.

'I'm so sorry,' I whispered.

'Don't be silly, Anna.' Her voice was crisp. 'It was my fault for not realizing quite how strong you evidently are. And, possibly, for choosing a less-than-wise test of your powers.'

Waiters were already hurrying round the room,

sweeping and tidying, and within five or ten minutes there was no sign of my outburst except for a rip in the wallpaper behind the sideboard where the soup tureen had shattered.

'It is of no consequence, darling.' My grandmother nodded round the room. 'The control will come, and look, no one is perturbed.'

It was true – they had all returned to their meals, except for those unlucky enough to have been still on their soup course, and they were swiftly being provided with fresh plates of soup by the waiters. The stains had gone and, as I watched, a waiter hurried over and smoothed the torn wallpaper back into place. When his hand passed over, the join was invisible.

'Where *are* we?' I asked.

'Do you mean what is the name of this place, or literally where are we? If you mean the latter, I can't answer that. We are in a place between, in a place we have created for ourselves. It draws its power from the lost rivers of London, trapped by men but harnessed by us. The Effra, the Fleet, the Falconbrook, the Neckinger, and all the others. The roots, the foundations for this place are in the rivers, which is why the entrances are always close to where those rivers surface – the Effra empties into the Thames under Vauxhall Bridge, at Saint Luke's gate.'

'And the name?' But as I said it, a woman stopped by our table and something seemed to grip me – a chill. Her face was familiar – and it made my spine trickle with fear. Why? *Why?*

'Chair Rokewood,' she said, 'Chair Corax asked me to mention the paperwork from the Sennite meeting to you before I left and to ask whether you'd had time to sign the accord.'

'Not yet,' my grandmother answered composedly. 'There are a few clauses I still need to consider.'

'I'm not clear what needs to be considered, ma'am. Chair Corax made his views quite plain.'

'Contrary to some beliefs, Corax is not the only person with an opinion on this accord.' There was steel under my grandmother's calmness, but I hardly listened to her words.

Instead I stared at the woman, gripped by the need to remember who she was, where I had seen her face, and why her presence here filled me with cold dread.

'Allow me introduce my granddaughter to you,' my grandmother said at last. 'This is Anna, Anna Winterson. Anna, this is Ms Revere, who works here for my colleague, Thaddeus Corax.'

And then I remembered.

I remembered where I'd seen the bird insignia

on my grandmother's calling card – and why it had disquieted me.

I remembered the face of the woman opposite and where I'd seen her before.

And I knew where we were.

'You!' I jumped up, rocking the table and causing the candle to totter and spill.

'I'm sorry,' said Ms Revere, and her voice was calm and light, though her eyes were wary. 'Have we met?'

'Yes we've *met*,' I spat. 'We met when you and Mr Peterson threatened to kill my friends and family.'

'What!' She gave a baffled laugh, but it sounded fake as hell to me.

'Anna, what are you talking about?' My grandmother stood too, looking from Ms Revere to me in consternation. I stared back at her, trying to read past that immaculate mask. Was her confusion real? Was this all a massive con, a trap? Was she even really my grandmother?

'Where are we?' I said through gritted teeth.

'In the dining room!' my grandmother exclaimed with a touch of exasperation. 'What on earth are you talking about, Anna?'

'Don't give me that,' I spat. 'I mean what's this place – this building? Who *are* all these people? Who are *you*?'

'But I thought you knew,' my grandmother said. 'This

219

is the headquarters of the Ealdwitan, of course it is.'

'*You're* part of the Ealdwitan?'

'Yes – I am one of the five Chairs. Surely you knew all this?'

'What do you mean? D'you think if I'd known you were one of *them* I would've let you anywhere near me – after what happened last year?'

'What happened last year? Anna, please calm down, you're becoming hysterical.'

'Calm down? Calm *down*?' I was almost sobbing. 'After you threatened my family, flooded my village, killed my *friend*, for God's sake! And you say calm *down*?'

Waiters were hurrying over to our table, ready, I supposed, to throw me out – but my grandmother made a motion with her hand and they paused, waiting for her command.

'Anna, there's been some misunderstanding,' my grandmother said carefully, 'some mistake.'

'Damn right there has.' I swiped at my cheeks – furious with myself for my weakness but unable to stop the tears of rage spilling out. 'My mistake was trusting you.'

'Anna, please.' My grandmother reached out with her hand and I backed away.

'Don't touch me. Let me out.'

'Anna—'

'Let me out of here, *now*. Or you'll regret it.' I meant it. I could feel the power rising inside me in line with my fear, and if I didn't get out soon we would probably *all* regret it. For a long moment we just stood, my grandmother and I, facing each other across the table, and then she let out a breath of defeat.

'Very well. There's an exit to your left as you leave the dining room, take the second turning and then it's the third door on the right-hand side of the corridor. But, Anna, please—'

I didn't wait to hear any more. I turned so sharply that my chair tipped backwards and banged on to the floor with a crash in the silent dining room. Then I left.

I walked as fast as I dared down the corridor, my heart beating painfully as I tried to ignore the startled glances from the secretaries.

Second left. I turned. One door, two doors, three. It was an unobtrusive thing sandwiched between two huge vases of flowers. I tried the handle and it turned – was it really possible they were going to let me go so easily? I glanced up and down the corridor; it was empty. I half expected Ms Revere to appear and block the way – but no one materialized and the door opened as smoothly as silk.

I found myself nose to nose with a man.

Behind him was a small sitting room, with no way out.

221

At the sight of the dead end I couldn't stop myself – my hands flew to my mouth and I stifled a cry. Was it a mistake? A trap? Had I misheard the directions or had they never intended to let me go?

I had no idea where to go. I turned, about to run, blindly, when the man grabbed my wrist.

'Hey, hey, what's the matter? Are you OK?'

'No!' I was too beaten and desperate to pretend any more. 'No – I'm not OK, please let me go.' I pulled at my wrist but he held me, not roughly, but his grip was strong. 'Let go!'

'It's all right . . .' He put his free hand on my shoulder and I felt his magic reach round me, a soothing immobilizing fug. 'Listen, just calm down—'

'Stop it, please, just let me go!' I tugged hopelessly at his grasp, hearing sounds from up the corridor and feeling the desperation of my predicament – entombed below London with the people I feared most in the world.

The man looked along the corridor and then back at me. He was young, I saw, only a few years older than me. In other circumstances I might have thought him handsome.

'Please,' I begged. The sounds were coming closer. 'Please, tell me how to get out of here.'

'OK,' he said, seeming suddenly to make up his

mind. He pulled me through the door and into the room, shutting the door behind us. Inside he let go of my wrist and turned to a long wall of books lining one side of the room. The books were behind glass doors and he took a key and unlocked one of the cabinets. 'In there.'

'In here?' I looked incredulously at the heavy shelves and he nodded impatiently.

'Yes.' There was a knock at the door and he raised one eyebrow. 'Well, do you want me to get that or do you want to trust me?'

'Who are you?' I said desperately.

'My name is Marcus,' he said. Then, as the knock came again, 'You have about three seconds to decide. One, two—'

I opened the door, stepped through, and someone slammed it shut behind me.

The other side was cold – incredibly cold – and for a moment I thought this was the last trap of all, and I'd been led into some oubliette of no return. There were sheer stone walls all around me, cold stone under my feet. Water dripped, the sound echoing around the walls, and high above a lightbulb flickered dully. I was just about to panic when I saw a familiar signpost pointing upwards, to Blackfriars tube station. I must be in an underpass on the Thames Embankment – probably under Blackfriars Bridge.

I started to walk in the direction of the sign, clutching myself against the cold. The thin silk dress was no protection against the January night air and I began to shiver. To make things worse, I was still wearing the stupid heels and they slipped and skidded on the steep concrete steps up from the underpass. But I was safe, out of that hellhole, and that was the main thing.

I thought bitterly about my clothes and boots, still lying in that office. Would I ever get them back? At least I had my handbag – I was still too much of a Londoner to leave valuables lying around in a strange place, no matter how posh. Without my purse and train ticket I'd have been royally stuffed. As it was, at least I'd be allowed on the train to Winter. If I didn't die of hypothermia or break a leg on the cobblestones first.

I'd never been so thankful to be on board a train. The meagre stream of warm air coming from the heating vents felt like a sauna after the freezing night air. I huddled into a corner seat and drew my knees up to my chest to try to get a bit of warmth into my chilled bones. Then I pulled out my phone and I tried Dad.

This time I let it ring until the answerphone cut in,

hung up, and then tried again. Still nothing. What was going on? It was long past his usual supper time. Surely he'd be home by now – I just couldn't believe he'd have gone for a night out without telling me, or without knowing whether I was home safe. It wasn't like Dad and I got the first chilly presentiment that there was something very wrong in Winter.

I tried Seth next. His phone cut out – but I'd been expecting that. He was probably at either the pub, or the hospital. Next I tried the bar phone at the Crown and Anchor.

'Crown and Anchor,' I heard in a half-shout above the bar noise. It was Angelica, one of the regular barmaids.

'Hi, Angelica. Is Seth there?'

'No, sorry, is that Anna?'

'Yes.'

'He's over at the hospital with Elaine.'

'OK, thanks.'

'Any message?'

'No worries, see you later.'

'Bye.'

She hung up and I texted Seth.

Will be Winter station 10ish if you want to give me a lift? No worries if not, can get cab. Ax

Then I let my head loll and waited for the train to carry

me back to Winter. The cold couldn't keep me awake. The noise of the station announcements didn't rouse me. Even the sound of my mobile beeping with Seth's reply didn't get through. I simply slept.

'Hey, gorgeous.' Seth was waiting at the ticket barrier as I trudged wearily up the steps. 'Christ, what are you wearing?'

'Don't ask.' I shoved my ticket bad-temperedly at the collector and we left the station.

'Anna, you're blue with cold.' Seth took off his jacket and I huddled into it gratefully. 'Where's your coat and stuff?'

'Oh, Seth.' I was so tired I could hardly think. 'I'll tell you tomorrow – but not now, OK? It's a long story.'

'OK. Just tell me one thing – you didn't get mugged, did you?'

'No, no, I didn't get mugged.'

I fell wearily into the passenger seat of Seth's car and let my head rest against the window as we drove down through the town to the harbour, and then began the climb up the cliff road, towards Wicker Wood and our house. My eyes were shut, so at first Seth's exclamation of 'Holy . . . Anna!' made no sense. I opened them blearily and looked around.

'What – what is it?'

'I don't know but . . .' He nodded out of his window and I peered past him into the black night. Except it wasn't completely black. There was a reddish glow above the forest. Right where Wicker House should have been.

CHAPTER FOURTEEN

I didn't really believe it at first. Not when we saw the dull, fiery glow above the trees. Not when the smell of smoke started to filter into the car's vents. Not even when we were bumping down the track in the forest and I could hear the crackle of police radios and see the blue pulse of emergency-vehicle lights.

But I had to believe when we drew up outside Wicker House and I saw the still-glowing embers, the fallen beams, the pools of dark water from the firemen's hoses and, worst of all, my dad, sitting on a broken-down fence with his head in his hands.

'Dad!' I stumbled from the car and took a few steps over the sodden ground, but my heels instantly sank into the mud, leaving me pinned. Impatiently I ripped them off and ran, hot cinders crunching beneath my bare feet.

'Anna!' His head shot up at the sound of my voice and

as I reached him he stood and put his arms around me. I buried my face in his fleece as I hugged him back. It smelt of smoke and my eyes welled with tears.

'What happened?'

'It's not as bad as it looks,' Dad said. 'The worst of the damage is to the barn and the garage. But the kitchen has pretty much gone. God knows how we'll pay for the repairs . . .'

'Oh, Dad.' My voice cracked. 'How? Was it the Aga?'

Dad shook his head wearily.

'Unbelievably, they think it was arson.'

'What!'

'I know. I know. But they found traces of accelerants – and there's that.' He nodded towards the end wall of the house, which was more or less untouched. It was illuminated by the lights from the fire engine, and I saw, to my horror, in blood-red letters a foot high: *EX 22 18 MM*.

Oh God.

'What does it mean?' I asked mechanically, even though I was pretty sure I knew what it meant. Not the text – but who'd done this, and why.

'Lord knows.' Dad ran a hand through his hair. Maybe it was the light, or the ashes in his hair and on his face, but he suddenly looked very old and very tired. 'Kids, probably. I told them about the other letters. They asked all the obvious: is there anyone who's got a grudge against us, did you have any suspicious ex-boyfriends, have I offended anyone in town . . . ?'

'What did you say?'

'What could I say? No, no and no. I said I had no idea.'

'This your daughter, sir?' A policeman was picking his way over the muddy, rutted field towards us. Dad nodded.

'Yes, this is Anna.'

'I'm Sergeant Whittacker, Anna. I'm very sorry to trouble you under these circumstances, but you'll understand I have to ask you some questions.'

I nodded wearily.

'OK.'

'That your young man?' He pointed towards Seth, waiting by his car, not wanting to intrude on Dad's misery.

'Yes, Seth Waters.'

'Seth Waters, eh? I know that name.' His lips thinned and I almost groaned. Not this again. Would Seth ever manage to live down that one dreadful fight? It was nearly four years ago, he'd been little more than a child, and he'd been picked on by a grown man who should have known better. But none of that seemed to matter to the police. They knew his name. That was that.

'I'll need to speak to him as well.' He motioned to Seth, who came over slowly.

'Been for a night out, have you, Anna?' the sergeant asked me.

'No – yes. Sort of. I've been up in London. With a friend. I was there all day, I just got back. Seth gave me a lift from the station because I couldn't get hold of Dad.'

'I see. And what about you, Seth?'

'I worked in my mum's pub this afternoon, then my mum and I went to visit my grandad. He's in Brighthaven Hospital.'

'I see. And you're old enough to serve behind the bar, are you?'

Seth raised one eyebrow and I could see his anger rising. I knew he was biting back a sarcastic retort. I took his hand and squeezed it gently and he exhaled and just nodded curtly.

'What time were you in the pub from?'

'Look, I didn't torch my girlfriend's house,' Seth said through gritted teeth. The sergeant said nothing for about ten seconds – just looked at him with unconcealed dislike.

'Just answer the question, son.'

'From about two. Maybe quarter past two. I was with another member of staff all afternoon, and then my mother picked me up. Is that OK?'

'We'll check it out,' the sergeant said flatly. Then he turned back to me. 'And what about you, Anna? Can you think of anyone who might have a grudge against you?'

Yes.

'No,' I lied miserably. 'No one who'd do a thing like this anyway.'

'Are you sure?' he pressed. 'People – specially kids – often do things for very trivial reasons. Small things get blown out of all proportion. No one at school you've offended?'

'No, honestly,' I said more categorically. 'I'm sure no one at school is connected to this.' That at least I could say honestly. But Seth was looking at me uncomfortably, biting his lip.

'What is it?' The sergeant, in spite of everything, was perceptive, and he saw that Seth was holding something back. 'Something you've remembered, Seth? If it's anything you think could help . . .'

'Well . . .' Seth turned to look at me and his lips silently formed one questioning word: *Caroline?*

'No.' I shook my head vehemently. 'No, no, no.'

'What is it?' Sergeant Whittacker pressed. Seth's face was miserable but he turned back.

'My ex. Caroline Flint. She was very upset when I got together with Anna; she said at the time she

232

was going to make Anna regret it.'

'No.' I shook my head again, frantic to shut him up. 'Seth, honestly, I'm *sure* Caroline's not behind this.'

'Anna, there are loads of other people who'll make the connection, you know. She threatened you – in front of the whole school. She said she'd make your life a misery.'

'She meant blanking me in the corridor and hiding my underwear after PE, Seth, you *know* she did. Come on, Seth – please, *please* don't do this.' I stared at him, willing him to understand, read my mind, *know* that there was something I couldn't say in front of Dad and the policeman. If I'd trusted my magic I would have tried to put the words silently into Seth's head – the way Caradoc had done in the bookshop. But I didn't. I might split Seth's brain, send him mad – kill him even – if I tried to mess with his mind. I could only stare beseechingly and beg him with my eyes to understand and *shut up*.

'Caroline . . . Flint . . .' Sergeant Whittacker wrote the name down in his notebook. 'Lives in Winter, does she?'

'Yes, out along the Anchor Road.'

'I see. Well, and you're sure there's nothing you can add for the moment?' He turned to me and my dad in turn, and we both shook our heads. 'Then I think we'll leave it for tonight, I'm sure you'll be wanting to get to bed. If you think of anything in the morning, here's my card.'

He handed Dad a business card with his number on and got into his patrol car along with his colleague, and they bumped slowly up the rutted track to the main road.

'Bed,' Dad said dully. His shoulders slumped and he leant back against the fence. 'Good Lord. What are we going to do about tonight?'

'Are our bedrooms OK?' I asked.

'Yes and no. The older bit of the house wasn't really touched, as far as I can make out. But there's no heating or electricity, and anyway the fire crew won't let us back in until they've okayed the structure.' He rubbed his face, leaving a smear of ash across his stubbled cheek.

'Come back to ours,' Seth said firmly.

'What?' Dad looked up, as if he'd almost forgotten Seth was there.

'You can't sleep here. Come back to our house. Tom, you can sleep in Grandad's room – he won't be using it in the near future – and Anna, you can sleep in my room. I'll sleep on the couch,' he added, as Dad raised an eyebrow.

'But what about Elaine?' Dad asked. 'Won't she mind?'

'Mind? Of course she won't mind. In fact, she'd give me an earful if she found out I let you go off to a hotel at a time like this. Please. Come on.'

'OK.' Dad looked too tired to argue, and I could tell he was relieved that we wouldn't have to start looking for hotels and B&Bs at this time of night. 'OK. Thanks Seth. We'll come. I'm afraid we won't be very good house guests though; all I've got is the clothes I'm standing in – and this.' He held up a carrier bag with his wallet and phone and a few pieces of paper and photos.

'Look, don't worry.' Seth put a hand on his shoulder. 'I'm sure Mum'll have a spare toothbrush. Anything else we can take care of tomorrow. Now, come on.'

So, wearily, we came.

It felt so strange lying in Seth's bed. I'd been in his bedroom many times of course, practically every day some weeks, but I'd never stayed the night. I'd never dared. Not because of what my dad or Seth's mum might say – they were both pretty liberal, and even if they refused, they wouldn't bawl us out for asking. But because of me. I didn't trust myself.

And now, here I was. Dressed in an old T-shirt of Seth's that skimmed my thighs and lying between cool sheets that smelt of his skin. I put my face to the pillow and shut my eyes, hot with longing for him. Don't lose it, I begged myself. Don't lose control, not here, not with Elaine next door and Dad in the spare room. But I felt my hold slipping and to try to anchor myself I opened my eyes, in spite of my tiredness, and looked round the darkened room, at the band posters on the wall, the revision Post-its above his desk, the crumpled clothes in the laundry basket. It was all so normal, so lovely after the mad, suffocating grandeur of the Ealdwitan headquarters.

My eyes fell on the grey silk dress lying, like the ghost of my shadow, draped over a chair. I'd loved it so much – and now it made me shudder to look at it.

The events of the night swirled and jostled in my brain, and I wished that my mind had a stand-by switch I could just press for a few hours. Dad's snores were audible even though the wall – it seemed so unfair that he could sleep in spite of everything: in spite of the shadows gathering around our lives, the Malleus, the Ealdwitan, our poor charred house.

Dad – oh, Dad. I felt sick at the thought of his narrow escape. I imagined the masked men creeping around the house with their lighters and bottles of fluid. If only I'd *been* there. My fists clenched and I felt the heat rise inside me and drew a deep shuddering breath.

Calm down. Calm down. There was no point in burning up Seth's bed as well as my own.

I sighed and turned Seth's pillow to the cool side as if

that could somehow soothe away the thoughts burning in my head. *EX 22:18*. The letters felt blazed into my mind and, unable to lie still any longer, I got up and opened Seth's laptop. Within seconds Google's answer flashed up. *EXODUS 22:18, THOU SHALT NOT SUFFER A WITCH TO LIVE*.

Suddenly there was a noise from the doorway.

'Anna?'

I jumped and whipped around, poised to slam down the screen before the intruder could read it.

It was Seth.

'Oh, Seth,' I choked.

He held out his arms, drew me on to the bed, and I put my face into the soft crook of his neck, and sobbed and sobbed. I don't know how long I cried for – but Seth just held me without asking any questions, and at last I lifted my head and he kissed my mouth very softly.

'Are you OK?'

I only nodded, and pressed myself closer, and he led me gently to the bed. We lay together, my head on Seth's chest, his arms around me, and I listened to the sound of our hearts, my frantic drumming beat slowing, slowing, until at last it matched Seth's slow, dreamy thud. I put my lips to his throat, touching the vein's slow beat beneath the hot skin.

'I love you.'

Seth's lips were warm against my temple and I closed my eyes and whispered, 'I love you too, oh, I love you so much . . .'

I felt his mouth form the words again, against my throat, my collarbone, the softness of my inner arm . . . My hands clenched and grew slack and clenched again, fighting the delight, fighting the urge to let go.

'Anna, what's wrong?' Seth pulled himself up on one elbow and looked down at me. His face was shadowed and he traced a path down the centre of my forehead and nose with his fingertip, smoothing out the frown lines I knew were there. 'You're so tense. What's the matter, sweetheart?'

'How can you ask that?'

'Oh God, I'm sorry. That was stupid. I know – your house, your dad.'

I sighed and sat half up.

'Look.' I pointed at the laptop screen. Seth read the words and then closed his eyes.

'The writing. Oh God, Anna. They came for you.'

'That was why I didn't want you to say anything about Caroline.'

'Screw Caroline. It's you I'm worried about. What are you saying – there are nutters out there persecuting

238

witches?' His voice was horrified. 'And they've tracked you down?'

I didn't nod. I didn't need to.

'What are you going to do?' he asked.

I shrugged. 'What can I do? Wait. Try to protect Dad. Hope they don't do anything else. They're only . . .' *Only outwith*, I thought. But I didn't say it.

'But, but you've got to do something – tell somebody.'

'Tell them what? That I'm a witch?'

'No, not that – but the rest.'

'Well, I have – we have. Dad called the police, didn't he? What else can we do?'

'Isn't there something magical you can do?'

'I don't know.' I rubbed my eyes wearily. 'I'll ask Emmaline. Maybe.'

'And what happened in London? What happened to your clothes?'

'Oh, Seth . . .' I wasn't really in the mood to go through it all again but Seth deserved some kind of explanation. 'It's complicated. I went up there to meet my grandmother – my mum's mother. Dad doesn't know,' I added warningly, 'so don't say anything. I'm waiting for the right moment to mention it. Anyway she took me out to dinner and I wasn't wearing smart enough stuff – so she lent me some clothes, but then we had an argument and I kind of stormed out. I forgot my bag.'

'An argument? What about?'

'Stuff. I'll tell you later.' I don't know why I didn't tell him, but somehow I wasn't quite ready to admit that my grandmother was a member of the secretive organization that had tried to kill us all last year. I didn't know what Seth's reaction would be. I hadn't even sorted out *my* feelings fully.

'She's got good taste, anyway.' There was a smile in Seth's voice, though his face was in shadow.

'What do you mean?'

'You looked *amazing* in that dress. When you came towards me at the station . . .' He stopped and I heard him swallow in the darkness. The sound made me shiver hot and cold. 'I just . . . I just wanted . . .'

I tried for a shaky laugh.

'Let me guess, drag me off to your cave and rip it off with your teeth?' It was meant for a joke, but my voice sounded strange and husky in my own ears. Seth's fingers were playing with the frayed hem of the T-shirt I was wearing. I felt everything slipping. 'I bet . . . I bet somehow your old PE T-shirt doesn't have the same effect, eh?'

'Actually . . . it kind of does . . .' He bit down gently on one sleeve and gave the fabric an experimental tug. The saggy neckline stretched and slipped, and one of my shoulders was bare to the cool night air.

'Seth . . .' I was torn between desire and the knowledge that Dad and Elaine were only feet away. And then, as my other shoulder slipped free, '*Seth*. Please . . .'

He groaned and rolled away from me, lying flat on his back.

'Oh, Anna . . .'

'I'm sorry.'

'It's OK. But you know, it would be nice. Some time. Don't you think?'

'It would be nice,' I said, and I couldn't keep the longing out of my voice.

'What is it, sweetheart?' He rolled over on one elbow and I felt him looking down at me in the darkness. 'I can tell you want to, don't you?'

'I do, I really do. It's just . . .'

'What?'

'I'm afraid.'

'I understand,' he said very quietly. 'I really do. But we could be really careful, take it really slow. Take, you know. Precautions and stuff.'

'What, condoms and things?'

Perhaps my surprise showed in my voice because he said, 'Yes, why, what were you thinking of?'

I bit my lip.

'Nothing. But that's not really what I was worrying about.'

'Then if it's not that – what?' He took my hand in the darkness and I felt his fingers rub the smooth stone of the seaglass ring. 'You love me, right?'

'Yes.' Oh God, yes.

'And you know that I love you?'

The silence stretched between us.

'Anna?' he said, and his fingers tightened on mine and then let go. 'You *know* that I love you, don't you?'

I felt for his hand again and interlocked my fingers with his.

'Yes,' I lied. 'I know.'

CHAPTER FIFTEEN

You could smell the house before you reached it. Dad and I stood in the dew-wet field, and looked at the blackened, water-logged ruins of our home. The sharp smell of charred wood mingled with the damp earthen scents of the wood.

As we watched, a gust of wind came off the sea, rustling the few brown leaves still clinging to the trees, and a piece of rafter shifted with a groan and crashed to the barn floor.

Dad sighed and we began to pick our way through the wet grass towards the front door.

Up close, the damage to the house wasn't quite as bad as it looked. Once you took out the smoke blackening, and ignored the charred ruins of the barn and the garage, the actual house hadn't come off too badly. It was wet and smoky, and the kitchen was completely gutted, but the firemen had pronounced it structurally sound, told us to keep away from the barns and outbuildings, and left us to argue it out with the insurers.

The one good thing, as far as I was concerned, was that the horrible corrugated iron lean-to had gone. Melted into a pile of scrap metal. The devil had taken his own and claimed that manky bathtub.

'Just as the house was starting to look ship-shape,' Dad moaned gently as we surveyed the ruined kitchen. Grey sky showed through the roof. 'As for the insurance money – it's like getting blood out of a stone. Heaven only knows when they'll finish their investigations.'

'What shall we do about cooking?' I was trying to be practical in the face of Dad's glumness. We moved through to the less affected part of the house and Dad looked round the living room, trying to assess the damage.

'I suppose we'll have to set up a camp kitchen in here, or maybe in the dining room. Get a microwave. What we'll do for washing up, I don't know.'

'Could we put a dishwasher in the downstairs loo?'

'I suppose so.' Dad opened the door and we looked at the space beside the basin, trying to work out whether one would fit. 'The sink's too small to be much use.' He ran his hand through his tousled wiry hair and I stopped him and smoothed it down affectionately. His hair had the same tendency as mine; to turn into a crazed bird's nest at the least provocation. Right now he looked like a dark-haired Einstein.

'Who would do this though?' he asked helplessly. 'That's what I keep asking myself.'

Guilt twisted my gut. Guilt and a strong desire for revenge.

'Hello?'

We both jumped as the shout rang through, echoing in the silence. Dad raised an eyebrow.

'Are you expecting anyone?'

'No.'

We both walked back through the smoke-smelling rooms towards the back of the house and I tried to ignore the fluttering nerves in my stomach. Having half the back of the house blown off made you feel weird, exposed, vulnerable. With no way of locking up, I felt horribly aware that anyone could just walk in. Though admittedly, burglars and rapists were unlikely to shout 'hello' when they arrived.

It wasn't a burglar or a rapist. It was Abe. He was standing open-mouthed in the burnt-out kitchen, staring around.

'Anna – Emmaline told me what happened. Are you OK?' He gave me a crushing hug, so hard his belt buckle felt imprinted on to my pelvis when he released me.

'I'm fine,' I said, slightly out of breath. 'I wasn't even here.'

'Who's this?' Dad said from the doorway, a slightly suspicious note in his voice. I suppose, looked at through Dad-vision, Abe wasn't exactly the boy next door. He was – well, I wasn't sure how old, but definitely the wrong side of twenty. He was also unshaven and dressed in bike leathers.

'Oh, sorry, Dad. This is Abe Goldsmith, Dad. His brother is Simon – you know, Sienna's husband? Abe, this is my dad, Tom.'

'Pleased to meet you.' Abe stuck out a hand and Dad shook it, thawing slightly. He liked and approved of Em, so Abe's association with the Pellers was a point in his favour.

'Likewise, Abe,' Dad said distractedly. 'Likewise. But listen, if you'll excuse me, I've got quite a bit of clearing up to do.'

'Yeah, of course, no worries.' Abe stood uneasily with his hands in his pockets as Dad left the shattered kitchen and then when he was gone turned to me. 'I'm here from Em. She got your text and she's worried about you. So am I.'

'Well, thanks for the concern but I don't really see

246

what either of you can do. I don't suppose Em's got any ideas, has she?'

'Maybe. She thought you might want to come over and discuss it, so I said I'd drive out here and pass on the message. Your phone's not working.'

'The landline's burnt out and there's no mobile reception out here. The hills cut out the signal. But I can't, I've got something else to do.'

'What, tidy up? Want me to help?'

'Well, I'll have to help Dad later, but actually no, I'm seeing Seth this afternoon.'

'Oh.' Abe's face set in almost comically disapproving lines. 'Him.'

'Yes, *him*. He is my boyfriend.'

'You deserve better.'

'What does that mean?'

'Just that.' He shrugged. 'You're remarkable. He's not. You're interesting. He's not. You're eminently kissable. He's not.' He saw my face at that and shrugged again. 'What? I'm just saying.'

'Well, don't. Say it.'

We stood for a moment, glaring at each other, and then Abe raised one eyebrow and laughed.

'You're the only girl I've met who gets arsey when you pay her a compliment. Anyway, what are you doing with the outwith? Apart from getting more bored by the minute?'

'Abe, don't be a dick,' I snapped. 'If you're going to be like this we can't be friends – and that'd be a shame. Some of the time.'

'OK, OK. Sorry.' Abe held up his hands. 'I'll behave.'

'OK. Well, if you must know, his grandad's being sent home from hospital tomorrow, so we've got to go and sort out his cottage.'

'What – he's going back there?' Abe's face showed his surprise. Castle Spit was a tidal island, cut off from the mainland for twenty-two hours out of twenty-four. It was barren and bleak and totally unsuitable for an invalid. I shook my head.

'No, he's going to stay with Seth and his mum. Indefinitely, so it means someone's got to get all his valuables and shut up the house and stuff.'

'Oh, I see. So you're giving Seth a hand?'

'That's about the size of it.'

'Hmm.' Abe looked dissatisfied. 'Well, whatever. But I don't really like you going out there.'

'What business is it of yours?' I was taken aback.

'Look, Seth nearly drowned you last time you went there. And the Spit is no place for our kind – we don't mess with Bran Fisher.'

'Seth didn't nearly drown me; I nearly drowned *him*,' I said crossly. 'And I agree the Spit is no place for our kind – it's no place for any kind of human being if it comes to that. But I said I'd help Seth, so stop being so melodramatic about it.'

'Hmm. Just be careful.'

I shot him a poisonous look and he raised an eyebrow.

'What? I can't tell you to be careful?'

'I'll be fine. I'll be with Seth.'

'Exactly,' Abe said darkly. And that was that.

When I arrived down at the quay after lunch Seth was already there, busy working on *Charley's Angel*. He was holding a blowtorch and doing something complicated with glass fibre, but he turned off the gas and pulled up his mask when he saw me, and leapt on to the quayside to give me a sticky hug.

'Are you OK? How was the house?'

'Not as bad as we thought. The bedrooms are fine. The living room needs a coat of paint and a new sofa, but it'll do. And Dad's got someone coming to reconnect the electrics this afternoon, so it looks like we should be able to move back in tonight.'

'Grandad couldn't have been kicked out of hospital at a worse time, could he?'

'No, don't be silly. We couldn't camp out at yours indefinitely. And anyway, I think Dad just wants to get back in there. He's worried about it lying empty with no way of locking up properly.'

Seth's face grew set at that and he shook his head.

'I know we've been through this, but I really, really don't like the idea of you being there at night with no proper security.'

Damn. I *knew* I shouldn't have mentioned that.

I sighed. 'Dad's reglazing all the windows. And he's going to get a proper lockable door for the living room, just until the kitchen's repaired. It's not like we'll be open to all-comers. He just doesn't want the place looking unoccupied for too long.'

'Did you talk to him about getting a burglar alarm?' Seth asked. I nodded. 'And?'

'I think he's going to.'

'Good,' Seth said shortly. I decided it was time to change the subject.

'So, anyway. Are we going to stand here all day, or are we going to get to the Spit before night?'

'Good point.' He looked at his watch. 'We should get going. Come on.'

We took Seth's little sailing boat, not the *Angel*, and I had the familiar feeling of fear, bordering on panic, as

Seth steadied the rocking little craft and beckoned me to jump on board. I wanted to shut my eyes – shut out the rolling seawater – but that would have been insanely stupid, so I jumped, eyes open, and crouched for a second in the bottom of the boat, waiting for the panic to subside. Then we were out on the waves and somehow it was easier to forget the fathoms of black water beneath us and all the horrors down there.

The landing on Castle Spit was even more impossible than last time – Seth tried half a dozen times, with me leaning out to fend off with an oar, and eventually we bumped up to the jetty with a slightly sickening crunch and Seth leapt out and whipped the painter through the rusty metal ring before the wind could veer again.

Up at Bran's cottage a repulsive smell greeted us as Seth hammered open the door with his boot.

'My God, what's that reek?' Seth covered his face with his arm and edged in, throwing open the narrow windows all around the single-room cottage.

'It's this bucket, I think.' I peered into a plastic bucket full of what looked like it might once have been fishguts and bones. Luckily the weather had been cold – too cold to turn the sludge to maggots and blowflies. But the stench was still incredible. Seth carried it at arm's length out of the cottage and chucked the whole load off the jetty, bucket and all. It bobbed away, the red plastic brave against the storm-grey waves, and then sank beneath the surf. The smell in the cottage had slightly lessened when we went back in.

'God.' Seth looked around him, a mixture of depression and disgust on his face. 'How can someone live like this in the twenty-first century?'

I knew what he meant. Barring a few things – an electric kettle, a single bare lightbulb – the cottage could basically have come complete from a Robert Louis Stevenson story. The frowsty bed, piled high with crumpled blankets stiff with stains, the smoke-blackened stove, the stone sink with its pump-handle hanging idle – it was all straight out of a novel about Victorian poverty and deprivation.

'At least he had running water,' I said, trying for a bleak laugh. I meant the stream running sluggishly from the pump and out of the door in a little black trickle, but Seth didn't smile. He only looked around him, his face hard with pity and anger.

'It never looked so bad when he was here,' he said, as if he hadn't heard me. 'Somehow when Grandad was here you didn't notice the filth and the cold. But now . . . now it looks like somewhere you wouldn't let a dog go to die.'

'Seth . . .' I put a hand on his shoulder and he took it

and turned it palm up, kissing the soft skin at the crease of my wrist. Then he sighed.

'Come on. Let's get started; I don't want to spend any more time here than we have to.'

We began sorting through Bran's meagre possessions. Seth picked through the clothes, salvaging wearable nightclothes, trousers and jumpers, discarding more than he packed.

Bran's stained and tattered underwear seemed unbearably personal and I felt suddenly sure that he would hate the idea of me poking through his belongings even more than he would hate me being on the island at all, so I turned to his paperwork, trying to do something practical without intruding on his privacy.

Most of it was in a small metal box under his bed and I began to look through it, trying to make sure we had his pension book, birth certificate, all the essentials he'd need to establish his new life at the Crown.

I had a carrier bagful of useful documents when I came upon something at the very bottom of the metal box. It was a piece of black fabric and at first I wasn't sure what it could be. I held it up, the folds fell out, and I saw.

It was a black hood, a mask, with holes cut out for eyes. Seth saw me looking and laughed.

'What's that? Grandad's Halloween costume?'

He picked it from my limp hand and, still grinning, slipped it over his head. The hood covered his head and face completely, blurring and mashing his face into a featureless mask. Only his eyes glittered, black against black, and full of hate.

I screamed.

I screamed and screamed and screamed, completely unable to stop, to speak, to breathe.

'Anna!' The voice came grotesquely muffled from the mouthless face. 'Anna! It's OK! Anna what's wrong? Stop, please stop.'

But I couldn't speak – the hooded stranger grabbed at me and I beat him away with terrified shaking arms. He finally got the hood off with a rip of tearing fabric and grabbed at my arms, gripping me so tightly I couldn't move, couldn't hurt him, could only shake with fear. But something in his strong grasp anchored me to reality, the shaking began to subside and I dissolved into sobs. Seth's warm hands stroked my hair in a comforting rhythm and I cried and cried while he held me wordlessly, as if he feared he'd lose me.

At last I raised my head from his chest and wiped my eyes and my nose and managed to choke out, 'I'm sorry – I'm so sorry.'

'I'm the one should be saying sorry. Oh, Anna, you silly thing.' His voice made the words a caress. I buried my face in his chest again and felt him say, 'But what scared you? It's only a bit of cotton.'

I couldn't explain. I could only shake my head and shudder all over again, feeling the horror I'd felt as I'd seen a stranger's gaze glitter black through the stabhole-eyes.

We stood for a long time, wrapped in each other's arms, my head on Seth's chest and Seth cradling me while my breathing returned to normal. But something else had caught my eye when I lifted out the mask and I pushed Seth's arms gently away and bent to look in the box again.

It was a small badge made out of stamped metal, with a hand-drawn design in black enamel. MM it said in irregular black letters and, beneath, the drawing of a crude hammer. It looked something like an old-fashioned Scout pin, the kind my Dad had worn.

For a long moment I stood, staring down at the small object in my hand, blind and deaf to everything else. What did it mean? Was it Bran's? If not, whose?

'Anna. *Anna.*' I heard at last and became aware that Seth had been speaking. 'What is it? Why are you looking like that?'

'Like what?' I said in a strange, dazed voice that didn't sound like me.

'Like that. Like someone turned you into a chunk of ice.'

'I'm sorry,' I said. I held out my hand with the badge on my palm. Seth bent over it and, when he looked up, his face was puzzled.

'What does it mean? I've seen that logo before, but I can't think where.'

'In red paint,' I said flatly. 'On the side of my house.'

His face went white and then he began shaking his head violently, as if he could shake the accusation out of his ears like water.

'No. No, no, no. Grandad was in hospital! How could it be anything do with him?'

'I didn't say it was.'

'But that's what you thought.'

'It's a group,' I said wearily, 'called the Malleus Maleficorum. The Hammer of Witches. Created to persecute and drive out witches.'

'This is not the sixteenth century,' Seth said angrily.

'No,' I agreed. I couldn't keep the bitterness out of my voice. 'Whoever burnt down my house is very much here and now and alive.'

We stood our ground, staring fiercely at each other.

Then Seth swore and turned away, deliberately hitting his forehead against the rough stone wall of the cottage.

'Shit. Shit shit *shit*.' He stood with both hands flat against the wall, his head bowed, refusing to look at me. 'That old bastard. It's never easy, is it? It's never simple. Why can't we just be together?' There was a furious bitterness in his voice that I didn't quite understand. I could only bite my lip as he kicked viciously at the cottage wall, as if Bran could somehow feel his violence. Then he crumpled the badge in his fist, flung it to the floor and ground it under his heel. I heard the enamel crack.

'What shall we do?' he asked at last, his voice harsh. I shrugged.

'I don't know. What can we do? I don't think Bran's strong enough to raise the subject, do you?'

'Ugh.' Seth rubbed his swollen forehead. 'I want to shop him to the police – but the stupid sod would probably have a heart attack just to spite us.'

'Anyway, chances are he won't be able to help us,' I said. 'He probably joined this group back in nineteen forty-something and hasn't had any connection since.' Seth said nothing, but the unspoken question hovered between us – then why had Bran kept the badge?

'It's getting dark,' Seth said at last. 'We'd better finish up here.'

I nodded and we began to pack up the clothes and papers into Seth's rucksack. As I tightened up the straps I saw, out of the corner of my eye, Seth pick up the black hood and crushed badge and toss them into the pile of rubbish. He handled them as if they were poisonous, with the tips of his fingers.

CHAPTER SIXTEEN

'OK. Well. What are you going to do?' Emmaline bit into a slice of soggy school pizza and stared at me accusingly. It seemed like every conversation these days was punctuated with someone asking what I was going to do. What to do about my grandmother. What to do about the Malleus. What to do about Bran. What to do about my leaky, imperfect power. How was I supposed to know? I was just seventeen. Eighteen. Whatever . . . I wanted someone to tell *me* what to do for a change.

'I don't know, Em. Happy? I have no idea. My grandmother is part of a secret organization who was trying to kill us last year. My boyfriend's grandad was part of a secret organization who seems to be trying to persecute me right now. My mother was so worried about my very existence that she tried to stamp out my magic before it even came in, for reasons I've yet to identify. I've lost my coat and my walking boots and I can't control my power. Apart from advocating compulsory euthanasia for the over-sixties, I really have no idea how to sort this out.'

'Look – you need a break from all this. Come over this weekend – stay the night, talk to Mum about it.'

This weekend . . . A cold feeling settled in the pit of my stomach and I said shortly,

'Can't, unfortunately. It's my birthday—'

'*Allegedly*,' Em interjected sarcastically.

'Allegedly,' I agreed. 'Anyway, Elaine wants to have me and Dad over for dinner to celebrate. While Bran's there. She hasn't exactly spelled it out, but I think she figures he can't kick up a fuss if she stages it as a big birthday-celebration-type thing.'

'Are you sure it's a good idea?' Em asked sceptically. I shrugged. Truth to tell, I wasn't entirely convinced myself – but Elaine wanted to do it and Seth wanted to do it and Dad wanted to do it. It seemed like Bran and I would have something in common at least. It looked like we were the only people who thought this was a bad idea.

I was about to say as much when a shadow fell over our table and Em and I both looked up. Mrs Redbird, the school secretary, was standing in front of us carrying a large cardboard box and wearing a thoroughly pissed-off expression.

'Anna Winterson, do *not* make a habit of this. I've put up with it this time, but my office isn't a parcel depot for your convenience.'

'I'm s-sorry?' I stammered.

'Here.' She dumped the box down on the table with a thump. 'I told the courier – any further deliveries for pupils will be returned to sender. Consider yourself lucky.'

She stamped off, back to her office, and Em and I were left staring at the box in bewilderment. It was done up in brown paper and string and had a white address label on it bearing my name and *c/o Winter High, Harbour Road, Winter.*

I turned it over to see if there was a sender's name. There was. It was from E. Rokewood. The return postcode was London W8 – Kensington.

'It's from my grandmother,' I said.

'Er, would that perchance be the same grandmother that tried to get us all killed?' Em poked the string with one cautious finger, as though the box might explode.

'Yup.' I hefted the parcel. It was heavy, but not too heavy. It wasn't ticking. No suspicious fluids were leaking out. 'What do you think?'

'Only one way to find out.'

With a feeling of mingled dread and curiosity I unthreaded the string and pulled away the paper wrappings. Inside was a cardboard box and a letter.

'Box first,' Em said bossily. 'If it's on a timer we need plenty of warning to decide which wire to cut.'

'Oh shut up, do.' I opened one flap and peered inside, and then had to laugh at myself as I realized I was holding my breath as if it really *was* a bomb inside. It was not a bomb. It was clothes. My clothes, to be exact. My coat – which had been dry-cleaned and pressed and looked smarter than at any time I'd owned it. My boots – cleaned and re-waterproofed. My jeans, my shirt, my socks – all beautifully laundered, ironed and folded with layers of tissue paper in between. I didn't flatter myself that my grandmother had done all this – she didn't look like she'd know one end of an iron from another. But it was, I supposed, kind of nice that she'd asked her secretary to sort it or something. But my clothes alone couldn't account for the size of the box and, peering underneath, I saw there were more layers of paper and more clothes. I shook out the top garment and sighed. It was the beautiful cashmere sheath dress, as soft as a black kitten against my cheek. Emmaline gave a groan of sheer envy and began to dig.

'Oh my God . . . Issey Miyake, Miu Miu, Alexander McQueen – what *is* this? Aid parcels for the poor relations?'

'Something like that.'

'Oh, oh, oh!' She pressed a mass of deep-sapphire pleats to her breast. 'Anna, I will die and go to heaven if you let me borrow this some time.'

'I thought you weren't into clothes?' I said sourly.

'Other clothes – no. These clothes – yes. If you can't tell the difference you don't deserve to wear them.'

I could tell the difference. At least, I could tell that eBaying this lot would probably pay for the repairs to the kitchen. At the very, very bottom was a small jeweller's box. I opened it and blenched. It was a pair of earrings, pretty hanging things each with a dark-blue stone the colour of the evening sky. I had a horrible presentiment that whatever they were, they were the real thing. I snapped the box shut and closed my eyes, and then opened them again and hastily started stuffing clothes back inside before anyone else could gawp.

'What are you doing?' Em was practically hopping up and down in agony. 'You're crushing them! Oh! You evil wench! Stop it now – it's a crime against couture.'

'Shut up,' I said briefly and yanked the string tight around the box. How the hell was I going to get this home? Then the bell rang and Emmaline was forced to go to her Philosophy class. I was luckier – I had a free, so I dragged myself and the bloody box off to the girls' toilets and locked myself in to read the letter.

Dear Anna, it began, *since I don't know your address I am sending this to Winter High where, I think you said, you attend school.*

Since you ran away from our dinner last week I have done some investigating and have made a few discoveries of my own about your experience with our organization. I can now quite understand your shock and horror at discovering where you were – and can only say how desperately sorry I am that you were put through such an ordeal.

But, my dear, please, please believe me – you are wrong to think that I had anything to do with those events. Maud Revere works for one of my fellow Chairs – it might be fairer to say, one of my rival Chairs. It was Thaddeus Corax who ordered the attack on Winter, advised by his agent Vivian Brereton, who, I understand, was working at your school.

I was completely unaware of the events and, to do him justice, I do not believe that Corax knew of our relationship. Had he known who you were, I am morally certain that he would have approached the issue very, very differently. You must remember that I did not know myself, until a week ago, that your surname was Winterson, or even that you were in England. All Corax knew was that someone had begun some rather indiscreet displays of power in Winter and that that person seemed unamenable to approaches.

I do not attempt in any way to excuse his actions, which were, let me state clearly, indefensible, regardless of our relationship. Unfortunately he is of another generation entirely – as you will discover if you meet him one day – and there are times when he forgets that summary justice is no longer our right to dispense, even if we wished to do so. And, too, he was not present at the attack, and some of his agents on the ground exceeded their powers. But all this sounds like I am making excuses for him, which is not at all what I set out to do in this letter.

Anna, please, please believe me when I say that I am distraught to think that Thaddeus Corax's high-handed actions may have sabotaged my chance to know my granddaughter. When I received Caradoc's call I felt as if I had been given a second chance, not only with you, but, by proxy, with your mother. To have that chance snatched away is too cruel – and I know, my dear, that cruelty is not part of your nature. I could see that from the first moment that we met.

Please, don't punish me in Corax's stead. And don't punish yourself. There is a great deal I can do for you – I can only guess how hard it must have been for you to have gone through the discovery of your nature without anyone to help you. You could do very great things, Anna – very great good. Perhaps I am naive in hoping that I can help you fulfil your destiny at this late stage, but I would like to do what I can.

And it is not only selfishness that prompts me to write to you – there is another, more practical, more political reason for my plea. It may be, if you will come to London and go over what happened last year, that Corax can be made to pay for his actions in Winter. I don't pretend that this is a certainty, or that the word of one young girl against a senior Chair of our organization would topple him instantly, but it might be a chink in his armour – and sometimes it is that first chink that is hardest to achieve.

So, dear Anna, for my sake, and for the sake of others who may come under Corax's thumb, please do reconsider.

Your very loving grandmother,
Elizabeth N. Rokewood

As I finished reading the letter, it seemed to twitch like a live thing in my hand, almost as if caught in a strong breeze, though there was no window open in the room. Then a corner of the paper began suddenly to glow and it burst into blue, heatless flames. Within seconds the page was just a handful of cold, grey ashes. I opened my hand and let them scatter to the floor.

Later that night, in my room, I tried to compose an email back.

Dear . . . Great. I was stuck at the second word. Dear what? Dear Granny? Dear Grandma? It seemed fake and cheesy to somehow claim a cosy relationship with this formidable woman I'd met only twice. Yet *Dear Mrs Rokewood* seemed like a deliberate snub and *Dear Elizabeth* was just impossible. In the end I deleted *Dear* and started again, ducking the issue completely.

Thank you for your letter, which arrived today, and for the clothes. I appreciate their return – though you didn't have to include the borrowed clothes as well.

I will think about what you said in your letter. Things are slightly difficult here at the moment – understatement of the year – *but I appreciate your point about bringing Chair Corax to account.* Two appreciates. Oh well, this wasn't an English essay. What to say next? Yes, I want a relationship? No, you cut my dad out of your life; you can't play happy families now?

It was impossible. How could I overcome eighteen years of silence? But at the same time, it seemed so wrong to let a moment's anger, nearly two decades ago and probably bitterly regretted ever since, dictate the rest of our lives.

I sighed and finished, *Your granddaughter*, Anna.

Then, before I could think better of it, I added an *X* for a kiss and pressed send.

As an afterthought I went back and sent a quick follow-up.

P.S., if you want to write again, please could you send it to my home address? The school was a bit cross at having to receive the parcel. My address is:

Wicker House

Castleton Road

Winter.

A

I was about to shut down the computer and go to bed when my emailed pinged and *1 message* flashed up in the corner of the screen. Surely not a reply so soon?

My heart was thumping as I opened up the inbox, but the email address was not my grandmother's, just a Hotmail address with a jumble of meaningless letters and numbers instead of a name. Probably spam, but I opened it up to check.

SAM AND ROG, 21st DECEMBER. WE KNOW, it said.

I stared, puzzled, and then deleted it and went to bed.

It was in the middle of the night that I made the connection and awoke in a pool of cold sweat.

21st December.

The night Seth had taken me out for dinner.

The night I'd left two boys half dead in an alley.

'What should I wear?' Dad looked anxiously down at himself. 'Will this do?'

We were getting ready to go to Elaine's for my birthday supper/welcome-home-Bran dinner. And Dad was nervous. It was weird – anyone would think *he* was the one going on a date. I was nervous too – but not about my clothes. No, I was nervous about what Bran was going to do when I crossed 'his' threshold, in spite of his warnings.

'You look fine.' I looked Dad up and down. 'It's maybe a bit formal though. It's only supper. How about you lose the tie?'

'Are you sure?' Dad wrestled with the tie and then pulled it loose. 'What do you think? I don't want Elaine to think we aren't making an effort. And I feel I have to match up to you.'

I was wearing the grey dress – kind of in spite of myself. I still hadn't quite resolved my feelings towards my grandmother's largesse, but it seemed a tragedy to leave such beautiful clothes lying limp in my wardrobe. And, too, there was the memory of the look kindled in Seth's eyes when he'd seen me in it last . . . But I'd kept the sapphires in their jewellery box. They were too showy for me, and the dress matched better with my mother's little silver drops, and Seth's seaglass ring.

'You look great. Without the tie is great. Let me just . . .' I leant up and undid his top button, pulling the shirt open at the neck. 'There, that's better.' I gave him a kiss on the cheek and he blushed unexpectedly.

'So what do you think – fit to meet the in-laws?'

'Dad . . .' Now it was my turn to blush. 'Whatever you do, please don't say that in front of Seth and Elaine! I'd be mortified.'

'Why?' Dad smiled at me, half teasing, half serious. 'Worried Seth might try to make an honest woman out of you? I wasn't much older when I met your mum, you know.'

'Yes, but it isn't the dark ages any more, thank God. Now, come on; we're going to be late.'

Angelica waved as Dad and I elbowed our way through the saloon bar and knocked on the door that led up to Seth and Elaine's private flat on the first floor.

'Just go up,' she called above the noise of the bar. 'They won't hear you with this racket down here.'

As we opened the door a fabulous, rich smell drifted down the stairs – garlic, onions, butter – making my mouth water. Dad's stomach rumbled audibly.

'Anna!' Seth met us at the top of the stairs. 'Hello, Tom, can I take your jacket?'

'Thanks.' Dad shrugged it off and looked around the flat. 'Very nice place you've got here. I've never seen upstairs. Where's your mum?'

'In the kitchen. Go in and say hi.'

Dad wandered off in the direction of the delicious smells and Seth took advantage of his disappearance to wrap me in his arms.

'Happy birthday. Are you sure it was a good idea to wear that dress?'

'What do you mean? Is there something wrong with it?' I craned over my shoulder to see if my hem was tucked into my knickers.

'No, quite the opposite. I'm just kind of worried I won't be able to keep my hands to myself at dinner.'

'Shut up.' I swatted him affectionately and then looked him up and down. 'You don't look so bad yourself.'

That was an understatement, of course. He looked, as usual, devastating, in low-slung jeans and a dazzlingly white shirt that made his tan seem deeper than ever. But, also as usual, he seemed completely unaware of

271

himself and just shrugged.

'You can thank Mum for that – she made me put on a shirt.'

'Where's Bran?' I asked. Seth sighed.

'Asleep in his room. Mum's going to wake him up for dinner – personally I'd be quite happy if he slept through the whole thing but . . .'

'It's his celebration too,' I said gently, but Seth only shook his head.

'Anna!' There was a gust of warm air from the kitchen and Elaine came over and gave me a hug. 'Happy birthday, love. Open your present.' She pushed a bag at me and I flushed.

'Elaine! You shouldn't have.'

'Of course I should!'

I opened it up and inside was a gorgeous pair of knee-high boots.

'I hope they fit.' Elaine eyed my face worriedly. 'It's always a bit of a gamble buying shoes but Seth said you usually take a six and I couldn't resist. I've never had a daughter to buy for.'

I took off my heels and stuck my feet in the boots. They fitted perfectly and I looked up at Elaine with a beaming smile.

'They're fab.'

'Not too tight?'

'No, the opposite if anything, but they'll be perfect when I'm wearing socks. Thank you.' I kissed her cheek and she gave me her beaming smile – the spitting image of Seth's. Just then we heard a rusty squeaking sound, and all the heads in the room turned towards the doorway.

It was Bran. He was hunched into a wheelchair and my first reaction was shock at how he'd changed. He'd always been on crutches since I'd known him, but he'd still been tall and wiry and strong, hobbling around his island kingdom in spite of the uneven rocks and pebbly paths. Now he was shrunk, wizened into his wheelchair. His white hair was wilder than ever, but his weather-beaten face had paled to grey and his eyes had lost their fire.

'Hello, Bran,' Dad said gently. 'Feeling better?'

'Eh?' Bran's head jerked up and he glared at Dad as if confused by who he was. 'Better? That's a damn fool question.'

'Dad,' Elaine said crossly, 'it's a perfectly good question. Tom was just being polite.'

'Better,' Bran was mumbling into his chest. 'Better, he says. I'll be better when I'm home, home at my own hearth.'

'Dad . . .' Elaine's voice was strained as if this was a

discussion they'd had a dozen times before. 'Dad, please. Not this again. You know what the doctor said.'

'Doctors – what do they know? I'm dying, girl – does it matter where I do it?' He pushed his squeaky wheelchair across the carpet towards the table and began trying awkwardly to manoeuvre into position. Seth set his hand to the back to help but Bran knocked his arm away roughly. 'Leave me be. I may be a cripple but I've not lost the use of my arms yet.'

Behind his back I met Dad's eyes and saw my own uneasiness reflected there. There was no way this dinner could turn out well. I had a strong desire to turn tail and run home, but I didn't. Instead, when Elaine went back to the kitchen to start serving out, I followed her, anxious to be out of Bran's sight.

'I'm sorry, Anna,' Elaine said wearily as she pulled sautéed potatoes and garlic chicken out of the oven. 'He's always been a cantankerous old sod, but he's got past bearing since his illness. I don't know whether it's the medication, or the frustration, or just sheer bloody-mindedness but I'm going to apologize now for his behaviour because it'll probably only get worse.'

'Elaine, don't apologize.' I took the plates she handed me. 'It's fine. He misses his home. I can see that.'

'Yes.' She stopped for a moment in the centre of the

kitchen, her face weary. 'Yes he does. It's more than that actually. He pines for it. He was never meant to live so far from the sea. He says it's killing him and I don't know, maybe he's right. But what kind of daughter would I be if I sent him back to live in that shack on the Spit?' There was desperation in her face, but I couldn't answer. I didn't know the answer to give. I just shook my head in mute sympathy and she closed her eyes for a moment and brushed back her straggling hair with a tea towel. Then she forced a smile. 'There I go again. This is supposed to be your birthday celebration and here I am moaning away and loading you up like a pack horse. It should be Seth acting the waiter, not you! You should be out there with your feet up.'

I'd rather be in here, I thought. But I didn't say it. Instead I followed her out into the dining room and began laying dishes out on the table and helping Elaine as she served out potatoes and fragrant chunks of chicken with garlicky lemony butter.

'Bran?' I asked timidly as the first plate was filled and he looked up, his eyes misted.

'Eh? What?'

'Is this OK? This portion? Can I help you to some potatoes?'

'Who're you?' he asked suddenly, gripping the table.

I looked at Seth, suddenly unsure what to say. Seth stepped in.

'Grandad, this is Anna. You know Anna. My girlfriend. It's her birthday, remember?'

'You!' His voice was shaking and he banged on the table with his fist. 'You!'

'Dad,' Elaine said sharply, 'calm down. We discussed this, remember? It's Anna's birthday. I explained – a dinner for Anna's birthday and your homecoming. Remember?'

'I will not have her under my roof!' Bran shouted suddenly. There was foam at the corner of his mouth and his eyes were wild. His hand shook as he banged it again on the table, catching the corner of the plate and sending chicken and sauce splattering across Elaine's carefully laid table. 'I will not!'

'It's not your bloody roof!' Seth shouted back, and suddenly I could see their resemblance, the likeness in their terrifying anger. Seth's rage had the same, dangerous quality as Bran's, the same air that any moment he might snap.

'Get her out!' Bran turned to Elaine and his voice was thunderous, unbelievably so for a frail old man in a wheelchair.

'No,' Elaine said, trying to be calm, though her voice shook a little. 'No, Dad. Calm down.'

'Steady on, Bran.' Dad put a hand to Bran's shoulder, but Bran shook it off as if shrugging away a fly.

'I will not share my bread, my table, my roof with a damned witch!' he roared, and to my amazement he was half out of his chair, his frail, trembling arms supporting his weight. His face was purple and veins threaded his forehead. He looked like he was going to have a heart attack.

'Bran!' Dad's face was shocked. 'Now, hang on—'

'Dad, it's OK,' I said. 'Elaine, I think I should just go.'

'Anna, no, it's your birthday!' Elaine said, but her voice was anxious. I shook my head.

'Please, I think it would be best.'

'Well . . .' Elaine looked from Bran's shaking frame, collapsed back into his chair, and back to me, and I could see she was torn. 'Well . . . Oh, I don't know. Maybe that would be best.' Her face was wretched, and I bent and gave her a kiss.

'Please, don't feel bad. It was a lovely idea.'

'Get out,' Bran said in a weak, shaking bellow, as I gathered my coat. 'Get out and good riddance.'

'Hang on.' Seth put out a hand to grip my arm. 'Anna's not going anywhere.'

'Seth,' Elaine said softly. 'I know, darling, but your grandad—'

'No.' Seth's face was set. 'This is my house, I live here. Anna has a right to be here – as much right as that cantankerous bastard in the chair.'

'Don't speak about your grandad like that,' Elaine said warningly.

'Mum, he damn near ruined your life – he's not going to ruin mine. He's got a problem with Anna? Fine, that's his business, he can stay in his room.'

'I will not have her kind under my roof!' Bran roared again. He rammed his wheelchair into the table with such force and frustration that the china rattled and plates fell to the ground with a crash.

'Bran,' Dad said warningly, 'I think you should calm down.'

'Get her out!' Bran bellowed, ignoring Dad as if he hadn't spoken.

'If Anna goes, I go,' Seth said, and his voice was very cold.

'If you want to go, that's fine,' Elaine said, relieved. 'Of course it is. Here, darling, help yourself to whatever cash is in my purse and take Anna out for a meal in Brighthaven or something.'

'That's not what I mean. If you let him force Anna out, I'm going. For good. I can't live like this.'

'What do you mean – for good? Where would you go?'

Elaine's face was astonished.

'Does that matter?'

'Of course it matters!'

'Let him go!' Bran said, and there was contempt in his voice. 'Let him go with his slut.'

'Shut up!' Elaine screamed, turning on him suddenly. 'Just shut up, Dad!' Then she turned back to Seth. 'Seth, please, don't do this. You can see what he's like – just let it lie, just this once.'

'It's not once though, is it? It's been like this ever since he came to stay. You may be able to put up with it, but I can't.'

'Please, Seth.' She put both hands on her son's shoulder and her voice was very low. 'Please, he's not going to be here for ever . . .'

'Good,' Seth said brutally. 'And when he's gone, I'll come back.'

'Get out,' Bran said, and then he laughed, a dreadful cackling, half-mad laugh. 'She's bewitched you, boy, can't you see that? You're tied to her like a dog to its master; she's got you right where she wants you.'

'Shut up, you old bastard,' Seth said viciously. And then, holding my arm in a grip so hard that it hurt, he pulled me down the stairs, out of the pub and into the cold, clear darkness.

CHAPTER SEVENTEEN

Seth drove like he was possessed, so fast I was terrified – not for myself, but for him, and anyone else we might meet on the dark coast road. I thought about telling him, begging him even, to slow down, but one look at his fury-filled face told me that my words would be a waste of time. In fact they might make things worse.

He did slow down at last and then stop, bumping the car off the tarmac and on to the short turf, where he turned off the engine and sat, his chest heaving.

'Seth,' I said, and he put his arms around me and buried his face in my hair. I felt his body shake with huge, agonizing sobs.

'It's OK,' I whispered, but I knew I was lying. It wasn't OK. What had Seth done? Elaine would take him back, I was sure of it. But I also knew Seth's stubborn pride, and doubted he'd ever ask, no matter how bad things got. 'It's OK. Oh, love, it's OK.'

At last he sat up and ran his hand through his hair, then swiped angrily at his wet cheeks.

'I'm sorry,' he said, and his voice was hoarse. 'I'm sorry you had to hear all that.'

'It's OK.'

'It's not OK. God! I hate him. I hate him so much.'

'Don't,' I said urgently. 'What good will that do?'

'None, but it might make me feel better.' He cracked a twisted smile and I managed to smile back.

'What are you going to do?'

'Well, actually it's not as bad as Mum's probably imagining. I can stay on the boat – the *Angel*.'

'Really? You sure the owner – what was his name? – you sure he won't mind?'

'Charles? No, he won't care. He's already said I can take it out whenever I want to. He's wintering in Morocco at the moment anyway.'

'It's all right for some.'

'We could go there,' Seth said, only half joking. 'Up anchor, sail away, just you and me . . .' He pulled a strand of hair behind my ear and I shivered with longing.

'Fish for food?'

'Mmm. And mussels. Lobster. Oysters.'

'I hate oysters. And I can't open them.'

'I can teach you. There'll be plenty of time to learn.'

'Shame we've got no money and a few boring things to think of like, ooh, exams, our futures, university.'

'Ugh, it's all so pointless.' Seth stared into the darkness and I saw that his hands on the wheel were clenched.

'What do you mean?' I asked in surprise.

'All these hoops. I feel like a circus animal. And for what? So I can go and work in some office, pushing paper all my life? But look at the alternative – work the sea like Grandad, end up disabled and broken and broke. I just want to be out there . . .' He looked out to the black rolling waves, endlessly crashing against the cliffs in the darkness, and I shivered. I could think of nothing worse.

'I should take you home,' Seth said at last. 'Your dad'll be worrying.'

It was true. Dad must have seen Seth tear away into the night at ninety miles per hour, and he was probably imagining us dead in a ditch. But Seth was more important right now.

'He'll be OK for a bit,' I said gently. 'I want to make sure you can get into your boat before I go home, and anyway—'

I broke off. My phone was ringing. I fished it out of my pocket; *Dad mobile*, it read.

'Hi, Dad.'

'Anna!' Dad's voice was a gust of relief. There was a lot of background noise and I had a hard time hearing him. 'Thank God. Are you OK? Is Seth?'

'We're both fine. He's going to stay on the boat he's been fixing for a friend tonight. I'll settle him in. Where are you?'

'In the Crown and Anchor.'

'Great, listen, if I go down to the boat with Seth could you pick me up on your way back?'

'Yes, sure. What time?'

'What time are you leaving?' I asked.

'I'm not sure. Elaine's here – we're having a drink in the bar. She needed to calm down. What?' He broke off, speaking to someone in the background, then came back on. 'She wants to talk to you. Let's say – what's the time now? – half eight. Let's say between half nine and ten, OK?'

'Fine. Bye, Dad.'

There was a short kerfuffle as the phone was handed over and then Elaine came on.

'Anna, I'm so, so sorry.' Her voice was full of wretchedness. 'You shouldn't have had to hear all that. And on your birthday – I feel dreadful.'

'It's fine,' I said. It wasn't – but it wasn't Elaine's fault, which was what I meant. 'I'm fine. Don't worry.'

'Is Seth there?'

'Yes.' I looked across at him, but he only looked out of the window, stony-faced. 'He's here.'

'Is he OK?'

'He's all right. Upset, but all right.'

'Can I speak to him?'

'Hang on,' I said. I put my hand over the receiver and looked at Seth. 'It's your mum. She wants to talk to you.'

'Tell her to go fu—' He stopped and shut his eyes, biting his lip. 'Tell her no thanks.'

'Seth, come on. She's worried about you.'

'Anna, not now. Not tonight.'

I looked at him for a long moment, taking in his haggard face, the dark bruiselike shadows around his eyes, the still-wet traces of tears in his lashes. He looked like he was at the end of his tether.

'OK,' I said. I uncovered the receiver. 'Elaine, I'm really sorry, but he doesn't want to speak right now.'

'I understand.' Her voice cracked slightly but she managed a cheerful, 'Tell him . . . tell him goodnight. I love him. And goodnight to you too, Anna. Happy birthday, sweetie.'

'Goodnight, Elaine. Thanks for the boots and everything.'

I hung up and Seth and I looked at each other. The moonlight reflected off the shifting waves, throwing shards of light into the car and giving a cold, sculptured beauty to his features. His expression made my heart feel close to breaking.

'Happy birthday,' he said bitterly.

'Seth, don't.' I buried my face in his shoulder. 'Please, please don't. It doesn't matter, I don't care about my stupid birthday.'

'But I do.'

He dug in his jeans pocket, drew out a thin parcel, and tossed it over to me.

'I'm sorry. I'm sorry it isn't more, better.'

I unwrapped it carefully and a very old book, bound in faded red silk, fell into my lap. There was nothing on the front, but gilt letters on the spine read *The Love Poems of John Donne*.

'Open it to the flyleaf,' Seth said.

I carefully opened the fragile, spotted pages and there was an inscription in fine copperplate:

I wonder by my troth, what thou, and I
Did, till we lov'd? . . .
If ever any beauty I did see,
Which I desir'd, and got, 'twas but a dreame of thee.

To my darling Emma, who has bewitched my heart,
   my soul, and every other part.

'Oh, Seth . . .' I leafed gently through the pages. 'It's beautiful. Where did you . . . ?'

'In a secondhand shop in Brighthaven. I saw the inscription and it seemed . . .' He looked at me, his face suddenly uncertain. 'You don't . . . The inscription – you don't mind, do you?'

'No.' I shook my head, swallowed against the stiffness in my throat. 'No, I don't mind. Oh, Seth, I love you.'

'And there's something else.' He leant over into the back seat of the car and picked up a carrier bag.

'Two presents!'

'Don't get too excited. This one's a pretty far cry from Tiffany. It's not even wrapped.'

I opened the carrier bag – and a rape alarm fell out.

'Please, Anna.' Seth looked at me in the moon-shadowed darkness, his eyes full of fear. 'Please, I want you to be safe. If something happened to you, it would kill me. These people—'

'I will be safe,' I said. I had smashed two boys into a brick wall, leaving them bleeding and unconscious. I had bigger weapons than a rape alarm. 'I can take care of myself.'

'I know you can – I know you think you can. But please, carry this, for me?'

'Yes, OK.'

Seth nodded, once. Then he started the engine and we drove into the night.

CHAPTER EIGHTEEN

In this interpretation, Macbeth is a mere puppet in the hands of the women who surround him, from Lady Macbeth right back to the three witches who precipitate his downfall. Try as he might, Macbeth cannot escape—

I stopped and rubbed my eyes. My English coursework was due in less than a week and it was the last thing on my mind. My brain seemed sluggish, weighted down with bigger worries, and every sentence was like getting blood out of a stone. Who cared about Macbeth and the bloody witches, anyway?

I stood, stretched my spine, and then made my way down the corridor to the toilet, feeling the stiffness leach from my muscles as I walked.

As I re-entered the room, drying my hands on my jeans, I noticed something on the bed – a scrap of paper. A stray sheet of revision notes? I picked it up.

It was a black-and-white photo ripped out of the school newspaper. It showed Seth, sweaty and grinning and celebrating some football victory or other, both hands above his head in a triumphant cheer. Someone had drawn crude manacles in biro around each wrist and a collar around his neck. Underneath was written *WE KNOW.*

I went cold all over.

They knew about Seth. They'd been in the house. In my *bedroom*.

When?

I ran to the window and opened it, but there was no sight or sound of any intruder, only the tranquil noises of the forest night.

The paper had lain in a fold of my duvet, hard to see from where I was seated at the desk. It might have been put there – when? Any time. While I was at school. While I was walking home. While we ate . . . ?

Chill fury prickled up and down my spine at the thought of hooded figures creeping quietly along the corridor, while down below Dad cooked so innocently. All it would take was a single sound, Dad coming up to investigate, finding them there . . . I felt suddenly sick.

Stalking me, endangering me, that was one thing. But involving Dad and Seth? This was too much. They'd gone too far. Screw principles. Outwith or not, I had to act.

My hands were shaking so much that I could hardly type.

Dear Grandmother,

You said in your last letter that you wanted to help me. Well, there's something I need your help with. It's urgent. Can we talk?

Anna

Then I pressed send. Up until now I would've said it would be a cold day in hell before I ran towards the Ealdwitan for help. Well, I felt very, very cold.

Seth was chatting to his friends at the school gate when I turned up the next day, but he broke off when he saw me. I saw him make a quick, hurried goodbye and then he jogged across the car park to sweep me up in a long kiss. Then he set me down and looked at me searchingly.

'Are you OK?'

'I'm fine.'

'I got your text. What did you need to talk about that we couldn't discuss on the phone?'

'This.' I held out the defaced photo of his football victory.

Seth swore.

'Hey, not so loud.' I put a hand across his mouth and looked around for teachers. 'You'll get serious trouble for that kind of language.'

'That's the last thing I care about right now. Look, don't worry about me. I can take care of myself. And as for this,' he held the photo with his fingertips as though it was soiled, 'chuck it in the fire. You're the one we should be worrying about.'

I let that slide, and only said, 'When are you going home?'

'I'm not.' Seth shook his head and his expression was grim. 'I've spoken to Mum and she's dropped off my clothes and my school stuff at the boat, but I'm not going back until Grandad apologizes.'

'Oh, Seth, please, *please* don't do this. Not for me. It's not worth it.'

'It's not just for you.' He touched my cheek. 'Honestly. You mean everything to me, Anna, but this isn't only about you. This is about Grandad learning he's not some tinpot king we've all got to kowtow to. It's about forcing Mum to stand up to him for once in his life. When he was strong he used that to force everyone to do things his way; now he's weak he's using his illness as a weapon instead. But I've had enough. Hey, hey . . .'

He cupped my cheek again and I realized I was crying.

'Come on, sweetheart, it's not that bad. I like the boat. It's actually quite comfortable – well, OK it's bloody cold, the shower doesn't work and I can't quite stand upright, but apart from that . . . You know, I can turn on the kettle in the morning without getting out of bed – how's that for luxury? Breakfast in bed every day!'

He'd succeeded in making me laugh in spite of my tears and now he wiped away the drops from my cheek and kissed me gently.

'I'm OK. Honestly. Now, tell me what we can do to sort out these bastards.' And he flicked the photo with his finger. His reminder brought all my anger flooding back.

'I'm calling in a favour,' I said. 'And I promise you this, when I'm finished, the Malleus will regret they ever meddled with us.'

It was about a couple of weeks later that Dad came into the kitchen with a piece of paper in his hand and a very strange expression on his face.

'What is it?' I said, catching sight of his face. 'What's going on?'

'It seems like I should be asking you that,' he said, sitting down at the kitchen table, still with that odd, nonplussed look. 'This,' he waved the piece of paper, 'is from your grandmother.'

Oh.

We'd exchanged emails over the course of a few days and I'd explained the situation in slightly coded language, not sure how private my grandmother's email address might be. Eventually we'd set up a time to ring each other. She'd been incandescent (her exact word) and had strongly urged me to come up to London and learn what she called 'some basic self-defence and divination skills'.

'We will track these people down,' she'd said grimly, 'and they will rue the day they ever interfered with a Rokewood.'

It had felt . . . nice. Her protective anger, her swift mastery of the situation – it had felt nice.

And now this – out of the blue. What had she said? I tried to read Dad's face. Was he angry? He didn't look it. He looked more – sad?

'I wish you'd told me,' he said at last. 'You should have known that I wouldn't mind your meeting Elizabeth. We've had our differences, but I'd never drag you into it. If you want a relationship with her, that's your right.'

'Really?' I said, and I couldn't stop the scepticism entering my voice. 'Then why did you keep her a secret for eighteen years?'

Dad rubbed the patch of skin where his glasses chafed his nose, and looked uncomfortable.

'All I can say is, I don't know, Anna. I really don't. I spent your whole childhood *wanting* to talk to you about Isla, I really did. But something was holding me back. Maybe I should have seen a therapist or something,' he gave an uneasy laugh, 'but back then that wasn't something men really did. I suppose I just had my own issues to work through, before I could talk about it with you.'

He put his hand on mine and the sadness in his eyes made my heart clench.

'And I thought . . . I told myself that perhaps the truth was too difficult for you to deal with. But I think now that was dishonest. What I really felt was that the truth was too difficult for *me* to deal with. I'm sorry, darling.'

Poor Dad. God knows, it wasn't his fault. I didn't know why my mother had bound him to silence. But she had. And now Dad was blaming himself.

'It's OK, Dad,' I said. 'I understand. But I would like to see Elizabeth; I've been up to see her in London – did she tell you?'

'Yes, she said that she met you for tea. She said your meeting was "quite unsought and accidental" – whatever that means. I suppose she's trying to tell me that she didn't go behind my back. Anyway, she's made a suggestion which, I might add, you are *entirely* free to refuse.'

294

'What's that?'

'She says she'd like you to come up to London for half-term. Stay with her. Meet your mother's side of the family. She's asked my permission to write to you about it. What do you think?'

'Well . . .' I was taken aback – but also quite admiring of Elizabeth's chutzpah. It was a clever strategy. 'Actually, I think I'd like to. Go, I mean. Would you mind?'

'Mind? No.' He folded up the letter. 'I'll miss you, of course. But you deserve a relationship with your mother's side of the family. I never meant to cut them off, you know – but they kind of disowned your mother when we got together. They were very well-to-do and disapproved of the match. I suppose they would have come around but, well, after Isla died it was too painful to pursue, I suppose. And I was very angry at first, which didn't help. But I'd feel bad if my cowardice ruined your chance for a relationship, especially as Elizabeth's obviously ready to meet halfway.'

'Dad . . .' I looked down at the table, unsure how to put this, not wanting to cause more hurt. But I wanted to know so much. I took a deep breath. 'You said she died – but do you ever think Mum might still be alive?'

'No.' Dad shook his head, his eyes bright and liquid. 'I'm sorry, Anna, I don't. The police searched high and low – papered the place with posters, put alerts out at the ports, they even showed her photo on TV. But there were no sightings. She didn't take her passport or bank cards. No money came out of her accounts. She didn't contact any of her friends.' He sighed and rubbed again at his glasses. 'She was very, very severely depressed. Psychotic in fact. And she didn't take her medication with her. She simply walked out of the house one day in her nightdress and was never seen again – well . . . except once. Possibly.'

'Once?' I prompted.

'Yes.' He sounded reluctant. 'There was one sighting. Unconfirmed. She was seen standing on the parapet of St Saviour's Dock in the East End. A passer-by ran to flag down a passing police car – and when they turned back, she was gone.'

My spine prickled.

'And you think . . . ?'

'Well, the police thought the obvious: suicide, and dredged the water. But no body was ever found. So perhaps she jumped, perhaps she didn't. Perhaps she was never there and it was a hoax or a mistake. I suppose we'll never know for sure. But one thing I am certain of – Isla would never have left us so long without word, unless something terrible had happened to her.' He sighed and then straightened his back with an obvious effort.

'Well, that's enough gloom for one day. What do you want me to do about Elizabeth then – write back and say you'll go?'

'Yes. Yes, that would be great.'

'I'll miss you, you know.' He ruffled my hair. 'The house'll seem very quiet without you. In fact, you know what, I might go away too. Then the workmen can have free rein to redo the kitchen while we're both out of their hair.'

'Where will you go?' I asked.

'Aha . . . research.' He tapped his nose. 'Remember my book? The history of fishing on the south coast? I know you thought I'd let it all drop, but I've just been biding my time, doing some reading around, sniffing out the lay of the land. Anyway there's a chap down in Polperro, local historian johnny, who's been very useful and I'd like to go down there and do a bit of nosying around. It's a bit far for an overnighter, so this might be just the chance to spend a few days down there.'

'That sounds nice.' I smiled at him, pleased to imagine him padding around sunlit fishing ports while I journeyed to London. It would be a nice thought, something bright to hold on to as I stepped into the shadows.

* * *

'It's all set,' I told Seth at school the next day. 'I'm going to stay with my grandmother for half-term. She's going to help me work out what to do about the Malleus.'

'Good.' He looked at me seriously and then nodded. 'Good. I think it's a good idea. You need to sort out some kind of plan, I've been going half crazy worrying about someone torching Wicker House again. When are you going there?'

'I don't know – Saturday, I suppose. Why?'

'Oh.' He looked down at his hands, rubbing at the permanent oil and paint stains. Something about his voice made me look up. His expression was remote, unreadable.

'What's the matter?'

'Nothing.'

'Come on.' I put my hand on his arm, letting my fingers caress the livid rope burn across his wrist. 'Don't be like that. Tell me.'

'Honestly, it's fine. It's just – you know – I'd kind of assumed we'd spend Saturday together.'

Saturday together . . . For a minute I was confused, then it clicked. Saturday. The fourteenth of February. Valentine's Day. My hand flew to my mouth.

'Oh, Seth, I'm so sorry – I forgot.'

'Honestly, it's fine. Saving your life is more important than some lame dinner.'

'No, wait. It doesn't matter if I postpone an extra day.'

'Are you sure?'

'Yes, totally. I'll ring my grandmother tonight.'

Grandmother was perfectly happy to see me Sunday instead of Saturday. She offered to meet me at the station, but I said I'd make my way to her house in Kensington. It wasn't like I was some tourist up from the country. I'd lived there all my life; I knew my way around London still.

But when I raised the subject with Dad, it was a different story.

'Dad, would you mind if we left Sunday, instead of Saturday?' I asked over supper. He shook his head.

'Sorry, sweetie, I've booked my ticket and it's not refundable. Why, was there something you wanted to do?'

'No, it's fine. Don't worry,' I said resignedly. I thought about raising the possibility that I could stay an extra night by myself, but I knew what Dad's answer would be: no way – not while the arsonists were still wandering around. And truth to tell, I didn't really fancy the idea myself.

That night I rang Seth from my room and told him the bad news.

'So I guess I'll have to reschedule my grandmother. Again. Unless . . .' I stopped.

'What?' Seth asked. In the silence that followed I could hear the slap-slap of rigging in the harbour and the sound of the waves filtering down his phone. I imagined his little boat bobbing on the dark waters.

'Well . . . you could . . . spend the night here. With me.'

I accompanied Dad to the station, my rucksack packed with all the things I thought I might need for London – all my meagre collection of smart clothes mainly. His train was first and we stood on the platform making chilly conversation while we waited. There was only a handful of other passengers on such a cold day – an elderly lady, three teenage boys probably off to Brighthaven, which was the next stop on the line, and a girl, with a curtain of ice-pale hair blowing in the wind. With a jolt, I realized it was Seth's ex, Caroline, and I turned my face so that she wouldn't recognize me. Fortunately at that moment the train drew up.

'Bye, sweetie.' Dad kissed my cheek and gave me a bear hug. 'Have a wonderful time. And remember – if you have second thoughts or get fed up just call me. I'm only a phone call away.' He patted the pocket with his mobile in.

'Really,' I said, only half joking. 'What are you going to do in Cornwall? Come up on your white horse?'

'No, I shall subcontract the white knight business to Ben and Rick, who will be only too delighted to sweep you off your feet and will probably do it with a lot more style than your old dad. But seriously, love, they're slightly odd people, the Rokewoods. I'm sure you'll have a wonderful time, but just in case—'

'Dad, don't worry. I've got your number; I've got Rick and Ben's number; I've got James and Lorna's number, and there are plenty of old friends I can call on in Notting Hill. Now, go on.' The train's engine was powering up. 'Go on, get on. You'll get left behind.'

'OK.' Dad hugged me again and then climbed on board. He moved up the train until he found a seat and I saw him mouthing through the window: *Bye, love you.*

'Bye!' I called back, as the train began to move. 'Have a great time!' And then he was gone.

I shouldered my rucksack and walked back along the platform in the direction of the London train. But I didn't stop. Instead I carried on up the stairs and out of the station.

I hadn't exactly lied to Dad – all I'd said was that my train was at 11.35, without mentioning that that was 11.35 on

Sunday, not Saturday. And chances were, Dad would probably have let Seth stay anyway. I was eighteen; we'd been going out for nearly a year. But it didn't stop me from feeling a slight pang of guilt.

Somehow the fact that he thought I was spending the night with my grandmother, and was being so nice about it, only made it worse. Instead I would be . . . what? My heart gave a strange, painful beat – a mixture of nerves and anticipation. I knew what Seth had thought – or hoped – when I'd suggested he stay the night at Wicker House. And part of me wanted to – desperately.

The ironic thing was, I was pretty sure everyone, Dad included, assumed that we'd done it a long time ago. Most importantly, I *loved* Seth. Loved him utterly and completely.

So why was I holding back? Why did the thought of this next step feel so terrifying, such a leap into the unknown?

I pushed the question down. I wasn't ready anyway. There was one last thing I needed to sort out before tonight. One last thing I had to do. Only, I couldn't do it alone.

I'd never been to Abe's place. I don't know what I'd expected – a shared lad-pad, maybe, knee-deep in takeaway cartons. Or a squalid bedsit with a fridge used for chilling beer and not much else.

Certainly not the reality. The bus dropped me on the main road, but it still took me nearly twenty minutes more to reach the cabin, tucked away in the depths of the forest, far up a winding track.

When I finally reached his porch I stopped, looking back while I caught my breath. I could see nothing but an unending sea of forest, stretching away and away to the horizon. If there was any civilization out there it was hidden by the rolling waves of trees. As it was, Abe might have been the last man alive.

I was about to knock, when a noise from round the side of the house made me stop. I followed the porch around and there was Abe.

He was digging. As I watched he thrust the fork strongly into the earth and turned over the soil, watching as it trickled through the tines. At the chink of a stone he leant down and picked it up, throwing it far into the forest with a hand that was brown with earth.

'Abe,' I said. He straightened, shading his eyes, then brushed his hands on his jeans and climbed the steps.

'Hi.'

'What are you doing?'

'Digging over the potato bed.'

'I didn't know you liked gardening.'

'I expect there's lots you don't know about me.' He kicked off his boots and then opened the door with a slightly ironic bow. 'But I haven't welcomed you to my humble abode. Please. Make yourself at home.'

'Thanks . . .' I said awkwardly, as I followed Abe into a sparsely furnished, almost Shaker-style room. 'Thanks for agreeing to help.'

'I haven't agreed to help. I told you to come over. I still don't know what you want my help with.'

While Abe washed his hands, I found myself a seat on a wooden settle and chewed my nail as I tried to think how to phrase it.

'Coffee?' Abe asked over his shoulder.

'Thanks.'

'Chuck another log in the stove, will you? It's burning down.'

I'd never operated a wood-burning stove, but while Abe ground coffee beans, and then put a pot on to filter, I managed to work the catch on the door and thrust another log into the glowing heart of the fire. Abe came over just as I finished and he expertly nudged the door shut with the poker and flipped the catch. Then he sat in the rocking chair opposite and fixed me with his steady black gaze.

'So. Spit it out.'

'It's Seth.'

'Great. Super.'

'I . . . I need your help. I need to make him a . . . a . . . protection charm.'

I waited, but Abe said nothing and I was forced to continue.

'I'm going away, tomorrow, for a week. And the Malleus have threatened him. I can't leave him unprotected, Abe. What if something happens while I'm away? What if they use him to punish me?'

I knew what Emmaline would have said, if I'd gone to her. She'd have laughed, told me I was being silly, that the Malleus had no argument with Seth. But Abe didn't. And somehow . . . somehow I'd known that he wouldn't.

He sat in silence, chewing his nail in an unconscious echo of my own edginess.

'That's serious magic,' he said at last. 'You want something that'll work while you're not there, is that right?'

'Yes – like a charm, or a talisman.' I thought of the package under my step and suppressed a shudder. 'Is that possible? I mean, do you know how?'

'Yes.' He bit his nail again, thinking. 'Yes it's possible. But it's indirect magic; it's much harder, because you're

305

not there to . . .' He paused and I could see he was struggling for an analogy. 'You're not there to charge it up – do you see what I mean? You have to get all the power into the object at the outset. For you to cast a protective spell over Seth – that's one thing. But imbuing an object to do the job in your absence – that's another. I mean, you need the object, for one thing.'

'I have one. This.' I held up a thick silver ring, very plain, like a sawn-off chunk of pipe. It was my Valentine's present to Seth. Or would be.

'I see. OK.'

Abe stood and paced to the window, looking out over the rolling, cloud-shadowed green, and then walked back to the coffee-maker. He poured two cups, handed me one, and then walked back to the window. I could feel him pacing out his thoughts, turning it over and over in his mind.

'It'll have to be blood magic,' he said at last.

'Which means?'

'What it sounds. It's not nice, Anna.'

'I don't care. I want Seth to be safe. I'll do whatever it takes.'

'Christ . . .' He looked at me, his face shadowed in the dim winter light. 'You don't do anything by halves, do you? You almost kill yourself holding back your powers for the best part of half a year, and now you're telling me you want to perform advanced magic on a Saturday afternoon – all because of some dumb outwith.'

'Don't call him that.'

'All right, I take that back. He's not so dumb, though it pisses me off to admit it. But he is an outwith, Anna. And he always will be.'

'I love him.' My throat was tight. 'I wouldn't expect you to understand.'

'How dare you.' Abe's face was suddenly hard, his jaw clenched stiff. 'You haven't got a clue what I understand.'

For a minute we both stood, facing each other. I felt if Abe were a dog he would have been snarling.

'Are you going to help me or not?'

'Yes.' His fury subsided as suddenly as it had come and he sank back into the rocker, rubbing his forehead tiredly. 'Yes, I'll help you. Douse the fire; this is magic best worked in the dark.'

While I knocked the logs down and drew the damper so that it was just a pile of simmering embers, Abe was collecting a small wooden bowl, a knife, a candle.

He set them on the table, lowered the blinds against the weak, setting sun, and then lit the candle.

As he set the match to the wick, it burnt high and wavering, giving his face a stage magician look, and for a moment I would not have been surprised to see him flourish a silken hat or a red-lined cape. Then it died down to a normal flame and he was regular Abe again – unshaven, with the candlelight glinting from his eyebrow ring, his coal-black eyes.

I watched as he passed the knife three times through the candle flame, each pass turning the bright blade darker with soot.

On the third pass he turned the hilt towards me and gestured towards the bowl.

'Put the ring in the bowl.'

I did so.

'Now tell it what it has to do.'

'It has to protect Seth.'

'Don't tell me, tell the ring,' Abe said impatiently.

I cupped the small bowl in my two hands and spoke, feeling a fool, but wanting this too much to care.

'Ring, please protect Seth. Protect him from harm, protect him from the people who want to hurt him. Please, keep him safe. Keep him alive.' My knuckles were white.

'Now,' Abe said, his voice very low. And he glanced at the knife.

Somehow . . . somehow I didn't need to ask any more. With a feeling of sick reluctance, I took the hilt in my right hand and stretched my left arm on the table. It looked waxen in the candlelight; white and soft and vulnerable, like a mannequin's, not flesh at all.

'Do you really want to do this?' Abe asked.

I didn't answer. Instead, I drove the knife into my arm.

The blood welled up, dark in the darkness. It ran down my arm and I angled my hand, letting it trace a snaking path down my wrist and fingers, and drip slowly into the bowl.

'Tell it,' Abe said. 'Tell it what you will give for Seth's safety,'

'Anything,' I said. My voice sounded strange in my own ears. The only sound in the room was the drip, drip of the blood in the bowl. 'I'd give anything. My life.'

Abe's breath seemed to catch in his throat and he stood, suddenly, so that his chair screeched on the wooden floor. For a minute I thought he was going to leave. But he only walked to the dresser at the other side of the room and pulled a clean cloth out of a drawer.

The blood was already slowing. When it finally stopped he handed me the cloth without a word. I wrapped it round my arm. I felt weak, shaky.

'Are you OK?' Abe asked.

I nodded. 'I'm all right. Did it work?'

'Yes. At least, you won't know for sure, until it's needed.

But it took the blood. That means that part of you, part of your power, is in the ring now.'

'Took the blood? What do you mean?'

For answer, Abe just held out the bowl. I peered into it, ready to pick the ring out of the mess of gore, wipe the blood off with the cloth.

But there was only the slightest pool of blood in the bottom; a few drops, no more. And as I watched, even that last trace soaked into the solid silver of the ring, until there was no sign. No sign of what I'd done, what I'd given.

Abe picked the ring out of the bowl and held it out to me on his palm. It looked . . . unchanged. Completely unchanged. When I took it and weighed it in my own hand it felt not one gram heavier. But something about it, something utterly indefinable, was different. I could feel it as it lay in my palm, emanating a power that was my own, and yet not my own.

I took it – and as I did, Abe put out a hand, catching my wounded arm. He held it for a moment, holding me close to him, his fingers pressing the bloody cloth. Then he let go abruptly.

I unwound the makeshift bandage. The cut was gone – the scar remained.

'Thank you,' I said to Abe. 'Thank you, I couldn't . . .'

But he'd already turned away, looking for his car keys.

The final candle was in place on the table and I looked at my watch – Seth would be here in just over half an hour and I'd only just finished laying the table. I hadn't showered or got dressed yet. I wanted everything to be *perfect*. I knew that was stupid – Seth had been over for supper enough times to know that we didn't normally dine off white damask and bone china. But tonight – tonight was different.

Pulling off my apron, I ran upstairs to the shower and stood under the steamy blast thinking about all the jobs left to do before Seth arrived. Wash hair – check. Shave legs – check. Change bedclothes – check. The thought gave me a funny little shudder: half anticipation and half terror.

As I got out of the shower and towelled my hair off I looked out of the window. Darkness had fallen and a creeping sea-mist had spread across the forest, turning the lighthouse beam into a strange ghostly halo over the wood. I hadn't bothered to draw the curtains – we had no neighbours; there was no one between us and the coast – but all of a sudden I was conscious of my nakedness and the unguarded window, and I shivered.

In my bedroom I scolded myself as I pulled on one of

the dresses my grandmother had given me. It was silly to be so jumpy. Just because Dad was away tonight didn't make it any more dangerous. And anyway, I was hardly some defenceless damsel. If it came to it, I could take care of myself a lot better than Dad could.

But all the same, as I smoothed the silky-soft material down over my hips and thighs, I was very glad that Seth would be here soon.

I looked at myself in the mirror as I pinned up my hair. The dress was lovely – it was made of a very fine silk jersey and started out deep, midnight-blue at the collarbones, fading through shades of cobalt and azure, until it ended just below the knee in a shimmer of pearly grey. It reminded me of the moon rising over Winter Harbour, and when I'd unwrapped it from its paper sheath I'd thought of my first proper date with Seth, when he'd taken me out on his boat for a moonlight picnic. The only snag was I couldn't wear a bra because though the front was very demure, the back was kind of low, nearly to my waist. Still, I thought I'd get away with it.

Then the doorbell rang and I ran downstairs barefoot to answer it.

'Ohhhhh my God . . .' Seth groaned when I opened the door. 'Don't do this to me, Anna . . .'

'What?' I looked round anxiously, wondering what

he'd seen, what had upset him.

'You expect me to sit through dinner while you're wearing *that*?' His cold hands crept around my waist. 'And . . . oh Christ, no bra . . .' His fingertips traced an icy path up my naked back.

'Ahhh!' I yelped. 'Your hands are like ice!'

'Sorry,' he grinned. 'It's very chilly out and there's no shower yet on the boat. I had to wash with a jug over the side.'

'Urgh.' I shuddered as I led him through into the living room. 'Rather you than me. Still, there's a fire in here.'

'If I warm up, will I be allowed to touch you?'

'Maybe.' I smiled to make it a joke, though his words set my insides fluttering.

I leant against the mantlepiece, trying to hide the sudden flush on my cheeks, and Seth stood beside me, his hands held out to the blaze. We stood in silence, side by side, not touching but very close. I turned to look at him, his skin flickering gold and red in the flames from the fire, his dark hair tumbled over his forehead, his eyes smoke-dark. Then, very slowly, he brushed his hand across my cheek.

'So . . . is that better?'

'Yes,' I said. My voice was husky.

'Still OK?' He let his hand trail down my jaw and the side of my neck.

'Yes.'

'This?'

His fingers skimmed underneath the soft midnight-blue hem of my dress where it dipped below my throat. I closed my eyes. The world shrank down to the heat of the fire, the slow touch of Seth's hands, his fingers . . . the white bed upstairs, waiting with clean sheets . . .

Something fell to the floor with a thud. We both jumped and I opened my eyes.

'What's this?' Seth bent and picked it up. He held out the small packet, wrapped in silver paper.

'Oh . . .' It was almost a struggle to remember. 'I . . . it's my present. To you. Happy Valentine's day.'

'Anna!' He looked stricken. 'I didn't know we were doing presents. I haven't got you anything – only a card.'

'That's OK. That's why I didn't tell you – it didn't seem fair. I've only just had my birthday. I didn't want you to have to get something else.'

'But . . . but now I feel . . .' His expression struggled between affection and irritation and then he gave up.

'Open it,' I said.

He began to pick at the wrappings with his oil-stained nails. I watched as he struggled with the tape.

'Should I get scissors?'

'No, wait, I've got it – oops!' The paper ripped suddenly and the ring shot out, skittering across the floor. Seth chased after it and caught it with a foot, then picked it up.

'What is it? It looks like a bit of plumber's pipe – reminds me of those sawn-off ends I used to find in my dad's pockets.'

'It's a ring. Do you like it?'

'A ring?' He looked at it curiously in the palm of his hand and then nodded. 'Yeah. I do. I don't know, I don't think of rings as being very blokey somehow but this – it's great. I love it.'

He slipped it on to the third finger of his right hand, matching the finger where I wore his seaglass ring, and then took my hand, interlacing our fingers. He pulled my hand to his mouth. His lips were warm and soft, and I felt them curve into a smile.

'Your fingers smell of fish. What's for supper?'

'Oh!' I groaned. 'I scrubbed them raw – but it's the bloody smoked salmon.'

'Smoked salmon? You're pushing the boat out.'

'Well, we're cooking off a gas bottle in the dining room, so I was a bit limited. The smoked salmon is for the main course, with tagliatelle. Dessert is chocolate mousse. And starter . . .' I led him through to the downstairs loo where the starter was sitting in a bucket of sea water. 'These.'

'Oh . . .' His broad grin became even wider. 'Anna, you star. Oysters. My favourite.'

Not my favourite – in fact I was only just learning to stomach them – but Seth adored them and would eat them by the bucket load.

'You'll have to open them,' I warned.

'Not a problem.' He picked the bucket up and took them back to the living room, where I'd laid out plates, napkins and lemon on the coffee table. 'So . . . are you trying to put me in the mood?' he teased.

'The mood?' I was deliberately demure. 'For fishing?'

'I'm always in the mood for that.'

Some two or three hours later and the fire had burnt low in the grate. I lay with my head against Seth's chest, enjoying the feel of his fingers lazily playing with my hair, long since tumbled out of its careful pins. The silver ring glinted in the firelight.

'Where did you learn to cook like that?' I heard his voice through his ribs, a deep, quiet murmur.

'Mmm . . . school . . . Dad . . . natural greed . . .'

'It was delicious.'

'Even the oysters?'

'Especially the oysters.' His chest shook with a quiet laugh and his hand stroked down my cheek and over my throat and shoulder. 'I like things that are hard to prise open. Perhaps that's why I love you.'

'What do you mean?' I twisted to look at his face, soft and golden in the light of the dying fire.

'Well . . . you are quite a private person, don't you think?'

I considered for a moment, surprised. I'd never thought of myself as particularly private but perhaps Seth was right. I could count my close friends on the fingers of one hand.

'And yet, you're so soft and lovely and tender inside . . .' He pulled me closer and I shut my eyes, and felt his lips on my forehead and my closed lids.

'Shame so many people get food poisoning from oysters . . .' I said with a shaky laugh.

'Not if you're careful,' he said softly, his lips on my cheeks, my jaw, the crook of my shoulder . . .

'You never know what's inside . . .'

'It might be a pearl.'

We stayed like that, completely still, for – I don't know how long. My eyes were closed, but I could feel his warm, sweet breath against my throat, the heat of his lips, barely touching my skin. The room was silent except for our ragged breathing and the sighing shifts of the logs in the grate. My heart was beating so hard that it felt painful in my chest. Was this what it felt like to die from a broken heart – not from desertion, but from a love so huge that it split your heart clean open?

'I love you,' I said to Seth, and felt my voice break with the impossibility of ever telling him how much I loved him – how purely and completely and utterly. How could three short words sum up all the glorious agony of being with him?

'I love you too,' he said and then he took hold of the hem of my dress. 'Is this OK?'

I couldn't speak, my heart too full to find the words. I only nodded. And then he tugged gently upwards and the dress lay on the hearth in front of the fire and he caught me in his arms and buried his face in my hair with a strange choking sob that might have been anything – love, desire, even pain. I pressed myself against him and all I could think was, please God, I'm empty. Please let it have been enough, what I did. If I can just get through this without hurting him, or burning down the house . . .

My fingers began to work the buttons of his shirt, awkwardly, slowly, one at a time, until at last it lay crumpled with my dress and we were pressed skin to skin, mine milk-white, Seth's tanned to deep gold even in the depths of winter. The firelight flickered off his torso and I looked at him, full of love, triumphant, finally fearless.

'Wait.' He put his hand to mine as I reached for his belt.

'What?'

'There's just one thing . . . I have to ask . . .'

I drew back a little and he sat up and ran his hand through his hair.

'I have to hear you say it.'

'What? Anything, you know that.'

'The other night,' his dark eyes searched mine, 'when I asked you if you knew that I loved you. You . . . hesitated.'

Oh God. Not this.

'And I have to know, do you honestly, *honestly* believe that I love you? You've put all that stupid stuff about the spell behind you, right?'

My heart began to thump again and I put my hand over it, trying to quell the pain.

'Seth . . .'

'That's all I want to know. Just promise me – that you believe me. Do you?'

'Seth . . .' I said again and then stopped, struggling, drowning, trying to find the words.

'Anna?'

But I couldn't speak.

It was terrible, chilling to watch – the soft openness of his face turning hard and cold; like watching a lake ice over in summer. As he saw me struggle to promise, saw that I *wanted* to, but that the words wouldn't come, that I couldn't frame the lie I wanted to utter, all the warmth left his face, leaving only a bleak anger.

He got up and began to yank his shirt on, buttoning it all askew, shaking his head in bitter disbelief. The sight broke my paralysis and I scrambled to my feet, clutching at him with hands that trembled.

'Seth, please, don't be like this.'

'I can't believe it; I can't believe it,' was all he said, still shaking his head.

'Oh please, don't be like this, don't ruin this.'

'*Me* ruin this?'

'I know.' I picked up my dress, clutching it against myself like a shield. 'I know, it's me; it's my fault, but please—'

'You were prepared to do *this* –' he flung an arm at the pile of crumpled clothes on the hearthrug '– and all the time . . .'

'I'm sorry,' I wept.

'So am I.' He caught up his shoes in one hand and pushed me away from him, not aggressively, but not gently either. I tripped and fell to my knees and caught my dress up in my hands to stifle my sobs.

At the door he turned and his face was horrible. Tears streaked his cheeks, though he seemed quite unaware of them.

'Goodbye,' he said. And something about the finality in his voice struck cold into my guts.

'What do you mean?'

'I'm sorry, Anna. This is it. I can't do this any more. I can't go through this again and again. I can't.'

'No – please no, Seth. Don't go . . .'

'I'm sorry,' he repeated. 'I'm leaving, for good. Don't come after me.'

'Seth!' I wept. But he only shook his head and began to walk away.

In the doorway he stopped for a moment, his back still turned, as if he couldn't bear to see my face.

'Was it all a lie?' he asked, and his voice cracked on the last word.

I shook my head, completely unable to speak, and he bowed his neck and walked into the night.

He walked away and it felt like there was a fish-hook buried deep in my guts. Seth was holding the line and every step he took he was ripping out my insides, step by step. And I couldn't say anything, I could only stand and gasp, wordless with pain, as part of my soul was ripped out of me.

At last, as his shadow mingled with the darkness of the wildwood, I found my voice.

'No!' I screamed, into the darkness. 'No!'

But it was too late.

CHAPTER NINETEEN

I lay for a long time, curled in front of the dying fire. It grew colder and colder until I began to shake, and I realized that if I stayed here I would probably be hypothermic by morning.

Seth's jacket was on the hearthrug where he'd left it. I shrugged my discarded dress back on, then picked it up and wrapped it around myself. Then I tried to stand, but I was so cold and cramped that my limbs gave beneath me. At last, with great difficulty, I dragged myself upstairs and crawled into bed, still clutching Seth's jacket around me. Then I pulled the covers over me and sobbed into my pillow, great tearing sobs that would have woken Dad, if he'd been there. But he wasn't there. I was alone. I pulled my knees to my chest, trying in vain to stop the great hole that Seth had torn when he left – but nothing worked. Every thought, every memory was agony.

What could I have said to stop him? *You could have lied*, my heart said bitterly. *You should have lied*. I'd spent so long trying to push him away – and now he was gone. I'd got what I'd wished for – but at such a price.

I wanted to be numb. I wanted to never feel anything again. Anything would be better than this feeling of having my heart and my guts and my soul ripped out through the hole in my chest.

The darkness pressed around me, nudging me, touching me, whispering bitter accusations in my ear until I screamed to shut them out.

Oil and water . . . oil and water . . . oil and water . . .

At some point – I don't know how long after – I fell into a half-sleep, dogged by strange dreams, where I relived our fight over and over, saying all the things I should have said, could have said. Then I was running, running through Wicker Wood, with Seth always a few steps ahead of me, just out of reach of my arms. I could hear his footsteps just ahead of me, the crack of sticks and branches, and the tearing of my own breath as I ran, twigs catching in my hair and ripping my clothes, but always unable to catch up. It was the last dream which was the worst. The one where Seth didn't leave and was in bed with me, his arms around me, his breath hot and harsh on my face. His grip was hard, so tight it was painful, and then, with a shock, I awoke.

It was no dream. It was real. There *were* arms around me – but not Seth's. The person bending over my bed, pinning my arms to my sides, stank of sweat, tobacco, beer. As I struggled to free myself a shaft of moonlight caught the intruder and I saw he was dressed in black, with a black hood over his head, and slit-eyes that glittered.

I opened my mouth to scream – and a hood was thrust over my head. Rough hands crammed the material into my open mouth so hard that I gagged and bile flooded my mouth. I could barely breathe, the material was stifling, and I drew desperate snorting breaths through my nose.

Someone was doing something to my wrists and with a huge effort I wrenched my hands free, clawing at the threads drawn tight around my neck, desperately trying to get some air, to see what was going on. They caught my hands and bound them too, and I was face down on my own bed, still fighting, but drowning in fear and sweat. I couldn't move, I couldn't breathe, I couldn't . . . *You can cast spells, you stupid witch!*, the voice in my head was like a panicked shout.

I gathered all my power for a huge burst – and a voice shouted, 'Oi! She's casting a spell! Stop her! Stick her now!'

There was a burning, stabbing pain in my thigh – and everything began to slow. It was a nightmarish feeling – everyone in the room was moving with normal speed but I was mired in tar, my limbs heavy and sluggish, my mind completely unable to gather . . . to gather . . . to think . . .

I felt my head loll, slip to one side, fall. There was a slithering rush and a blinding crack. My skull hit the floorboards. I slid into black.

I awoke to darkness and a pounding pain in my head. I was cold and stiff, but the worst was that I was unbearably thirsty. It hurt to move. When I tried, the pain sent little flickers sparking across my vision, but I couldn't lie here and wait for them to come and find me.

Ignoring the stabs of pain, I tried to move my hands. They were still bound, but only with rope, and there was some room for movement. My feet – loose . . . No, wait, there was something round my ankle. A chain, but a long one. That was something at least – I could kick, even though the movement sent red flashes of agony searing across the blackness.

Cautiously I tried to move my hands up to my face. I could feel from the cold stone against my cheek that the hood was gone, but something felt wrong – there was something in my mouth, on my face. Something hard and cold, digging into my skin. My fingers met metal.

For a second I was puzzled, then as my hands moved across my skin, I realized what it was. A wave of fear and revulsion threatened to overwhelm me – but anger won. I grabbed and yanked, trying bodily to rip the thing off me. The movement was agony, sending red and black shards of pain ripping through my head – but I gritted my teeth and carried on.

Only after a long, agonizing eternity did I let my hands fall. I lay trembling on the ground, waiting for the pain and the blinding lights to subside.

The thing was a scold's bridle – a witch's bridle. I'd seen one in Winter Museum – a horrific rusty thing of indescribable misogyny and hate. *Used to silence the tongue of a scolding wife or punish women suspected of witchcraft* read the little dusty card. Even as a relic from the past it had made me shiver, trying to imagine the pain and fury of the women forced to wear the contraption.

Now I was wearing one myself. Bands of metal bound my head, forcing a steel bit between my teeth, pressing down my tongue so that I could barely swallow, let alone speak or call for help. Instead I made the only sound I could – a wordless bellow of fury that echoed around my small prison.

No one came. No one answered me. I was alone in the

darkness with the cold, and the pain, and the thirst. I huddled my arms against myself, trying to pull my clothes tighter against the cold, and found I was still wearing Seth's jacket. I buried my face in the collar, breathing in his familiar smell until I thought my heart would crack, and the tears leaked out through the metal bridle, and into my hair.

I must have slept, because when I awoke there was a tiny chink of light coming from a grille in the wall and I could see a beaker on the floor. Water. Water at last.

I scrambled to my knees and crawled across a stone floor to the beaker, trailing the chain behind me. It was just within my reach, the chain almost taut at my ankle, and I picked up the beaker carefully with my bound hands and drained it, painfully trying to swallow around the choking bit of the bridle. Half of it trickled through the metal-work and sloshed down my front, but it was the best drink I'd ever had – and for a moment I was too thankful to worry. They didn't intend me to die of thirst, at least.

It was the strange aftertaste that warned me: an odd bitter flavour. It wasn't unpleasant – but whatever was in the cup, it wasn't just water. As my head began to swim, I put both hands on the floor to steady myself. But it was too late. The stuff was taking effect. I had just time to look up and see a face peering through the grille, a grotesque, masked face grinning in triumph, and then the drink took hold and I collapsed to the floor again.

The next day, and the next, and the next, were all the same. They waited until I was too thirsty to resist and then offered me the drugged water. Sometimes it was a knockout dose, designed to put me under. Other times just enough to make me disoriented and confused, and then they would push food through the grille and disappear. I tried to resist, growing weaker and weaker as the thirst took over, feeling my lips begin to crack and my throat burn. But soon, pathetically soon, I cracked and drank.

I had no idea what was in the drink – or the food – but I knew what the effect was. It did something to my magic, kept me in a half-waking, half-sleeping nightmare where I couldn't focus enough to shape a spell. The witch's bridle, I guessed, was for the same reason, designed to stop me saying words of power, or calling spirits and demons to my aid.

The third day – or maybe it was the fourth or fifth or sixth – I held out a particularly long time, gritting my teeth and refusing to drink, until at last I fell into an exhausted doze. I woke to find someone in the room. Hands held my jaw open and they were pouring liquid down my throat. I choked and gulped against the flow – but it was too late. I could feel the lethargy begin to take hold . . . But before it dragged me under I had just enough strength to stagger to my feet and lash out with all my force.

Electricity crackled across the room and the hooded man yelled in pain and reeled back, swearing and clutching his arm.

'Bitch!' he bellowed. 'Help! The witch shocked me!'

Figures came running, crowding into the room and I collapsed to my knees. The hooded man aimed a kick at my side and I fell, hearing the bridle clang as it hit the floor.

'I've got the syringe,' one of the new arrivals panted.

'Bit bloody late,' the hooded man said crossly. 'She's going under now.'

My head was lolling and the room was swimming in and out of focus, but I could hear through the roaring in my ears that their accent was local. These men were from Winter, Brighthaven, maybe Easthead. Not much further. They sounded like the traders in the market, like the fishermen who called to each other on the quay. Through the open door, the air smelt of the sea.

'Why are you doing this?' I tried to say, coughing the words painfully around the bit. The figure in black just shook his head.

'Shut up, witch. You'll have your say at the trial, soon enough.'

The trial . . . I closed my eyes and he aimed a last kick at my spine and left.

That night I lay between waking and nightmares and tried, desperately, to scrape together enough magic to release myself. I'd been stupid to waste my power shocking the guard. I'd been too weak to do any serious harm. But how to escape?

The room I was in was small and built of thick stones, and it stank like a pigsty. Maybe it *had* been a pigsty, once upon a time. The door was thick wood and I couldn't reach it; my foot was chained to the far wall and the chain was too short to let me near. But the roof – the roof was the weak spot. It was made of slates, haphazardly piled on each other with gaps and chinks that let in daylight and rain. I doubted I could manage to blast my way out of the cell – but maybe, just maybe, if I could keep this stupor at bay for long enough, I could do a transformation spell. Witches could transform into animals and birds – I'd seen the Ealdwitan do it. I didn't know if I could do the same – and even if I transformed myself, would I be able to transform back? But it was my best hope – to transform into something small enough to slip my chains and squeeze between the tiles to freedom. I had no choice. It was that or lie here and wait for my 'trial' – and I had no illusions about what the outcome would be.

As I lay there, I realized I could hear a dripping sound, like water over stone, and I dragged myself across the floor in the direction of the noise. It was coming from the corner of my cell and, when I got there, I found the stones were slick and slimy to the touch. A thin stream of water oozed down the wall. I tried to put my mouth to the trickle, but the bridle got in the way. It was so frustrating – I could feel the water just centimetres from my lips and I couldn't touch it.

I lay back for a moment, trying to think, and then I sat up, feeling along the walls for something sharp, any kind of hook, a bit of sticking out stone or metal. My fingers touched something jagged – rusty metal, it felt like – and I hooked the hem of my dress over the projection, and then pulled and ripped until a piece of fabric tore free.

I crawled back to the damp patch and stuffed the piece of fabric between the cracks in the stone and waited until it was wet. Then I sucked. The water was disgusting – it tasted bitter and full of mould and slime. But it was wet. And it wasn't drugged.

When the scrap of dress was sucked dry I pushed it back into the slimy crack until it was soaked again, then I sucked it, repeating the actions again, and again, until my thirst was slightly less.

Then I tried again to cast a spell. There was almost nothing there – I could feel that. Just as my muscles were weak and limp, with no power to kick and fight, I could feel there was no magic inside me, nothing to fight with. At last by straining every fibre, I managed to conjure a little witchlight, a pathetic thing really. It burnt very low, very dim, against the stone floor, and I cast my eyes up and round the cell, gazing at the mossy walls and stained floor.

The sight was so depressing that I let the light burn out and then I lay in the dark, wondering how long I'd been here and whether I'd ever see my home again.

Emmaline had been right. The Malleus had got me at last, as they'd said. And I'd been too stupid, too proud, too sanctimonious to protect myself. I remembered my words to Emmaline: *They're only outwith, right?* The memory made me want to cut out my own tongue. Stupid Anna. Stupid, conceited, ignorant Anna.

I'd underestimated them – just as Emmaline had tried to tell me. And what now?

No one would miss me for at least a week, perhaps longer. Dad would think I was with my grandmother. So would Emmaline and Abe. My grandmother would wait for my arrival – and then what? Phone the house, I guessed. But Dad wasn't there. She didn't have his mobile number. She didn't know where he was. And in any case, she'd probably just assume I'd changed my mind.

And worst of all, Seth . . . my heart failed me as I thought of Seth. What would he think? Or maybe he'd already left Winter and wouldn't even know. Would he care?

I let my head fall to the stone floor and wept.

When I awoke, some time later, the gaoler had come as usual and had left more water and some bread and dry cheese. There was a chink of light through the grille so I fell on the beaker, pretending to gulp it down just as ravenously as before, but I let a bit more than usual drip down my front. The room turned hazy and began to slip away, and I fell to the floor, hearing, as if from a long way off, the clank of the iron bridle as it hit the stones. But I didn't slip into complete unconsciousness quite as fast as usual. As I lay on the floor, somewhere between waking and sleeping, I heard voices from outside, strangely distorted, but recognizable as human.

'How long d'you think then, till the trial?'

'Not yet – she's still got too much fight in her, the bitch. We don't want her trying that electricity thing again.' The voice was bitter and I guessed that this must be the guard I'd shocked. 'But soon. Coupla days maybe?'

'And they've got the witnesses all lined up, have they?'

'Yeah. Them boys identified her, said it was definitely her in the alley.'

'What about the other girl – the one who turned her in? She's ready, is she?'

'Oh aye, she's ready. More than ready. She's been keen to see justice done for a *long* time.'

There was a grim laugh in his voice that made me shudder, and the first voice said sharply, 'D'you see that? Did she move?'

There was a silence and even with my eyes shut I felt their gazes piercing the murk. I lay very still and tried to suppress even my breathing.

'You're imagining things,' said the second man at last. There was something familiar about his voice, and I strained to try to think where I'd heard it before, but my drug-wasted brain wouldn't cooperate. It put impossible faces into my head – boys from school. Bran.

Seth. Tears leaked out of my closed lids.

They stood, watching, and then the same voice said, 'Nah, she may be a witch, but she'd have to be a rhino to withstand that dose. It'd knock out someone twice her size.'

'She looks pretty small, doesn't she? Doesn't look like she could hurt anyone much.'

'Don't be soft. She put two good lads in hospital; it's not her fault they weren't killed. She's got another running around after her like a chained dog frightened of a whipping, and she's done more harm to Winter than a year's worth of disasters. Storms, accidents, floods – all her.'

'And her so young . . .'

'So evil, you mean.'

'*Faugh*, makes me sick.' The voice hardened. 'Lying there like butter wouldn't melt.'

'Evil like that, dressed up as innocence. It's the most dangerous kind.'

'I don't understand why we couldn't go after the other one – the other girl.'

I caught my breath – not . . . not Emmaline? Please God, don't let me have dragged Emmaline down with me . . .

'You know the rules,' said the second voice. 'They

leave us alone, we leave them alone. But if they step over the line . . .'

'Yeah. Fair game,' the first man said. Then his voice dropped. 'I heard her . . . You know, crying. But the book says they can't weep.'

'Faking,' said the second voice with a sneer. 'They'll do anything for a bit of sympathy. She probably never met a situation she couldn't wheedle her way out of. Like the book says: *If she be a witch she will not be able to weep: although she will assume a tearful aspect and smear her cheeks and eyes with spittle to make it appear that she is weeping; wherefore she must be closely watched by the attendants.*

'Well, we're watching.' He banged on the grate, almost making me jump, though I managed to hold still, clenching my teeth around the bit of the bridle. 'Do you hear that, witch? D'you hear that? We're watching!'

There was the sound of laughter and then a scraping crunching sound, and they drew the cover over the grate and left me in darkness.

I woke thirsty and confused some hours later and for a moment just lay there. I stank. I literally stank. I'd been lying in the damp in the same clothes for days now and they were rank with the stench of fear and sweat and blood – and worse. They'd put a bucket in the corner of the room which was sometimes emptied, but I hated to think what had happened during the long hours of unconsciousness.

My hair itched; so did my skin beneath the bridle. I could feel sores starting to come up where the metal chafed my skin. But worst of all were my lips: dry and cracked and bleeding. In the end the feeling forced me to my knees and I crawled across the cell to the trickle of water.

The cold water seemed to help me shake off some of the lingering stupidity of the drugs and, when I'd drunk enough, I sat up and gathered my magic around myself like a warm blanket and tried to think. I needed to change – to change into something that could get through that roof. The spaces were small and there was no foothold on the slimy stone. So it had to be something that could fly – but not a crow, a crow could never fit. I thought of the house martins squeezing in and out of their nests under the eaves at Wicker House and a lump rose in my throat. Dad – oh, Dad . . . But I shoved the thought back down. Tears wouldn't be any help. I had to be strong, practical.

I shut my eyes and pictured the house martins, slim and lithe, swooping through the dusk with their joyful exuberance. All of a sudden, something prickled at my wrists, across my cheek . . . I raised my fingers, and felt the down of feathers on my skin. Then, just as quickly, they were gone. But my heart was pounding with triumph. It was a start.

I was gathering my strength for another try when I heard voices approaching from along the corridor and hastily lay down, pretending to sleep.

'Tomorrow, is that the plan?'

'That's right. The witnesses are arriving at dark.'

'And she's safe to go?'

'What, the witch? The Inquisitor reckons so. She's got precious little fight left in her, but we'll keep a syringe of that stuff handy in case she pulls any tricks. *All wickedness is but little to the wickedness of a woman*, as the book says.'

'What'll be the sentence, d'you reckon?'

'Well, I'd say we burn her. House fire probably, to cover up the evidence. Her house is in the middle of nowhere so it shouldn't be hard to arrange.'

I lay there, prickling with fear. Tomorrow. They were doing it tomorrow. That meant changing tonight. Could I do it? My power was coming back – but *tonight*? And such a big change. What if I had enough magic to change, but not enough to change back? But I had to – it was my only chance.

My thoughts were interrupted by the sound of footsteps

outside and the man's voice ringing out, sharp with alarm, 'Who's that?'

'It's me,' said a third voice, crisp, clipped, with only a trace of the local accent; one I'd never heard.

'Inquisitor!' There was a shuffle, as of backs being straightened. 'Any news?'

'Unexpected development. Another witness has turned up. The boy. He wants to testify.'

'Eh?' There was surprise in the first man's voice. 'Him? There's a turn up for the books.'

'Quite. With evidence from Waters – well! All I'll say, lads, is keep your torches alight. You'll be needing them tomorrow.'

They moved off up the corridor, still talking, but I still lay, with my hands pressed over my mouth to stifle my sobs. If I'd been alone, I would have screamed.

Seth had turned against me. Nothing mattered any more.

CHAPTER TWENTY

I awoke with a start, sweating and shaking. The guard was in my cell, standing over me with his legs apart. His face was covered with a black hood and he was holding something in his hand – a kind of stick, about a foot long. It was yellow and if I hadn't been so afraid I would have laughed; it looked like a toasting fork. But there was nothing funny in his stance, or the way he held the stick out towards me

'You,' he snapped. 'Up.'

His voice was familiar – maddeningly, itchingly familiar. Why couldn't I place it?

'I know you,' I said, the words coming thickly around the metal bit. 'I know you – but who are you? Why are you doing this to me? Please—'

'Shut it,' the guard snarled. And he shoved the prongs of the stick against my bare leg.

Pain ripped through me, pulsing up from my leg as if I'd been stabbed with a red-hot knife. I arched and screamed, hearing the noise ricochet around the tiny cell, echoing up and down the long tunnels outside. Then, just as suddenly, the pain stopped, and I slumped to the floor, panting and gasping, my breath sobbing in my throat.

'D'you know what this is now?' He showed it to me again and I flinched and then managed a painful nod.

'Right. A cattle prod. High voltage, low current. Maximum pain, for minimum damage. Now, here's how I'm gonna use this. If you try any spells, you get this. Try to run, I'll shock you. If you speak, except to answer questions, I'll shock you. If I don't like one single thing about your attitude, I'll shock you. Understand?'

I opened my mouth to say yes and then thought better of it. Instead I nodded. When the man spoke again, he sounded like he was smiling beneath the hood.

'Good.' He kicked me with his boot and I flinched again. 'Now, get up. We're going to your trial.'

Suddenly I knew. I knew where I'd heard it before. It was the man on the quay – Greg. The one who'd told Seth to flemish his line. The one who'd picked a fight with a kid half his age and borne a grudge ever since.

But before I could think what to do, what to say, the cell door opened and two other men came in, both

342

wearing hoods. In their hands were a collection of chains and manacles.

'Undo the ropes,' Cattle Prod instructed – I found it hard to think of him as anything else, while he was holding it out like a weapon – and the smaller of the two stepped forward, holding a knife. He sawed through the bindings and for a glorious moment my hands were free of the heavy itching rope and I could stretch and wriggle my fingers. But then, all too quick, the other man seized my ams and pulled them behind me. I felt metal cuffs close around my wrists and heard the clank of a chain. Greg – Cattle Prod – yanked on the chain, making me stagger and nearly fall, and the small man stifled a giggle with his hand.

They unlocked the cuff around my foot. Then the other man stepped forward with a black hood. This one was eyeless.

'No,' I said involuntarily, but Greg stepped forward threateningly. Then the bag closed over my head and everything was dark.

'Come on,' he said brusquely. 'The Inquisitor's waiting.' He pulled my chain and I stumbled forward, out into the cold night air.

We walked, I don't know how far. It felt like a long way.

My feet were bare and I stumbled over stone cobbles, through puddles of water. I could smell the sea, a painful familiar smell that made my stomach twist, and I could feel sand and grit beneath my feet. Then a door opened, someone yanked viciously on my chain, jerking my wrists painfully, and I stumbled forwards into a room.

After the dark monotony of the pigsty, the smells, sounds and sensations were like an assault. The room was warm, hot even. Above my own stink I could smell the sweat of working men, woodsmoke, dust – and petrol. The crackle of a fire came from my right, the flames heating my side and casting little sparkling shards of orange through the coarse weave of the hood.

There was a flurry as I entered, breaths drawn, low guffaws. Then rough hands pushed and pulled me across a stone-flagged floor and up a wooden step, a door slammed and there was the clanking sound of chains being secured and the grinding noise of a padlock key turning.

'The girl is secured, Inquisitor,' said a guard in a formal, respectful tone.

'Good.' The voice was the cold, clipped one I recognized from my cell. 'Let the trial begin.' There was a shuffle of papers and he spoke again, suddenly formal, as though reading from a script. 'Men of the jury, we are here today to decide on the guilt or innocence of the girl you see before you, Anna Winterson. Do you solemnly swear to judge her according to the evidence you will witness here today and give a true and faithful verdict before God?'

There was an answering rumble from my right.

'Defendant, state your name for the court.'

For a long moment I said nothing and the Inquisitor repeated impatiently, 'Are you Anna Winterson of Wicker House, Winter? Yes or no?'

For a brief, crazy moment I wondered what would happen if I said no – if I told them I was someone else entirely, some innocent bystander. But then sanity returned. The worst thing I could do would be to lie so obviously. My only chance lay in convincing them that I was telling the truth when I said I was innocent – perhaps not innocent of witchcraft, but innocent of any intent to harm.

'Yes,' I said thickly, trying to speak around the bit of the bridle.

'You are here to answer the following charges: using black magic to summon storms, causing harm to the village of Winter and to your neighbours. Using black magic against two boys, Samuel Evans and Roger Flint, with intent to cause their deaths. Bewitching Seth Waters, with intent to cause him to break with his friends and love you against his will. Setting fire to a rival, one Zoe Eldwick, from jealousy. Using black magic to summon evil demons to your aid, to do your bidding. How do you plead, guilty or not guilty?'

I swallowed. It sounded dreadful, piled crime upon crime like that. My head swam and the bridle bit into my skin viciously. But I gritted my teeth and held on to the wooden rail in front of me.

'Not guilty.'

'Not guilty to all charges?'

'Yes.'

'Let the girl's plea be noted,' the Inquisitor said with a heavy note of irony in his voice. Then he turned back to me. 'Remember, if you plead guilty now, your sentence will likely be more merciful. You can't escape death, but we can make it painless, drug you unconscious before we set fire to the house. If you persist in your lies and are still found guilty, then your death will be long and painful. We will chain you and leave you to burn. This is your last chance to change your plea.'

'No,' I said. But my voice cracked. There was a murmur and the Inquisitor banged something – a hammer by the sound.

'Silence!' he roared and the whispers subsided. 'Call the first witness.'

I heard the sound of footsteps as someone entered the room and walked to the far side. My heart was thumping in my chest so hard that I could barely swallow, and bile rose in my throat. I was about to be sick.

But my body realized why I was so terrified before I did – with a rush of relief as I heard the voice giving the oath. My knees felt weak and I clutched at the wooden rail to hold myself up. It wasn't Seth. It wasn't Seth. I didn't have to face the worst, not yet.

'. . . the whole truth, and nothing but the truth, so help me God.'

'Very good. State your name.'

'Samuel James Evans, Inquisitor.'

'Tell us what happened on the twenty-first of December last year.'

'Well, sir, my cousin Rog and me, we was walking home from the pub—'

'What time?'

'About elevenish, sir. And we took a wrong turn, down a blind alley. They was waiting for us.'

'Who?'

'The witch and a bloke. Youngish, with dark hair.'

'Did you know them?'

'No, sir, least not at first. But afterwards we asked around, Rog and me, and we was pretty sure we knew 'who they was.'

'How would you describe them?'

'Well, him, he was about six foot and he wasn't a big type, but he was strong, he packed a punch. Round my age, maybe a bit older – nineteen, twenty say. Dark hair, kind of dark-skinned. Like he did something outdoors. But it was the scar that did it.'

'What scar was that?'

'Across his wrist, like a burn or summat. When Rog asked around someone said they knew a lad from Winter had a scar like that – Seth Waters.'

'And the girl?'

'The witch, sir? Well, she was smaller, like. Just a little thing really, looked like you could snap her wrist with one hand. Dark hair, curly like. And these dark-blue eyes.'

'No identifying features?'

'No, sir, but I'd know her again.' His voice was grim. 'When someone near as kills you, you remember their face.'

'Explain what happened.'

'Well . . .' He shifted, uncomfortable for the first time. 'We got into a fight, like.'

'You and the girl?'

'No, me and Rog and the Waters bloke. He had the upper hand at first, but then Rog pulled a knife, self-defence like, and that was when the girl lashed out.'

'It's a lie!' I shouted, goaded beyond endurance. 'They attacked us, they attacked Seth, they—' My words were cut off by a jab to my leg and the searing electrical jolt of the cattle prod ripped through me. I slumped forward, only a wooden rail saved me from pitching to the floor. As the pain ebbed I heard my own gasping, sobbing breath, loud inside the hood, and beneath that the harsh voice of the Inquisitor.

'You speak when spoken to and not before – do you understand?'

I tried to control my tearing breath and gritted my teeth.

'Do. You. Understand?' the Inquisitor said slowly, and with indescribable menace.

'Yes,' I whispered through clenched teeth.

'Good. Let's get on with this. What happened, Evans?'

'I can't rightly explain it – but it was like a bomb. She kind of *crackled* with energy, all her muscles stood out, and her face had this terrifying expression. I've never been so scared in my life. And then she let go this *blast*, like. It knocked me backwards and the next thing I knew was waking up in Brighthaven Infirmary with concussion.'

'And you're sure the blast came from the girl?'

'Yes, completely sure. I can't explain how I know, I

just . . . I just do.' He paused, groping for a meaning, and said, 'It's, it's like when someone speaks – you just know it's them, don't you? You . . . you *see* them do it. You can *hear* the voice comes from them. Well, she *made* that blast – and I saw her do it, as sure as if she'd slapped me. That's as near as I can put it.'

'And your attacker, is she in this room?'

'Yes, sir.' There was a rustle and I felt heads turning to look at me. 'Her. She's the witch all right. The one who tried to kill me and Rog.'

'Are you sure now? Look at her properly. Guard, take off the hood.'

I felt a hand seize my shoulders and another hand grip the rough material of the hood. Firelight blinded my eyes and I had a confused flash of a cramped room full of dozens of bodies; a man on a rough wooden throne with scarlet robes and a beak-nosed mask; a boy, wearing a grey hooded top, his face filled with a mixture of fear, hate and shame. He nodded, and then the hood was yanked back down, and it was in darkness that I heard the words.

'Yes, it's her. It's the witch. The witch who tried to kill me and Rog. I'd know her anywhere.'

The chain was too short for me to sit, but as the hours

wore on my legs grew so weak I leant on the wooden rail, feeling my head droop and then snatch up again as they questioned me again, asking me to change my plea to guilty. I shook my head, the weight of the bridle dragging against the movement.

'Speak up!' barked my Inquisitor.

'Not guilty!' I choked the words around the bridle and he gave a huff and turned back to the legal arguments. They had been watching us for some time, that much was plain. They'd seen Emmaline and me together, heard us talk of magic, seen snow fall in strange places when I was there. One of the guards had even been in the pub the night that Zoe's hair had burst into flame and spoke about the pass she'd made at Seth, and my look of hatred.

I thought again of the footsteps in the snow around our house, of the eyes that had been watching for so long. I'd thought myself at home in Winter and all the time . . .

'Defendant, will you change your plea?'

'No,' I said, trying to keep the sob from my voice.

'Then call the next witness.'

More footsteps, the now-familiar sound of feet across the flagged floor. Then a voice, a girl's voice, very low and uncertain, as she muttered the oath. She spoke so quietly I could hardly hear her through the folds of the hood.

'State your name for the court.'

Another murmur.

'Now, it was you who originally lodged the accusation of witchcraft against the defendant, is that correct? You said that you believed a girl in your school had practised black magic against a boy called Seth Waters, had bewitched him, and forced him to love her against his will?'

'Yes.' Very low.

'And once again, can you tell us, is the witch in this room?'

'I – I . . .' She stopped. 'I can't see . . . I mean, I can't tell . . .'

'Guard, take off the hood,' the Inquisitor said shortly. My head jerked back as the hood was ripped away and then, as my eyes adjusted to the light, I found myself staring into the white, set face of Caroline Flint.

She gasped and put her hand to her mouth as she saw me, and for the first time it hit home what I must look like – barefoot, filthy, in my ripped evening dress, Seth's jacket still clutched pathetically round me. I put my hand to the obscene metal bridle and Caroline touched her own face in unconscious imitation. She closed her eyes as if she couldn't bear to see any more and then opened them as if she couldn't look away.

'Is this the witch?' the Inquisitor asked. But Caroline

said nothing – she only stared at me in horrified silence.

'Is this, or is it not, Anna Winterson, the girl you accused of bewitching Seth Waters?' the Inquisitor asked, impatience in his voice.

'I – I – I don't . . . I didn't mean . . . No. No.' She shook her head. I saw that her hands were trembling.

'No, what?' There was annoyance now in the Inquisitor's voice and he turned to stare at her through his strange black beaked mask, his eyes glittering through the holes. 'No, this is not Anna Winterson? Or no, Anna Winterson did not bewitch Seth Waters?'

'I don't know . . .' There were tears in Caroline's eyes. She shook her head. 'Please, I didn't mean . . . I didn't want . . .'

'It's a simple question,' snarled the Inquisitor. 'Is this the witch, yes or no?'

'No!' Caroline cried. She looked at me and her blue eyes swam. 'I want . . . I want to retract my accusation. I take it back.'

'It's not yours to take back,' the Inquisitor spat. 'You made an accusation – it's for the court to decide the outcome, not you. You have no say in the matter now.'

'Then I refuse to give evidence,' Caroline said. Tears spilt down her cheeks, but she held her head high and spoke courageously. 'I won't testify.'

'No matter.' The Inquisitor looked away. 'You're not important. We've got sufficient evidence from other witnesses to convict. Take her away, guard.'

'Oh!' A cry escaped Caroline's lips. 'Please no! If I'd known . . . I thought . . . I thought . . .' Her voice dissolved into sobs and she covered her face. There was a hurried conference between the ranks of hooded men and then a guard stepped up and led Caroline away, still weeping. As she passed the rail where I was chained she stopped and wrenched herself out of the guard's grasp for a moment.

'Anna, I'm sorry, I'm so, so sorry, I never meant—'

'Be quiet!' the Inquisitor roared. The guards began to propel Caroline forcibly out of the door.

'I was angry,' she called back, twisting to get free. 'I thought they'd just scare you, I'm so—' The heavy door slammed shut and there was a shocked silence.

'Kindly make sure,' the Inquisitor said in a low voice that shook with rage, 'that we have no more scenes like that one.'

'Yes, Inquisitor.' The murmur ran through the ranks of hooded men and their heads bowed. Then the Inquisitor seemed to dismiss the matter from his mind and his beaked mask swung back to face the room.

'Very well. Call the next witness.'

'Call the next witness,' echoed the guard.

The door swung open.

And Seth walked into the room.

CHAPTER TWENTY-ONE

I gasped and only just managed to bite back a cry as the guard stepped forward, his cattle prod threateningly raised.

With a superhuman effort I controlled myself, but my fingers bit into the wooden rail as Seth walked across the floor towards the makeshift witness box.

I expected him to avoid my eyes, to hang his head, look away. But he walked in calmly, his face untroubled, his gaze steady, and when his grey eyes met mine, they were like a draught of cool water. He held my look for a long moment and I felt a sob rise in my stomach. Accusations choked in my throat: *Traitor, bastard, murderer.*

But I said nothing. Not just because a guard stood behind me, with his cattle prod inches from my bare neck. But because the only thing that could condemn me, from Seth's lips, was the truth. And how could I blame him for telling the truth? If I burnt, it would be for a crime I *had* committed. It would be for my crime against Seth. Everything else, every other piece of magic I'd worked had been in self-defence, or involuntarily, or for some other good, necessary reason. I could put my hand on my heart and swear that I'd only ever done what I had to, what I'd been forced to do. All except for Seth. All except for that one, stupid, criminal act.

I couldn't ask Seth to lie for me, not now. But the truth, from his lips, would kill me.

They were putting the book under his hand now and he spoke the words of the oath, so that my heart twisted inside me.

'The truth, the whole truth, and nothing but the truth, so help me God,' he finished. His voice was steady and his grey eyes met mine without fear. Cool. Clear. Unutterably, unbearably lovely. I looked away.

'State your name for the record.'

He turned back to the Inquisitor and spoke quietly, but I had no difficulty in hearing him across the silent room.

'Seth Waters.'

'Grandson of Bran Fisher?'

'That's right.'

There was a murmur from around the courtroom and the Inquisitor banged his hammer for silence. He spoke again as the sound died.

'Please tell the court how you first met the defendant.'

'She moved to Winter about a year ago and we were in the same year at school. We were seated together in Maths.'

'And you felt no initial attraction to her?'

'I was curious about her, I suppose. I mean, she was a new girl and I thought perhaps she'd be interesting to have as a friend, but that was it. I wasn't looking for anything more. I had a girlfriend.'

'Ah yes, Caroline Flint.'

'Yes.'

'And then? What changed your mind?'

'I woke up one day and felt . . . I felt . . .' He stopped and, for the first time, he looked shaken. I saw the movement of his throat as he swallowed.

'Yes?' the Inquisitor prompted. 'You felt – what? An attraction? Would you call it a *violent* attraction?'

'Violent, yes. I'd call it an obsession actually. I was completely obsessed with her. I couldn't think about anything else – I couldn't eat, I couldn't sleep. My school work suffered. I broke up with my girlfriend and more or less stalked Anna. I behaved totally out of character.'

'And this wasn't, in your opinion, the normal behaviour of a man in love?'

'No, definitely not. I've had other girlfriends, other crushes. I know what it feels like. This was something else. A kind of . . . madness.'

'And how did the defendant react to this? To your behaviour? Did she seem surprised? Pleased?'

'Well, she didn't act pleased. At first she refused to go out with me.'

'Seriously, in your opinion?'

'I think so.'

'But she did eventually agree?'

'Yes.'

'Quite.' There was a rustle from the jurymen as they drew their own conclusions. But the Inquisitor was pressing on. 'And it was your opinion that she loved you?'

'Yes.' His eyes met mine fleetingly and then he looked away. 'At least, she said so.'

'Hmm. Well, moving on, what made you eventually believe that you'd been bewitched?'

'Oh, she told me.'

At this there was an audible hiss from around the room and the Inquisitor dropped his hammer and looked more closely at Seth and then at me.

'She *told* you?'

'Yes.'

'You swear, under oath, that the defendant admitted her witchcraft, admitted bewitching you with a love spell?'

'Yes.' Seth nodded. His face was completely without expression; a cold mask that might have been carved of marble.

I shut my eyes. My knees were suddenly weak beneath me and I held on to the wooden rail to try to hold myself upright. It was all over. It was all over.

'Well . . . Well, well, well.' There was the sound of a smile beneath the beak now. 'I don't think we need to waste any more time here. Gentlemen,' he turned to the massed black ranks to his right, 'can we agree on a verdict in view of this evidence?'

There was a murmuring in the ranks as they consulted with each other and then one man stood and nodded his hooded head.

'Yes, Inquisitor. We are unanimous in finding the defendant guilty.'

The room rustled again, a desiccated sound like wind through dry leaves.

'Guilty,' the Inquisitor repeated, dwelling over the two syllables. Then he turned back to the courtroom, to face me, and if the curved black beak could have smiled, I'm sure it would have.

'Anna Winterson, you have been tried and found guilty of the crime of witchcraft. Your sentence is death by burning. You will be taken to the place from whence you came, to face your execution. May God have mercy on your soul.'

I hardly heard his words. There was a strange roaring in my head and my heart was thumping, painfully loud. I didn't see the men in black crowding round, nor the Inquisitor raise his hammer and bang it for silence; my eyes were fixed on Seth. I had loved him. No, that was wrong. I still loved him.

'Seth . . .' I tried to speak, but the bridle cut my tongue. The guard started to unlock the padlock chaining my hands to the rail, ready to take me back to the pigsty, and from there – where? To my death?

'Seth . . .' I tried again, but my words were drowned out by the hubbub in the court. And then I realized Seth was saying something, calling something above the noise.

'Sir – Inquisitor, sir.'

'Yes, Mr Waters?' The Inquisitor turned his head, motioning for hush. 'Do you have something to say?'

'She's wearing a ring I gave her. Can I take it back? I don't want it to be destroyed.'

He took a few steps towards me, his face questioning. The Inquisitor gave an impatient nod and Seth crossed the flagstones to stand in front of me.

I couldn't look at him. I thought if I did, my heart might crack. Instead, I looked down at my hand, clenched on the wooden rail. The seaglass ring hung loose, now, on my dirty emaciated finger, and there was blood in the grooves of the metal. My throat choked with bitterness. Seth couldn't even leave me with that one thing of his. Well, if he wanted it back, he'd have to rip it off himself.

I shut my eyes. I thought about punching him, about smashing my manacled hands into his face. But I didn't. I stood very still, I waited, and I trembled as his hands touched mine. They felt just as they'd always done. They felt like Seth, *my* Seth. His grip was warm and strong. His large hand closed over my smaller one and I felt something hard and cool press against my knuckles. My ring. He was still wearing my ring.

His calloused thumb stroked, very gently, across the soft inner skin of my wrist.

And then there was a stabbing, searing pain and he drove something sharp deep, deep into my forearm.

I opened my eyes in shock and looked down to see a syringe full of a dark liquid sticking out of my arm. Seth looked up at me and his eyes seemed to beg me to understand something – and then he pressed the plunger.

* * *

For a minute nothing happened. And then it was like wildfire ripping through my veins, pumping through my muscles and bones and arteries. It was agony. Burning and biting and searing. And then I felt the stuff – whatever it was – reach my heart and something inside me seemed to explode. I think I screamed – a howl ripped through the room – and everything slammed into colour.

I was back. I had my power back.

It had all happened far, far faster than it takes to tell. In the same instant, Seth had wrenched the cattle prod off the unsuspecting guard and stunned him with a vicious butt end blow to the side of the skull. Another guard came running up behind and Seth whipped the cattle prod right way round and jabbed him in the neck with both prongs. The guard dropped like a felled tree, with a cracking thud as his skull hit the stone floor. More guards were coming but Seth took a step forward, holding the cattle prod out in front of him to stop anyone else from closing in.

'Keep back!' he shouted. 'Now, listen – Anna doesn't want to harm you, but she will if it's what it takes to get us out of here. Either you let us go, or people will get hurt.'

'She doesn't have any powers,' snarled the Inquisitor. 'Don't listen to the fool. Guards – grab her.'

A hooded guard came running towards us, intending to vault the rail, and almost without thinking I raised my hand and flung a spell at him. He staggered back, crashed into a bench and then fell to the floor completely motionless. There was an echoing crash as my manacles fell away and I raised my hands to the witch's bridle, ripping at the straps. There were cries and yells from around the room, screams of 'She's working spells!' and 'The witch is loose!'

Behind me I saw Seth stabbing with the cattle prod at the guards trying to close in from behind, and heard him gasp, 'Anna, I can keep them at bay, but this is up to you. Get those chains off and get us out of here.'

With a wrench I pulled off the bridle, letting my hair stream free, and I looked out, over the black sea of struggling, hooded forms, clawing at each other in their desperation. I shut my eyes and drew a long breath.

Then I opened my eyes and blew.

At first it was just a breeze, that ruffled the long black gowns and made the flames in the chimney rise up like fiery spectres. But I blew again and the wind picked up, swirling round the confined space, plucking at hoods and stools and papers – anything not fixed to the ground. I saw the Inquisitor, his scarlet robes flapping, holding on to the rough-hewn throne with one hand and clutching at his beaked mask with the other.

Still the wind rose, and now those guards not running for the door were holding on to each other, on to furniture, doors, anything that would anchor them down. But the wind was whipping into a spiralling maelstrom. Soon nothing would be able to resist it.

I grabbed Seth and together we jumped over the rail and huddled in the centre of the whirlwind, in the tiny stillness at the eye of the storm. Objects flew past, just inches from our heads – boxes, benches, ripped black shreds of gown. I saw a flailing silver snake flash past and recognized the chain that had manacled me to the rail. A black hood whipped by, flapping like a misshapen crow, and now for the first time I could see naked faces, contorted with panic. My captors no longer looked like hooded nightmares, but men, ordinary men. Workers, fishermen, dads, uncles. Ordinary folk you might see on the quayside at Winter any day, only their expressions were twisted with fear.

I couldn't see Greg anywhere but I caught glimpses of other faces I half recognized – a man, was he a sailor? And beneath a torn mask, a red beard that I was sure I knew. But this couldn't go on – the room couldn't hold. I could hear great tearing, rending noises, as if the building itself was being swept into the whirlwind. I didn't even try to stop it – I didn't want to. A fierce destructive delight was raging out of me – raging out of control. I had the sense that I could do anything, shape this stormwind into anything I chose.

'Anna!' Seth shouted. 'Anna, focus!'

And then there was a shriek like nothing I'd ever heard before, a crashing, rending screech of wood and stone and metal. Tiles began to rain down into the swirling, spiralling mass – and I felt Seth's arms tighten around me.

'Oh hell!' His yell was barely audible above the screaming wind. 'The roof's going. Get down.'

He pulled me down to the floor and crouched with his arms around me, and I knew he was trying to protect me, futile as that was. But I didn't need protection. This was *my* storm. Everything, every particle of air, would do my bidding. I was completely focused as I wrenched it back under my control – and then sent it spiralling up.

A strange, tearing exhilaration flooded through me, as the roof ripped away and the storm was free. I felt like a seagull must feel when they're whipped and tossed by the sea winds, just escaping the murderous waves beneath. The roof lifted, the tiles fluttering away like scattered leaves, the beams flipping up and outwards like matchsticks.

I caught a glimpse of the Inquisitor in his scarlet robes,

his beaked mask ripped free, his face deformed into a snarl of terror.

'Damn you, you bitch!' he screamed. But I didn't quail. I could have laughed – his face beneath the imposing mask had the fat, white jowls of a middle manager. I'd never seen him before – but I knew I'd never forget his face, forget the hate in his eyes as he leapt over a table, running towards us with his gavel raised above his head like a war-hammer. His other hand swung a length of rusty chain like a medieval flail.

Seth raised his arm, warding off the vicious blow – but it never came. Instead the tall chimney shivered, tottered . . . and then it began to crash slowly down, stone by stone, in a fiery explosion of shattered embers, ash ballooning up in a mushroom cloud.

The first stone hit the inquisitor on the back of his skull and he dropped full length, the gavel flying from his hand into the storm. Then stone after stone rained down on his body, spraying across the room like murderous hail.

'Hold on,' I said to Seth, and his arms gripped my waist with a fierce strength.

I felt my feet lift from the floor.

And then we flew.

* * *

We shot out of the middle of the storm into a deep-blue sky, streaked with rosy clouds and dawn-bright contrails, and hovered twenty or thirty feet above the wreckage. It took a minute for me to make sense of what I could see – which was nothing. Nothing but choppy blue and orange, reflecting the sunrise. It was only when I looked down that I realized we'd been on an island. Below us was a small rocky outcrop; a stone building in the centre being ripped apart before our eyes. As I watched there was a deafening explosion. Roof tiles scattered into the air like confetti, chunks of masonry flew outwards to land in the sea with great splashes, and clouds of sea birds rose into the air with angry screams.

As their shrieks died down, silence filled the air, broken only by the crash and wash of the waves against the rocky shore of the island. Below us the building was just a pile of rocks and ashes, with thick black smoke drifting in the sea wind, and the stench of petrol filled my nostrils. It seemed impossible that anyone could have got out alive – I found it hard to care about the fate of the guards, but had Caroline got away?

I scanned the sea for a boat, but all around us the empty blue stretched away to the horizon.

'Seth,' I gasped, 'where are we?'

'Holy shit.' Seth's arms were wrapped so tightly around

me that it hurt. He weighed a ton. 'Anna, you're *flying*. We're flying.' He risked a glance down and then closed his eyes looking sick.

'I know,' I said, trying not to let my desperation show. 'I know we're flying, but I don't know where. Where are we? Where do we go?'

'It's OK, I know this island. It's a bird sanctuary – you're not supposed to land but there's good fishing off the rocks, so some people do. It's only a few miles off shore.' He opened his eyes slightly and then closed them again hastily. 'Christ. Anna, did I ever tell you I'm not good with heights?' I felt his sweat trickle down my cheek.

'We've got to head north,' he said.

'Yes, but which way *is* north?' I felt as sick as Seth looked. The massive adrenalin rush of the storm and the fight was wearing off, and I felt bone tired. We could be flying in circles for ever, with Seth a dead weight around my neck – until my strength gave out and we both plunged into the sea.

'It's OK.' Seth was breathing deeply, trying to calm himself, nerve himself to look down again. 'It's dawn, the sun'll be nearly due east. So keep that to your right and you'll be heading in the right direction.' He opened his eyes and I felt his fingers tighten. 'Ugh. OK, look, there, see that dark shape on the horizon?

369

That's Castle Spit and the lighthouse.'

'It's miles away.' A sob rose in my throat.

Seth must have felt my panic for he raised his head painfully to look at me and the belief in his calm grey eyes anchored me.

'Anna, you can do this. You've got to do this. It'll be OK. Just fly.'

So I flew.

It seemed to take for ever. The waves skimmed beneath us, an insouciant blue that belied the depths beneath and the merciless cold of the water. I flew and flew, the sun rose in the sky, and still the distant smudge of Castle Spit stayed just out of reach. I could feel my strength beginning to fail. Seth's weight grew heavier and heavier, and we flew lower and lower, until the cold spray of the waves splashed against my bare legs and the crash of the breakers was very near. Soon the fishing boats would be leaving the harbour, but I had no choice; there was nothing I could do but keep going.

I was cold. I couldn't feel my feet; only the heat of Seth's body against mine stopped me shuddering convulsively. And still we flew, now just inches above the waves.

Seth said nothing, but I knew that he must be able to

hear the way my breath tore in my throat, feel my heart beating harder and harder. He said nothing and I loved him for it. I wasn't sure if I could have kept silent in his place, watching the waves get closer and closer. And I knew that he must be suffering himself, the muscles of his arms must be screaming in protest from hanging on to my neck for so long.

He turned his head and I knew he was looking at the distance to the Spit, calculating if I could last. Could I? My breath sobbed in my ears and my vision was breaking into fragments of black and red. Everything hurt. My arms hurt, and my lungs hurt, and my heart felt like it was going to beat itself to death.

'Anna, you can make it,' Seth said urgently.

'I can't,' I gasped. But I knew I had no choice.

'You can, if I do this,' Seth said. He drew a breath. And then he let go.

CHAPTER TWENTY-TWO

'Seth!' I screamed as he plunged towards the dark waves. But it was too late, he hit the water with an almighty splash and disappeared.

For a moment I hung in the air, paralysed with shock. There was a roaring in my ears and my limbs felt like jelly. I watched in horror as the dark waves closed over Seth's head, like a nightmarish replay of the events last year.

There was only one thing I could do. I took a deep breath – and plunged in after him.

For a minute there was a confusion of roaring water and crashing waves, and a tearing pain in my lungs. I felt myself tumbling over and over – and then I opened my eyes to the stinging salt water and saw Seth's body floating in the deep, his eyes wide with shock. The roaring in my ears grew louder, the red and black fragments in front of my eyes shook apart, plunging me into a swirling darkness, and I thought, *So this is what it's like to die.*

I didn't die. But as I lay on the beach, choking salt-water phlegm into the sand, for a while I wished I had. At least if I was dead I wouldn't be so cold, and so tired, and everything wouldn't hurt so much.

But something kept dragging me back, a hand shaking me, a voice saying, 'Anna, oh, Anna! You fool, you bloody idiot. Come on, sweetheart. Sit up, get *up*!'

I choked again, great gouts of salty foam, and the hand stroked my spine as I vomited up the meagre chunk of bread and dry cheese that had been my last meal.

'Seth,' I croaked, and opened my eyes. He was there. He was alive. Blue and shivering, but alive.

'Anna, you fool,' he said, and his voice cracked. 'Why did you dive after me?'

'Couldn't . . . couldn't let you die.'

'I wasn't going to die, you idiot. I was going to swim and let you fly the last bit alone. I knew I'd be all right; I just didn't expect you to fall out of the sky like a dead seagull after me and have to tow you back as well.'

Great. I let my head fall back and tears leaked out to join the salty vomit.

'I'm s-sorry . . . I d-didn't . . .'

'Hey, hey.' He put an arm round me and pulled me up against his chest. I felt like a sack of potatoes in his arms. 'It's OK. Don't be silly, you were fantastic. You got us out of there.'

'You came back for me,' I said. I put my head against his shoulder, feeling the stupid, weak tears come again, but powerless to stop them. 'You came back.'

'Yes,' he said quietly. So quietly that I should have realized, even then. I should have known there was something wrong. But I was too tired, and too relieved to think straight. I just let my head rest against his shoulder and I shut my eyes as Seth gathered me up and carried me up the beach. Somewhere before we reached the land, I fell asleep.

When I woke up I was in bed, my own bed. Someone had stripped off the filthy, ripped evening dress, and it lay draped over my desk chair like a dishrag, with Seth's jacket beside it. I was wearing a clean cotton nightshirt – and it felt amazing. I thought about weeping with gratitude. Instead I yawned.

'Anna?' A dark head poked round the door and Emmaline came into the room wearing an expression of worried delight. 'You're awake! How do you feel?'

'Like crap.' I stretched. 'But kind of fantastic all the same.'

Everything hurt, everything was stiff. There were weeping sores on my wrists and ankles, stinging with dried sea-salt, but I had a goose-feather pillow under my head and that made up for a lot. Plus I could hear the thunder of bathwater in the tub and the most unbelievably mouth-watering odours were coming from downstairs. It was as close to heaven as I was likely to get – at least for the moment.

'Oh, Anna.' Emmaline sat on the bed and then, in a most uncharacteristic gesture, she leant over and hugged me. I felt her chest heave as she struggled to contain tears and then she straightened, wiping her eyes determinedly. 'Well. Gosh. OK, by the way, you stink.'

'I bet I do.' I lifted a lock of my matted hair, stiff with seawater, blood and various other gross bodily fluids, and sniffed. 'Urgh.'

'There's a bath waiting next door.'

'I can't wait. What day is it?'

'Saturday. Your dad's due back tomorrow. So don't worry.' She grinned. 'You just scraped in under the wire.'

Saturday. So that whole endless nightmare had been only a week. *A week!* It seemed incredible. Impossible.

'Honestly?' I asked uncertainly. 'I was only gone a week?'

'Honestly. It felt like a lot longer to us though.'

'You're telling me.' I put a hand to the sores the bridle had left on my face and then sat up painfully. 'Owwww.'

'I'll put a slug of antiseptic in,' Em said, eyeing my various cuts and scrapes and bruises. 'Christ, they really put you through the ringer, didn't they?'

'Pretty much, yup.' I ran my hand cautiously through my hair, trying to ignore the pain that the movement caused. 'Em, what *happened*? How did Seth find me? And what was that stuff in the syringe?'

'Well . . . it's a kind of long story. Are you up to it?'

'Yes, I think so. At least, maybe I should have a bath and some food first.'

'Tell you what,' Em said, 'I'll bring you up something to eat in the bath and I'll tell you while you wash. Don't worry,' she said, seeing my face. 'I'll turn my back. I've got no desire to see your lady-bits, believe me. But the state you're in, you look liable to sink without a trace and Mum would be pretty pissed off if we got you all the way back from the Malleus, only to let you drown in the bath.'

'Just one thing,' I asked before she left. 'Have you . . . have you seen Caroline? Recently I mean?'

'Yes.' Emmaline gave me a funny look. 'She was waiting at the bus stop this morning actually. Why?'

'It doesn't matter.' I felt suddenly weak. Weak with

relief, relief that it was all over, that I didn't have any more blood on my hands. 'It doesn't matter now.'

I couldn't suppress a whimper of pain as I lowered myself into the scalding water. The mixture of antiseptic and bath foam stung every scratch and cut – and there were plenty. But once I was in, the water felt so good I wasn't sure I ever planned to get out. When Em handed me a plate of toast and a mug of hot chocolate, there really didn't seem much reason to move ever again.

I began to demolish the toast with wolfish bites and Em settled herself on the floor with her back against the side of the bath and prepared to tell her tale.

'So, I expect you worked out what happened after you left – which, at first, was not a lot. We all thought you were in London, so we were pretty surprised when Mum got a call at the shop asking where you were.

'It was your grandmother. She got worried when you didn't turn up in London, and at first she thought you were just late, but when she couldn't contact you or your dad she decided there must be something seriously wrong.

'Well, Ma had no idea what was going on, but she offered to go round to your house and see if you were there. As soon as we got there we knew something had happened. We let ourselves in . . .' Emmaline broke off at my questioning look and shrugged. 'What? It's magic, not rocket science. Locks are not a big problem. Anyway we could hear your phone beeping as we walked through the door, which was our first clue that something was wrong. Then we found your rucksack was still in your bedroom, along with your purse and your train tickets, and it looked like there'd been some kind of scuffle. There was a window broken at the back and stuff knocked over. It didn't take much to work out the Malleus were responsible.'

'So what did you do?'

'Well, first of all we panicked. Ma called Abe, Sienna and Simon, and we all sat round in our kitchen with your grandmother – which was pretty uncomfortable, I can tell you. Then we panicked some more. We tried everything – spells, charms, scrying. And between us we got some answers – but they weren't the ones we were hoping for and they weren't pretty.

'So we were busy crapping ourselves, metaphorically of course, and pondering the weirdness of being in an alliance with one of the senior Ealdwitan after what happened last year, when Abe realized he'd seen you *after* you were supposed to have left for London, on your way to meet Seth.'

She stopped, significantly, and I hunkered down in the bath and took a gulp of hot chocolate, refusing to be drawn on that one. The silence stretched, broken only by the drip, drip of the hot tap, and I knew Em was waiting for my account of things. But eventually she gave up and sighed.

'So we rang Seth,' she continued. 'He was slightly . . .' She gave me a sideways look over the edge of the bath, 'Hmm. Well. You know.'

Yes, I knew. Too many adjectives sprang to mind.

'And rather rude to me into the bargain,' Em added primly. 'But when he understood what we were going on about, he was the only one who came up with a plan. And it was a bloody good one. It just terrified the bejaysus out of all of us.

'Basically, Seth's argument was that he was the only person who stood a chance of getting anywhere near the Malleus without getting killed – and the only person with a cover story. His idea was that he'd offer to give evidence against you. He'd get to wherever they were hiding out, try to get in contact with you, and then chance it from there.

'Well, the first part of the plan seemed OK – it was dangerous for Seth, no question, but he was right that he was the only person with a chance of getting close to you and getting out alive. But the second part was suicide. There was no question of chancing it – we knew they'd have drugged the magic out of you and that left one girl, probably in a pretty bad state, and one guy, alone against a whole army of nutters. No, he'd be pulverized and you'd end up being fried just the same.'

I shuddered. It had come too close to that for comfort.

'It was your grandmother who came up with the second part of the plan. At first we didn't think it was any better than Seth's idea of chancing it – it wasn't suicide, but it was pretty close to it. But the more we talked and argued, the more we realized it was the only option available.'

'The syringe,' I said, suddenly understanding.

'Yes.'

'What *was* in it?'

'Magic,' Em said. But her voice made the word sound closer to 'poison'.

'What do you mean?' I asked. Em shifted uneasily and cleared her throat.

'Look, there's stuff. Scary stuff, about w—' She flinched and then spat the word out. 'About witches. Things you don't know. Things *I* didn't really know – just rumours.' She shuddered against the side of the bath and the surface of the water trembled in sympathy. 'And it turns out it's all true.'

'What do you mean? Stop skirting round this – what

happened? What did you do?'

'Have you ever heard of transfusions?'

'What, blood transfusions?'

'No. Not blood. Magic. We'd all heard the rumours, that . . . well, that some witches can take the magic from one person and transfuse it into another, to give them the ability to do stuff beyond their own power.

'It was your grandmother who first suggested it – and at first everyone said she was crazy – that it was too dangerous, that you could die.' Em sighed, and ran her hand through her hair. 'We all skirted around the truth, too chicken to say it, until eventually it was your grandmother who laid it on the line: we didn't have any choice. If we didn't do this, you were going to die anyway.

'After that it was only a matter of finding the most compatible person. The problem was, they still don't really understand the matching process. That's one of the reasons it's considered so incredibly unethical, because it's so dangerous.'

'Dangerous how? For who?'

'For everyone. I don't know how they do it, but I know it's not like taking blood. They kind of . . . drain them. And because they haven't completely worked out the compatibility issues there are a lot of deaths. The person they inject often dies. Their body rejects the stuff and shuts down. I mean, clearly you're fine, so I think . . . but it was a huge, huge risk.'

'And the other?' I whispered. 'The person they take it from?'

'Yes. They often die too.' Em said. She put her head in her hands. 'They go into shock.'

'Who . . . ?' I stopped. I wasn't sure I wanted to know.

Emmaline spoke. Her voice was a whisper.

'Abe.'

'Abe?' I swung round in the bath to face her, water slopping over the sides to the floor. '*Abe?* Is he OK?'

'Not really. Not at the moment. Your grandmother reckons he'll recover.'

'Oh God, Abe! But why? Why would he risk his life – for me?'

'Why?' Emmaline's voice was weary and she refused to look at me. 'For God's sake, Anna, why do you think? Why did you risk your life for Seth? Why does anyone lay down their life?'

She got up, her back still turned, and draped the towel she was holding over a chair.

'I'll go now. Let you get out.'

The door clunked shut behind her. And I was left alone and bewildered.

I pulled the plug and watched the cloudy water swirl

down the plughole, leaving a silt of filth and grit and blood in the bottom of the bath. Then I turned on the tap and soon not even that remained, not even that evidence of what I'd been through.

I looked down at my arm, at the spreading black bruise on my forearm where Seth had jabbed the needle in to save my life, and suddenly it all made sense – the storm, the sense of flooding power, of possibility. Abe . . . Abe had given me all that. He'd done more than just offer me his life – he'd offered me his power too.

I found I was crying, tears streaming down my cheeks. For a long time I just stood there in the steamy bathroom, weeping into my towel. Then I heard voices outside the door, and heard Maya's voice through the wood.

'Anna? Are you coming? We've got supper on the table.'

'Come out, darling.' My grandmother's warm, rich tones. 'We're all longing to see you.'

I straightened, scrubbed at my face, unlocked the door, and walked out into their welcoming arms.

I wasn't surprised to find that neither Seth nor Abe were there. The house had that indefinable sense of release when a place is inhabited solely by women. What was surprising was Maya and my grandmother's new-found camaraderie. They sat and chatted like old friends over the kitchen table as I stuffed my face with stew and dumplings, clucked together over my injuries, and colluded in persuading me to larger and larger helpings of apple pie for pudding.

At last I laid down my spoon and said, 'I want to see Abe.'

They exchanged a look, all three of them, and then Maya nodded.

'OK. He's at our place. Sienna's over there with him. Well . . . you may as well know. She's nursing him. He's not very well.'

'Because of the transfusion,' I said; a statement, not a question, but Maya nodded.

'Yes.'

'But he will recover.' My grandmother put her hand over mine. 'He's not in shock, which is the real danger. He's just very weak. He gave more than was perhaps advisable. We rely on the donor to tell us when to stop, when they begin to feel weak, and he . . . well, he carried on perhaps a little too long.'

'Oh, Abe.' I put my head in my hands and Maya stroked my shoulder.

'Darling, we're not saying this to make you feel bad.

384

It was his choice. But I just didn't want you to go in there unprepared.'

'And Seth?' I asked. 'Where's Seth?'

Maya shook her head.

'I don't know. Maybe Emmaline does.'

But Emmaline didn't.

'Christ, witch. You look like shit,' Abe said in a hoarse voice. 'What did they do to you?'

I had to laugh, though it came out shakily. It was so exactly what I'd been thinking about him.

'I was about to say the same thing to you.'

He shrugged.

'Yeah, well. I'm just malingering.' He coughed and then nodded at the open laptop propped on a footstool beside his makeshift bed. 'It's really just an elaborate excuse to work from home. I'll be up and about tomorrow.'

I looked at him sceptically, not so sure. He was lying on the sofa, completely limp, and there were dark bruises under his eyes and shadows in the hollows of his cheeks. His normally olive skin was clay-coloured and even his snapping dark eyes were dull and lustreless.

'Abe,' I twisted my fingers, 'Abe how can I ever . . . I mean, I owe you—'

'Anna, leave it.' He cut me off uncomfortably. 'Don't make this into a big deal.'

'But it *is* a big deal. You saved my life – you and Seth.'

I knew straight away the coupling of their names was a mistake. His face twisted in disgust and he looked away, out of the window.

'Yeah, well,' he said distantly, 'I'll leave the white charger and the shining armour to him, thanks. Look, it worked; you're alive; I'm pleased. I'll be good as new in a few weeks; there's nothing to owe. Can we leave it at that and forget it?'

'Yes,' I said quietly. 'Sure. Consider it forgotten.'

But of course that wasn't true. Even after Abe's strength and magic came back, it would always be there – this huge thing between us. Abe was part of me now – I'd felt his magic pulse through my body. There was no going back from that.

He softened and pulled me down beside him on the sofa, tracing his fingers over the half-healed welts on my wrists and then tilting my chin gently to angle my face to the light. I heard his breath catch in his throat as the sunshine lit the cuts and sores, illuminating them to full effect. Then he swore very quietly and looked away.

'Anna, what did they . . . what . . . ?' He broke off.

'A bridle,' I said shortly. 'A witch's bridle. And manacles

on my hands. Don't worry, they didn't torture me or anything.'

Well, not unless you counted drugging, electrocution and imprisonment as torture. But I guessed the kind of thing Abe was thinking of. At least I could be thankful I'd escaped that.

'No?' He tilted my face to his again and looked at me. 'Are you sure? You wouldn't – you know – be *brave* about this?' Hide things, I suppose he meant. Try to protect people from the truth of what had gone on.

'I'm sure,' I said. I met his eyes and he must have seen that I meant it, for he let go and nodded. I managed a laugh. 'They barely spoke to me, in fact – I think they were so terrified I'd turn them into toads. So no, no torture or interrogation. Just lots of drugs and not a lot of food.'

'You've lost weight,' he said, sounding like a pernickety great-aunt. 'It doesn't suit you. You're too thin. I can see your hip bones, for goodness' sake.'

'So are you,' I retorted, hitching up my jeans crossly to cover the offending bones. 'Your cheeks are hollow. You look cadaverous.'

'Nonsense, I look distinguished. It's my Kafka look.'

'Kafka? That's your style icon?' I snorted. 'I think you can do better.'

He laughed and then hit me gently on the arm, and I

pursed my lips and pretended to sulk.

'So, be honest, was it cool?' he asked slyly.

'Was what cool?'

'Having my magic instead of yours. I hope you made the most of it. I'm curious – was it different?'

'It kind of was,' I said slowly, trying to think back. 'It was the weirdest thing, because you know what I did to get us out of there?'

'No, tell me.'

'A wind. A whirlwind.'

Abe nodded slowly, and then shrugged.

'Well, I've always been good with the weather.'

'And so was I – just for a bit. It was kind of amazing actually. I felt . . . strong. Practised. I just *knew* the storm would obey me. It's never been like that before.'

'Anna.' Abe's hand gripped my arm. 'You could have that, you know. You just need to trust yourself. Look at what you've done – there're plenty of witches who'd give their right arm for your power. You don't need mine or anyone else's. You just need to let it out.'

'I know.' I looked down at my hands. 'I know. I let myself in for this and dragged you down with me. It was my fault. If I'd taken your advice, yours and Em's, and practised – learnt how to defend myself—'

'That's not what I'm saying; I'm not blaming you.' He

heaved himself painfully up on one elbow. 'I'm just saying . . .'

He stopped. His face was grey and tired and for a minute I thought he was going to faint.

'Yes?' I asked.

'I'm just saying,' he said wearily, 'you don't have to choose. Between love and magic. You could have both.' He looked me in the eyes and my heart skipped a beat. 'There are people who could give you both.'

I found my throat was dry and my heart was beating painfully. I don't know what I would have said – but at that moment Sienna came in. She looked from me, to Abe's gaunt, grey face, and shook her head.

'Anna, you need to go home and rest. You look dreadful. And Abe, you *need* to sleep. No buts!' she added crossly, as if this was an argument they'd had before. 'I don't want to hear it. I'm taking away your laptop and if I get any more gyp I'm going to put powdered Valium in your coffee.'

I shuddered. It was a little too close to the bone for comfort. Abe saw it and put out his hand.

'It's all right,' he said. 'It's over. Go on. Go home and rest.'

But I couldn't go home, not yet. I had to see Seth.

CHAPTER TWENTY-THREE

I found him right where he always was these days. Down at the quay, working on the *Angel*.

He was stripped to the waist and the sight made me shiver, in spite of the thin spring sunshine. I was wearing two layers and still had goosebumps. But Seth was bent over, sanding something furiously so that the dust flew, and as I watched he straightened and wiped the sweat off his forehead with his balled-up T-shirt, and then rubbed his eyes as if he was very tired.

'Seth,' I said. He didn't hear me at first, and then he turned around and something in his face changed.

'Anna.'

'Seth, I—' I moved towards him but he took a step back.

'Just a sec, I'm all sweaty and covered in varnish and crap. Just let me . . .' He picked up a bucket and leant over the side to pour the contents over his head and shoulders, rubbing off the dust and dirt with his T-shirt. It made me feel cold just to watch, but Seth shook himself like a dog and then disappeared inside the boat's cabin.

Taking a deep breath, I jumped the gap between the boat and the quay and ducked my head to follow him. He was standing in the middle of the small cabin pulling a fresh T-shirt over his head, and my heart thumped painfully at the sight of him struggling to get it on. He looked peculiarly vulnerable and endearing with his face concealed; just his long, lean belly sticking out the bottom of the T-shirt and a shock of dark hair sticking out the neck hole. Then, with a wrench, he dragged it over his head and his face appeared again and he was my Seth. Tired and damp, but my Seth.

'Seth—' I started, but he held up a hand.

'Wait, listen, before we talk about anything else I just wanted to say – it wasn't Grandad. Who turned you in to the Malleus, I mean. I'm sure of it. I asked him outright and he hadn't a clue what I was on about. He's an old bastard but I don't think he'd lie.' I opened my mouth to try to speak, but Seth ploughed on. 'He'd be more likely to boast about it. And in fact he was the one who told me where to find the leaders – and if he had anything to hide there's no way he would have done that. He'd have wanted me as far as possible from them if he knew what was going on—'

'Hang on, hang on.' I'd been trying to interrupt his flow of explanations and finally he stopped. 'It's OK. I know it wasn't Bran.'

'You do?'

'Yes. It wasn't him turned me in.'

As soon as the words were out of my mouth, I realized what a mistake I'd made. At the same moment Seth realized too and pounced.

'So you *know* who it was? Who?'

Oh God. I stared at him for a moment, trying to work out what to do.

'*Who?*' He took a step forwards, fists clenched. I knew he'd never hurt me, but his still fury frightened me.

'WHO?' he shouted, and I flinched. He banged the counter with one fist. 'For God's sake, Anna, I've got as much of a right to know as you have. I nearly died there too, you know. Or doesn't that mean anything?'

'Of course it means something!' I cried, stung into retort. 'How can you say that?'

'Then who? They were getting revenge on me as much as on you. And if you won't tell me, presumably it's someone we know, is that right? Come on – who? Matt? Chris Meeks? Angelica?' He began reeling off names at random – friends, colleagues from the pub, fishermen down the docks. I shut my eyes as the realization struck home. If I didn't tell him, he'd always wonder which of his friends had betrayed him.

'It was Caroline,' I said at last. For a minute I thought Seth hadn't heard. Then I realized he was simply too angry to speak, or even respond. For a moment he just stood there and I could see a vein throbbing in his throat.

'I'll kill her,' he said very quietly. Then 'I'll *kill* her!' in a furious bellow. He swallowed and flung his head back, his chest heaving in wordless rage. 'Shit! *Shit!* The calculating, cold-hearted, evil bitch, I'll kill her . . . I'll – I'll . . .' Then he just swore.

'Seth,' I said, but he was too angry to listen, or even hear me. 'Seth, Seth, listen to me. Seth, she was sorry. She said she was sorry. She took it back. She asked them to drop the charges. Seth, are you listening to me?'

'I don't care!' he shouted. Then he put his head in his hands and began to weep. 'I don't care. I don't care what she did afterwards. There are some things you can't take back.'

I didn't understand it. He was distraught out of all proportion. Yes, what Caroline had done was pretty bad but then from her point of view what I'd done to her was

393

pretty bad too. And it had worked out OK – we were all here and alive. I moved across the cabin and tried to take him in my arms.

'No!' He pushed me away with a violence that made me stagger.

For a moment I stood, gasping with shock, and then, not understanding, I took a step forward with my arms outstretched, trying again.

'No!' Seth said, and his voice was a sob. 'Anna, no, you'll only make this harder.'

'What? What do you mean? Make what harder?'

He turned away as if he couldn't bear to look at me and put his hands over his face. Then he pushed back his hair, wiping at the tears with his sleeve, and when he spoke his voice was weirdly calm.

'Listen, Anna, I love you. But I meant what I said.'

'What you said?' For a minute I didn't have a clue what he was on about. Then, suddenly there was a pain, an actual physical pain in my gut. I remembered the fish-hook and put my hands over my midriff. 'What you said? When?'

'When . . .' Seth stopped and took a shuddering breath. 'When I said goodbye.'

'No—'

'Why didn't you stop them, Anna? You could've done.

You know you could – if you'd practised, if you'd let yourself.'

'No.'

'Yes, yes you could. But you're so screwed up over what happened with us that it's poisoning everything. It's poisoning your magic. It's poisoning both of us. You're trying to be something you're not – you're turning yourself into a half-person. And for what? Because at the end of the day, you still don't really believe I love you. You'll never believe you deserve this, deserve to be loved. You'll never believe me until I walk away. So that's what I'm doing. I'm going away, completely. I'm leaving Winter.'

'No.' I held my stomach, knowing that if I let go my guts would spill out on to the polished boards of the *Angel*. 'No.' My voice was so weak that I could barely hear it myself. I wasn't even sure if Seth knew I was speaking. He wasn't even looking at me.

Suddenly I had the crazy idea that if I could just get him to look at me, get him to meet my eyes, it would all be OK.

'Please,' I said. 'Seth, please, please look at me. Please tell me to my face that you're going to do this.'

Then he looked at me. His eyes were full of tears, but clear and calm at the same time.

'Goodbye, Anna.'

I gasped. I think I put my hands over my mouth, to try to stifle a cry. I don't know if I said anything – I don't think I did. I know there were tears streaming down my face but I don't remember making a sound.

CHAPTER TWENTY-FOUR

'Anna.' Emmaline sat down beside me in the library with a weary sigh. 'Anna, you need to stop this.'

I said nothing.

'I know you're there. And I understand why you're doing this. But it doesn't work on me, and you can't do it for ever.'

Ms Wright walked past and looked at us curiously.

'Are you OK, Emmaline?'

'Yes, fine, thank you, Ms Wright. Just talking to myself.'

'Mmm, so I noticed.' Ms Wright gave a slightly mystified shake of her head, as if to say *Kids today*, and then walked on, leaving Emmaline and me alone.

'See?' Emmaline said, when Ms Wright's footsteps faded. 'You've got to stop this – if nothing else I'm going to get banged up in the local bin for hearing voices.'

I smiled reluctantly, and let myself flicker back into

view. Emmaline grinned.

'That's better.' She gave me a half-hug, half-shoulder-pat. 'Look, I don't blame you. *I'm* sick of people wanting to talk about Seth leaving,' she ignored my flinch at his name, 'so I can't imagine how pissed off you must be. But you can't stay invisible for ever – and it'll get better. I promise.'

As if to contradict her, a lower-sixth girl sidled up.

'Hey, you're Seth Water's girlfriend, aren't you?'

I bit my lip and didn't answer. I couldn't lie. But I couldn't quite bear to say the truth yet – not to strangers.

'I think it's so cool what he's doing.' She made cow-eyes at me. 'Don't you, like, massively miss him though?'

'It's not *cool*,' Emmaline snapped, mimicking the girl's reverential tone with cruel accuracy. 'He's dropped out. It's bloody stupid. He's messed up his A levels and screwed his chances at uni.'

'But he's sailing to *Morocco*,' the girl said breathily, as though it was Zanzibar or Tasmania. 'By *himself*.'

'Yeah well, whoopi-do,' Em said sourly. 'Most normal people get a plane. Pity Waters was too dense to work that one out.'

'Em,' I said wearily, 'be fair. He didn't just drop out – Charles Armitage is paying him to take the boat down to his summer house. There are people who have actual careers in boat transport, you know. It's not a holiday.'

No. It's a coward's way out, Emmaline said silently inside my head. I still hadn't got used to her mental broadcasts, but it was all part of her ongoing campaign to get me witched-up to the max.

'We're not going to discuss this,' I said shortly and, ignoring the lower-sixth girl, I stood up and shuffled my books together.

I saved the tears for night-time mostly. It's hard to keep up an invisibility spell when you're crying, and I didn't feel like suddenly flickering into view with red eyes and snotty nose in the middle of the school playing field.

But at night there was always the risk of Dad hearing, no matter how hard I muffled my sobs with the pillow.

The knock came around eleven, and at first I just groaned and pushed my face into the duvet, but I didn't want Dad to worry. I sat up and wiped my eyes, trying to look like I'd been doing my homework, as I'd claimed.

'Come in,' I said, wishing my voice wasn't so cracked and hoarse with crying. Dad put his head around the door.

'Are you OK, sweetie? I thought I heard . . .' He trailed off, seeing my swollen eyes. I shrugged wearily. There was no use pretending, not really. 'Oh, lovie.' Dad came and sat on the side of my bed with a creak of springs and put his arm around me. 'I know. I know you miss him.'

'Oh, Dad.' I put my face in his warm shoulder and he held me close. 'I love him so, so much. It *hurts*.'

'I know.' Dad rested his chin on the top of my head and I felt his stubble graze through my hair and heard the slow comforting rhythm of his breath. And he did know. Of course he did. It had been even worse for him.

'How did you manage?' I raised my face at last and looked up at him. 'When Mum left, how did you cope, Dad? How did you not go mad, not knowing where she was and how she was doing?'

'I don't know.' Dad shrugged sadly. 'I don't know. Maybe it was because I always knew she loved me, loved us both. I never doubted that. I came to believe that sometimes people leave, not because they don't love you, but because they love you too much. They believe that you'll be better off without them – however impossible that seems to the people left behind. Maybe it was because I always thought, deep down, that she might come back. And I held on to that hope, silly though it seems now. Or maybe . . .' He stopped.

'Yes?' I asked.

'Maybe it was because I had something to do. Something important.'

'What was that?'

'I had you to raise. And I concentrated on that. On being your dad.'

He sighed and kissed the top of my head and then stood, his knees creaking audibly.

'Oh dear. Time this old man went to bed, I think. Good night, sweetie. It does get better, I promise.'

Long after he left that night, his words hung in my mind. *I had something to do. Something important.*

I opened my bedside drawer and took out the faded snapshot of my mum. This time I didn't use my witchcraft, didn't search for any hidden meaning at all. I just lay and looked at her smiling face, her blue-grey eyes, warm with love and life. Perhaps . . . perhaps I had something important to do as well.

Turn the page
for a
sneak peek
of

A WITCH ALONE

The final novel
in
Ruth Warburton's
WINTER TRILOGY

CHAPTER ONE

It was dark, but I could tell someone was there as soon as I opened the barn door.

'Hello?' My voice echoed in the rafters. 'Hello?'

I waited for a moment, listening. Nothing. But I wasn't alone. I didn't need witchcraft to tell me that; someone was there; a living, breathing someone, and the knowledge made the hair on the back of my neck prickle.

A long shriek broke the silence and I jumped, but it was only the barn door slowly swinging to behind me, the damp wood groaning as it went. Then it clunked shut and darkness engulfed the vast space.

I wasn't afraid. If I was blind, so was he. I stood, waiting.

The blow hit me like a blindside, slamming into me so hard I staggered and saw stars. I stumbled against a wooden beam and clutched at it, holding myself upright as I tried to gather my wits for a counterspell.

'*Sl-*' I tried. But the blast of lightning came too quick, sending me sprawling to my knees in the straw.

In that brief, blinding instant, I saw him – standing on a rafter in the centre of the room. It was a vantage point, but a dangerous one. For a minute I lay face down on the filthy barn floor, trusting that he'd be pulling himself together, readying himself for another go.

Then I leapt up.

'*Ábréoðe!*' I yelled.

There was a deafening crack from the beam he was standing on – then a bone-cracking crunch and a cry of pain as a body hit the floor.

I stood, panting, waiting to see if he got up. He didn't, and for a moment I felt triumph. Then a suffocating web of threads began to drop from the darkness, sticking to my hands, my eyes, my mouth. The more I struggled the closer they clung, like a giant spider's web, binding me in their grip. In a panic I struck out, useless curses right and left, countercharms that did nothing but singe my skin and rip my clothes. I heard laughter, mocking laughter, shiver through the dark, and fury rose up in me.

'*Unwríð!*' I screamed. The bindings sizzled into shreds and I concentrated all my rage into a spear of anger and flung it through the darkness in the direction of the laughter. It hit – I heard his cry of pain.

Now it was his turn on the defensive. I pushed home my advantage, hitting him again and again, punching him with every ounce of magic I could muster.

But I was tiring and he wasn't. I could feel his energy and the strength of his magic as he pushed back my blows. Then he began to force his way across the floor of the barn towards me. Now I was concentrating not on hurting him, but on keeping him back. And I couldn't. He forced me back, back, until my spine was against the rough wooden wall of the barn. He was so close I could feel the crackle of his magic, the heat of his skin, smell his sweat.

'No!' I panted. 'No!'

But it was too late – I was trapped into a corner, and he was inches away, crushing me. I felt him lean in, closer and closer in the hot blackness. It was all over. He'd won.

'OK,' I said, my voice shaking with exhaustion. 'OK, I—'

His hand closed on my shoulder, the other gripped my hair, and he kissed me.

For a minute I couldn't think – I just stood, shattered, all my defences down, and let him. All I could think about was the soft heat of his mouth, the hard strength of his body, the harshness of his unshaven skin against mine.

For a long, long minute I did nothing, just stood and trembled as he kissed me.

It was only when I felt his hand slip beneath my shirt that clarity broke through. A vicious blast of magic shook the barn. His body was flung backwards, crashing against the opposite wall with a terrible cracking sound.

And then there was silence.

When love is tangled up in magic, how do you know what's real?

Immerse yourself in the story of Anna, whose life changes
for ever when she moves to the small town of Winter. In Winter
she meets Seth Waters and unleashes a chain of events that
leads them from love, to heartbreak, to mortal danger.

'This is not a fluffy romance tale; it's also an exciting story of
a deadly power battle ... there's plenty in this debut for teenage
readers who like romance, exciting battles and magic.'
The Telegraph

bookswithbite.co.uk
if you've got a thirst for fiction, join up now

www.hodderchildrens.co.uk

Hodder
Children's
Books

Ruth Warburton
Online

Ruth's blog, book news, reviews, FAQs and loads more can all be found on her website.

For all things Witch, Winter and Ruth Warburton, there's nowhere better!

www.ruthwarburton.com